Andrea H. Japp

Born in 1957, Andrea H. Japp trained as a toxicologist and is the author of twenty novels. She is the French translator of Patricia Cornwell and has also written for television.

Lorenza Garcia

Lorenza Garcia translates from French and Spanish. Her two most recent translations are *The Montmartre Investigation* by Claude Izner, which she co-translated with Isabel Reid, and *The Season of the Beast* by Andrea H. Japp. She currently lives in London.

THE BREATH OF
THE ROSE

Second in the Agnès de Souarcy Chronicles

THE BREATH OF THE ROSE

ANDREA H. JAPP

Translated by Lorenza Garcia

GALLIC BOOKS
LONDON

This book is [...] f the Burgess
program [...] London.

First published in France as *La Dame sans terre 2 :*
Le Souffle de la rose by Calmann-Lévy

Copyright © Calmann-Lévy 2006
English translation copyright © Gallic Books 2009

First published in Great Britain in 2009 by Gallic Books,
134 Lots Road, London, SW10 0RJ

A CIP record for this book is available from the British Library

ISBN 978-1-906040-21-5

Typeset in Fournier MT by SX Composing DTP, Rayleigh, Essex
Printed and bound by CPI Bookmarque, Croydon, CR0 4TD
2 4 6 8 10 9 7 5 3 1

Gentle Pye,
go to your brother,
with no pain

CONTENTS

AUTHOR'S NOTE

Words marked with an asterisk are explained in the Historical
References and Glossary starting on page 294.

SUMMARY OF BOOK ONE
SEASON OF THE BEAST

Winter 1294, Comté du Perche. The recently widowed Agnès de Souarcy takes under her wing Clément, the newborn infant of her lady's maid, Sybille, who has died in childbirth.

Cyprus, 1304. The Knight Hospitaller Francesco de Leone is sent to France. His official mission is to gather information that will help the Hospitaller order anticipate the political machinations of France's monarch, Philip the Fair. However, Leone is guided by a secret quest.

Paris, 1304. Philip the Fair aims to free himself of the Church's authority. Pope Benoît XI is fatally poisoned, and the Pope's personal guard – the twin orders of the Knights Templar and Hospitaller – comes under threat. Philip the Fair, with the help of his most influential counsellor, Guillaume de Nogaret, advances his pawns. He needs to find a docile pope.

Souarcy-en-Perche Estate, 1304. Clément has grown into a young boy with a lively intelligence. He gains entry to a secret library at Clairets Abbey. There he devours all the ancient texts forbidden by or unknown to the Church, and stumbles on a journal belonging to the Knight Hospitaller Eustache de Rioux, which refers to a mysterious Vallombroso treatise, two birth charts and a series of incomprehensible runic symbols . . . Is there a link between these discoveries and the Knight Hospitaller Francesco de Leone's extraordinary quest?

The body of a man lies in Souarcy Forest. It appears to have been burnt and yet there is no trace of any fire in the vicinity. An emissary of the Pope delivers a message to the Abbess of Clairets, Éleusie de Beaufort. The message contains a reference to the divine blood that washes away all sins. More corpses are discovered, as well as a series of clues pointing to Manoir de Souarcy and Agnès.

On her estate, Agnès, Dame de Souarcy, must also cope with the incestuous desires of her half-brother Eudes de Larnay, who dreams of forcing her to submit to him and is quick to throw her into the clutches of the Inquisition and the bloodthirsty Nicolas Florin. The only person who might save Agnès is Artus, the Comte d'Authon, who has fallen in love with her . . .

MAIN CHARACTERS

Agnès, illegitimate recognised child of Baron de Larnay, widow, Dame de Souarcy, aged twenty-five.

Clément, ten years old, posthumous 'son' of Sybille, the lady's maid to whom Agnès gave refuge, unaware that she was a heretic.

Mathilde, Agnès's only daughter, eleven years old, shallow and capricious, frustrated by the harsh life at Souarcy.

Eudes de Larnay, Agnès's half-brother and overlord.

Francesco de Leone, member of the order of the Knights Hospitaller, which has retreated to Cyprus.

Artus, Comte d'Authon, Eudes de Larnay's overlord. Agnès is his under-vassal.

Éleusie de Beaufort, Abbess of Clairets and Francesco de Leone's aunt.

Honorius Benedetti, the Pope's camerlingo (treasurer and secretary)

Nicolas Florin, Dominican friar, Grand Inquisitor in the Alençon region.

Esquive d'Estouville, a young girl who crosses Francesco de Leone's path without his suspecting that she is his protector.

A unknown figure, perpetrator of base acts, but in whose interests?

NICOLAS Florin was adamant that Agnès de Souarcy should be installed in the stout wooden wagon that gave the impression of a tomb on wheels. Minute arrow slits on each side allowed the occupants a limited view of the outside world. These were covered by leather curtains so that in the event of an attack no arrow could pierce the narrow openings. Four Perche horses were needed to draw the wagon.

The five men-at-arms requested by Nicolas Florin sat beside the driver or were jostled about on a cart trundling along behind. Agnès's belongings were contained in a small chest while, in an astonishing display of extravagance for an inquisitor, those of Nicolas filled an enormous trunk. An escort of five men-at-arms for one woman seemed an exaggerated precaution, but the Dominican was fond of such excesses. He saw them as visible proof of his newly acquired power.

His eyes were glued to Agnès, watching for the slightest sigh, the merest tensing of her jaw. Indeed, it was the reason he had given the order for her to travel with him in the wagon instead of in the cart. Did she regard the gesture as a mark of respect for her social status? Florin could not tell, and the thought had irritated him from the outset of their journey. Things were not going according to plan and had not been since the day of their first encounter when he had gone to notify her of the beginning of her period of grace. Did she really think she could get the better of him? Or that he would show her mercy? If this were the case, she would soon be disappointed. He lifted the leather flap and peered out at the sky. Night was falling. Since sext* they had been advancing at the horses' slow but steady pace. She had not once raised her eyes from her hands clasped upon her lap, or uttered a single word, or even asked for water or a halt in order to relieve herself – something Nicolas would have been only too glad to agree to in the hope that she might be humiliated into wetting her shoes or the hem of her skirts in the presence of one of his guards.

A vague feeling of unease crept into the Grand Inquisitor's irritation. Had his victim received guarantees of protection? If so, from whom? From Comte Artus d'Authon or the Abbess of Clairets* or someone more highly placed? But who could be more powerful than the man behind the imposing figure who had paid him a visit at the Inquisition* headquarters in Alençon? No. He was behaving like a scared child. The bastard was adopting the haughty air of the sort of lady she aspired to be, nothing more.

She raised her blue-grey eyes from her hands, which were joined in prayer, and stared at Nicolas. He felt an unpleasant warmth suffusing his face and diverted his gaze, cursing himself as he did so. There was something peculiar about this woman – something he had not taken the time or had been unwilling to see. He tried now to analyse what he felt, but without much success. At times he had experienced the thrill of terrifying her, just as he did the others. But then all of a sudden another woman appeared, like a secret door leading to a mysterious underground passageway. And that other woman was not afraid of him. For some reason, Florin was quite sure that Agnès had no control over these transformations. Had he been an unthinking fanatic like some of his brothers, he would no doubt have seen it as proof of demonic possession. But Florin did not believe in the devil. And as for God, well, he had little time for Him. The pleasures life had to offer to those who knew how to take them were of greater concern to the Grand Inquisitor. Among the many he had condemned to death for sorcery or possession, Florin had never come across any convincing proof of the existence of miracle workers or witches.

His annoyance got the better of his cunning and he blurted out:

'As I am sure you are aware, Madame, the inquisitorial procedure* permits no other counsel than the accused himself.'

'Indeed.'

'Indeed?'

'I am aware of that particularity,' she said in a voice whose confident tone humiliated the inquisitor.

He stifled the anger welling up in him and the accompanying urge to slap her. He knew he should have held his tongue, but the desire to watch her face turn pale was too overpowering, and he continued, forcing himself to speak softly:

'It is not customary to reveal the identity of the witnesses for the prosecution, any more than the content of their accusations . . . However, because you are a lady, I may grant you this privilege . . .'

'I have no doubt that you will do all that is necessary and correct, Monsieur. If you do not mind, I should like to take a short nap. The long days ahead require me to be rested.'

She leaned her head against the back of the wooden bench and closed her eyes.

Florin's eyes filled with tears of rage, and he pursed his lips for fear he might utter an oath that would reveal his agitation to Agnès. He was vaguely consoled by the words of one of the most celebrated canonists: 'The aim of trying and sentencing the accused to death is not to save his soul but to uphold public morals and strike fear into the hearts of the people . . . When an innocent refuses to confess, I resort to torture in order to send him to the stake.'[1]

Agnès had no wish to sleep. She was reflecting. Had she won a first victory in the long battle for which she was preparing herself? She sensed this man's puzzling hostility towards her and his exasperation.

Is it your still-innocent soul that protects me even now, Clément? Thanks to him Agnès knew that Florin was using the first of many tricks in the inquisitor's arsenal.

Many months before, on a July evening when it was nearly dark, Clément had returned in an excited state from one of his frequent forays. It was already late and Agnès had retired to her chambers. The young girl had scratched at her door and asked to see her for a moment.

No. She must never think of Clément other than as a boy or she risked making a blunder that would endanger both their lives. She must continue to refer to him only in the masculine.

The child had tapped at her door and asked to see her for a moment. He had stumbled upon a copy of *Consultationes ad inquisitores haereticae pravitatis*[2] by Gui Faucoi, who had been counsellor to Saint Louis before becoming Pope Clément IV. The treatise was accompanied by a slim volume, or, rather, a manual of bloodcurdling procedures. He had stammered:

'M-Madame, Madame . . . if only you knew . . . they use trickery and deceit in order to obtain confessions, even false ones.'

An inscription at the head of the slender manual read: 'Everything should be done to ensure that the accused cannot proclaim his innocence so the sentence cannot be deemed unjust . . .'[3]

'What an abomination,' she had murmured in disbelief. 'But this is about trial by ordeal . . . How is it possible? Where did you come across these works?'

The child had given a muddled explanation. He had mentioned a library and then skilfully evaded Agnès's questions.

'I see in it a sign from God, Madame. Knowing and anticipating your enemies' ploys means avoiding the traps they lay for you.'

He had described them to her: the technique of coercion and humiliation aimed at breaking down even the toughest resistance, the scheming, the manipulation of witnesses. The wretched victims were questioned on points of Christian doctrine. Their ignorance should have come as no surprise to anyone and yet was used as proof of their heresy. Clément had also listed the few possibilities of appeal at the disposition of the accused. As almost no one was made aware of them they were rarely invoked. It was possible, for example, to appeal to the Pope – though such appeals had every chance of being mislaid, often intentionally, unless an influential messenger delivered them directly to Rome. An objection to an inquisitor could be made on the grounds that he harboured a particular animosity towards the accused. However, the process was liable to miscarry since it required judgement, and very few judges were willing to risk getting on the wrong side of an inquisitor or a bishop associated with the Inquisition.

Clément had managed to dash any last hopes his lady might have entertained by adding that the majority of inquisitors, although they received a wage, rewarded themselves with the confiscated property of the condemned men and women. It was therefore against their interests for the latter to be found innocent, and wealthy victims, although more difficult targets, were desirable prey.

The knowledge Clément had acquired from some unknown source had allowed Agnès to forge what she hoped would be her most reliable weapons when confronting Florin.

The inquisitors' initial ploy, then, was to swap the names of the witnesses and their accusations. Thus the first accusation would be attributed to the fifth witness, the second to the fourth, the third to the first, and so on . . . In this way the accused would appear clumsy in his defence against each informer. Cleverer still, they added the names of people who had never come forward as witnesses to the list of actual informers. But the subtlest, most convincing and preferred method was to ask the accused in a roundabout way whether he was aware of having any deadly enemies who might perjure themselves in order to bring about his downfall. If the accused failed to mention the most fervent of his accusers, their testimony was placed above suspicion since by his own admission they could not be fabrications. In each case the protection of witnesses was considered essential for the very good reason that 'without such a precaution, nobody would ever dare testify'.

Curiously, these revelations, which had so shaken her that night, now came to her aid. Had she believed that she was about to be dragged before impartial judges whose sole concerns were truth and faith then her resolve would have been weakened. She would have searched inside herself for the failing that could justify such harsh punishment. Clément had helped her to understand the wicked nature of this farcical trial. Only a noble enemy deserves a fair fight.

Her thoughts had been wandering in this way for a while when Florin's voice almost made her jump. He thought he had woken her and this gave him further cause for alarm. How was she able to sleep at a time like this?

'Owing to the limited space at the Alençon headquarters, you will be subjected to *murus strictus* while you are in custody, unless that is . . . the midwife attests that you are with child.'

'Perhaps you have forgotten that I have been a widow for many years. Is not *murus strictus* a severe punishment rather than a . . . temporary accommodation?'

He seemed surprised that she would have knowledge of such things; the secrets of the Inquisition were jealously guarded in order to further demoralise the accused. The 'narrow wall' was simply a gloomy, damp dungeon the size of a cupboard where it was possible to chain prisoners to the walls.

'Madame . . . we are not monsters!' he exclaimed with feigned indignation. 'You are allowed brief visits from members of your close family – at least before the beginning of . . . the real interrogation.'

The torture, she thought. She tried to respond in an impassive voice:

'You are too kind, my lord.'

Agnès closed her eyes again in order to end the conversation, whose only aim was to frighten her. Her heart was pounding in her chest and it took a supreme effort of will for her to control her breathing. The only way she could control or stifle her mounting terror was by clinging to the thought that she had managed to place Mathilde and Clément out of harm's way.

Half an hour later, Florin shouted: 'Stop!' causing Agnès to start.

'We shall make a brief halt, Madame. Would you like to use the opportunity to stretch your legs?'

Despite her determination not to give in, she needed a moment to herself. After a second's hesitation she replied:

'Gladly.'

He leapt nimbly to the ground and refrained from offering to help her down. One of the guards hurried over and handed him a package, probably containing food and refreshment. The inquisitor studied her for a moment and asked:

'Do you require a little privacy, Madame?'

Stifling a sigh of relief, she accepted:

'Indeed, my Lord Inquisitor.'

'I think we all do. Hey, you over there, escort Madame.'

A big brute with a squashed face walked up to them. Agnès was on the verge of changing her mind, of saying that she preferred to wait until they reached Alençon. She was dissuaded by the smirk on Florin's face and the pain that had been searing her belly for hours. She spotted a thicket of bushes and walked over to it. The brute followed.

Once she was out of view of the others, she waited for the man to turn away, but his eyes were glued to her. His moist lips spread in a lecherous smile as she lifted her skirts. Agnès squatted, her anger eclipsing any embarrassment she might have felt, and stared straight at her escort. The man's smile dissolved and he lowered his gaze. This small victory comforted the young woman. It was a sign that she could prevail.

She did not remain outside enjoying a little more fresh air, but climbed straight back into the clumsy wagon. She could smell through the crack in the door the faintly acrid odour of bracken and the soothing forest air, heavy with humidity.

Florin glanced down at the hem of her dress as he sat down opposite her. Agnès fought back the urge to point out that she had not wet her gown. She had hitched up her skirts and if his man-at-arms had glimpsed her calf or her knee then much good might it do him. She was beyond such foolish concerns, though at other times and in other places they would have seemed of the utmost importance to her.

When they finally reached Alençon, Agnès's lips were parched with thirst.

The wagon rattled over the cobbled courtyard of the Inquisition headquarters. Florin announced in a hushed voice:

'We have arrived, Madame. You must be exhausted after the long journey. I will show you without delay to what will be your . . . lodgings over the coming weeks.'

Agnès was in no doubt as to his motives. He wanted to see the distress on her face, and she prepared for the worst – or so she thought.

Despite the enveloping gloom, the inquisitor strode confidently towards a small flight of steps leading up to a heavy door reinforced with struts. She followed, aware of two guards some yards behind her.

An icy cold pervaded the hallway. Florin ordered a few candles to be lit, and in the flickering light it occurred to Agnès that he resembled a beautiful vision of evil.

'Come along,' he chivvied, the excitement becoming evident in his voice.

They crossed the low-ceilinged room, which was devoid of any furniture except for a vast table of dark wood flanked by benches. Florin walked over to a door on the right of the enormous room.

Suddenly, a young man appeared as if from nowhere and stood at Agnès's side.

Florin declared in an alarmingly gentle voice:

'Why, Agnan, you look only half awake. Could it be that while I was crossing hill and dale for the greater glory of the Church you were sleeping?'

Out of all the clerics, Nicolas had chosen Agnan to be his secretary because the young man's unredeemed ugliness suited him to perfection. Ugliness. What a splendid example of injustice. Agnan was the sweetest, gentlest creature, honest and pious, and yet those beady close-set eyes, that bony protruding nose and receding chin were deformities that inspired immediate mistrust in the onlooker. On the other hand, who would have believed that Nicolas's long slender frame, his gentle slanting eyes and full lips concealed a soul whose darkness would have struck fear into the heart of any lay executioner? And so Agnan suited Nicolas down to the ground, and moreover he was easily intimidated.

'Indeed not, my Lord Inquisitor. I have been busy assembling the various pieces of evidence for the forthcoming trial in order to further you in your task,' explained the other man timidly.

'Good.' Nicolas gestured towards Agnès without looking at her, and added: 'Madame de Souarcy is to be our guest.'

Agnan glanced nervously at the young woman then quickly lowered his head. And yet she could have sworn she saw a flicker of compassion in the secretary's eyes.

'Very good, run along now and keep up the good work.'

The other man bowed, stammering his agreement, and left with a rustle of his dowdy habit made of homespun wool.

One of the men-at-arms rushed to open the low door. A stone spiral staircase plunged into the murky blackness. The guard went ahead to light the way. As they descended into the cellars, the damp, acrid air caught in Agnès's throat and soon combined with the lingering odour of mud, excrement, pus and rotting flesh.

The staircase opened onto a floor of beaten earth that had

turned into sludge with the first rise in the water level of the river Sarthe. Agnès breathed through her mouth in an attempt to quell her feeling of nausea. Florin declared cheerfully:

'After a few days one grows accustomed to it and the stench is no longer noticeable.'

The underground chamber seemed vast; bigger, Agnès thought, than the surface area of the Inquisition headquarters. The supporting pillars were joined up by bars that demarcated the cells. They walked alongside the cages, which were too cramped for a man to stand up in. Occasionally, the flickering light from Florin's candle briefly illuminated an inert figure huddled in a corner, asleep perhaps, or dead.

'We are not accustomed to receiving ladies of your standing,' Florin said ironically. 'Although I am a monk, I am still a man of the world and as such have reserved one of the three individual cells for you.'

Agnès was perfectly aware that this gesture was not motivated by any consideration for her wellbeing. His aim was to deprive her of all contact – even with her fellow prisoners, who admittedly were in no position to offer her any solace. For the first time she found herself wondering whether he might not be afraid her. Nonsense. What could he possibly fear from her?

The floor sloped gently downwards, and they passed beneath the vaulted ceiling and alongside the remaining cells enclosing the poor tortured, terrified souls. Agnès's shoes sank into the thick mud. They were certainly close to the river. A damp, unhealthy chill caused her to shiver, and the idea that she would soon be alone, shut in with this foul odour, undermined her resolve not to allow her fear to show. Strangely, even Florin's evil presence felt preferable to this void full of horrors that awaited her. All of a sudden something slippery gripped her ankle and she screamed. A guard rushed over and, pulling her roughly to one side, stamped his heavy wooden clog onto a hand . . . A bloodstained hand drooping through the bars of one of the cages. There was a wail, then whimpering ending in a sob.

'Madame . . . there is no hope of salvation here. Die, Madame, die quickly.'

'What foolishness!' exclaimed Florin, and then in a voice that had regained all of its cheerfulness he warned the shadowy figure of a man hunched against the bars: 'Pray, but pray in silence; you have offended our ears enough with your griping!'

She remained motionless a few steps away from the cage, peering into the darkness that the candle flames struggled vainly to illuminate. Could those two blue openings surrounded by what looked like raw flesh be eyes? And was that gaping wound a mouth?

'Dear God . . .' she groaned.

'He has forsaken us,' responded the feeble voice.

'Blasphemy!' Florin shrieked, pulling her by her coat sleeve. 'And he protests his innocence.'

A few yards further on they came to a door that could only be entered by bending double. It had no peephole. One of the guards drew back the bolt and stepped aside. The inquisitor walked in, followed by Agnès.

'Your chamber, Madame,' he announced cheerily, and then in a voice suddenly filled with loving sadness: 'Believe me, my child, there is nothing quite like peace and quiet for putting one's thoughts in order. I hope that you will have time in here to reflect, to see the error of your ways. My overriding desire is to help you return to the Lord's fold. I would give my life in return for saving your lost soul.'

The door slammed, the bolt grated. She was standing alone in total darkness. She began to walk tentatively, sliding one foot after the other. As soon as her leg touched the primitive bed she had been able to make out in the gloom, she collapsed on it in a heap.

She was gripped by a sudden panic, and it was all she could do to stop herself from screaming and hurling herself against the door, pummelling it with all her might, begging them to come back for her.

And what if they left her there to rot, dying of hunger and thirst? What if they waited until she went mad and then declared her possessed?

That man, that wretched soul who had grasped her ankle and implored her to die quickly. He knew. He knew that years of detention awaiting trial could turn into a lifetime on the pretext of further inquiries. He knew about privation, humiliation, weeks of torture. He had learned to live with the fear and certainty that few ever escaped the Inquisition's clutches.

Silence! He wants you to give up and let go of life. I order you to stand firm! Baronne de Larnay, Madame Clémence would not have given in. Stand firm!

If you plead guilty, you will languish here until death comes to claim you, and Mathilde and Clément will be doomed. They will endeavour to declare you a relapsed heretic – the most heinous of crimes in their eyes.

14

Remember, you will be shown no mercy, he will not be moved to pity. Stand firm!

Even as she admonished herself, she was struck by the terrible certainty that Florin was enjoying himself. However absurd the idea might seem, Florin was not driven by material gain, still less by faith. He took pleasure in torturing. He enjoyed causing suffering, lacerating and disembowelling. He rejoiced in making his victims scream. She was his latest toy.

An acid saliva rose in her mouth and she bent double as she cried out.

Clémence . . . Clémence, my angel, bless me with a miracle. Show that you deserve the miracle by standing firm!

Château d'Authon-du-Perche, September 1304

JOSEPH, Artus d'Authon's old Jewish physician, masked his contentment. He felt flattered that young Clément possessed such a rare ability to learn and could express his awe so openly to him.

And yet it had taken all of the child's powers of persuasion and the Comte's insistence to convince him to take the boy on as an apprentice. The mere idea of having to explain, repeat, din the beauty of science into the young boy's head exhausted him.

Joseph had soon been surprised by how much Clément already knew. He had even lost his temper with the boy, ordering him to be silent when he mentioned certain medical facts known only to a small number of scholars – facts which, if openly talked about, ran the risk of provoking religious reprisals.

'But why lie when one possesses true knowledge that could prevent suffering and death?'

'Because knowledge is power, my child, and those who control knowledge have no wish to share power.'

'And will they always control it?'

'No, because knowledge is like water: you may try to cup it in your hands but it will always slip through your fingers.'

As the weeks went by, Joseph had allowed himself to

16

become enchanted by the boy's keen intelligence, and perhaps also by the desire, by the hope, of being able to pass on the vast knowledge he was afraid would die with him.

Why had he left the prestigious university at Bologna? He was honest enough to admit that he had been motivated by foolish arrogance. The works of the great Greek, Jewish and Arab doctors of medicine had been translated in Salerno and Bologna. However, despite the wealth of knowledge generated by these previously unheard-of works, the West had persisted in using practices that owed more to superstition than to science. Joseph had gradually convinced himself that he would be the harbinger of this medical revolution. He was mistaken. He had settled in Paris in 1289 in the belief that his wish to propagate his art for the common good would protect him from the anti-Semitism that was rife in France. Again he was mistaken. A year later, the situation grew worse after the case of Jonathas the Jew,[4] who was accused of spitting on the Host, even though so-called witnesses were unable to describe the exact circumstances in which the supposed sacrilege had taken place. Jews were once again portrayed as enemies of the faith in the same way as the Cathars. Besides the everyday humiliations and official discriminatory measures, they lived in fear of being stoned by a hostile mob that would readily tear them apart with impunity. Abandoning his possessions, like so many others, he had chosen the route to exile. He considered going to Provence, which was known for its tolerance, and where many of his people already enjoyed a peace they mistakenly believed would be lasting. But

Joseph's age had caught up with him and his journey had ended in Perche. He had set down his meagre baggage in a small town not far from Authon-du-Perche, and had tried to remain inconspicuous. He had occasionally treated people, though without employing his full knowledge for fear of arousing suspicion, and yet was so much more successful than the local apothecaries and doctors that news of his reputation soon reached the château. Artus had summoned him and Joseph, not without trepidation, had obeyed. The tall, withdrawn, broken man had stood before him and studied him in silence for a few moments before declaring:

'My only son died a few months ago. I wish to know whether you could have saved him, esteemed doctor.'

'I cannot say, my lord. For, although I am aware of your terrible loss, I do not know the symptoms of his illness.' The tears had welled up in the old physician's eyes and he had shaken his head and murmured: 'Ah, the little children. It is not right when they die before us.'

'And yet, like his mother, he had a frail constitution and often became ill and feverish. His skin was deathly pale and he bled profusely even from the smallest scratch. He complained of tiredness, headaches and mysterious pains in his bones.'

'Did he feel the cold?'

'Yes. To such an extent that his room had to be heated in summer.'

Artus had paused before continuing:

'Why did you, a Jew, choose to practise in this part of the world?'

Joseph had simply shaken his head. Artus had gone on:

'To be a Jew at this time in the kingdom of France is a frightening thing.'

'It has long been the case and in many kingdoms,' the physician had corrected, smiling weakly.

'Together with the Arabs you are reputedly the best doctors in the world. Is such a reputation justified?'

'Our patients must be the judges of that.'

For the first time in many months, Artus, whose grief had been unrelenting since Gauzelin's death, allowed himself a witty rejoinder:

'If they are able to judge, it is because you have cured them, which is more than can be said for the majority of our physicians.' He had taken a deep breath before asking in a faltering voice the question that had been plaguing him all along: 'He, my physician, was fond of bloodletting. It worried me and yet he swore by its effectiveness.'

'Oh, how fond they are of bloodletting! In your son's case it was pointless, I fear, though, judging from your description of his symptoms, the little boy would have died anyway.'

'What was he suffering from in your opinion?'

'A disease of the blood mostly found in very young children or those over sixty. It is quite possible that the same sickness in a less severe form also took your wife. The condition is incurable.'

Strangely, Joseph's diagnosis had eased the Comte's terrible suffering. Gauzelin's death had not been due to his physicians' – and consequently his own – shortcomings, but to a twist of fate that they had been powerless to prevent.

Joseph had subsequently found sanctuary at the château.

The Comte granted him full use of the library and the freedom to come and go as he pleased and this, together with the Comte's influence, made him feel secure. Gratitude had gradually given way to respect, for Artus d'Authon was a man of his word and, one day, in the course of conversation he had said to Joseph:

'Should your people's plight worsen – as I fear it may – then I strongly advise you, for appearance's sake, to convert. My chaplain will attend to it. Should the idea prove abhorrent to you, Charles II d'Anjou, King Philip's* cousin, whilst complying in Anjou with the monarch's severe treatment of the Jews, is far more tolerant in his earldom of Provence and his kingdom of Naples. Charles is a cautious but shrewd man and the Jews bring him wealth. Naples seems far enough away to offer more safety. I would help you travel there.'

Joseph could tell by the solemn look in the eyes gazing intently at him that, come what may, he could trust this man's word.

The Comte enjoyed such robust health as to make him the despair of any doctor wishing to practise his art. And so Joseph treated the minor ailments of the Comte's household or the more serious illnesses afflicting the serfs, which were mostly caused by deprivation or lack of hygiene. The old physician had long given up trying to fathom the contradictions in man and had reached the conclusion that it was a futile search. His patients showed their gratitude by bringing him small gifts and bowing as they passed him on the street. They took him for an

Italian scholar or powerful sage, called upon by their master to look after their health. Children would run along behind him, taking hold of his robe as though it were a lucky charm. Women would stop him, shyly informing him in hushed tones of a recovery or a pregnancy, and slip him a basket of eggs, a bottle of cider or a milk roll sweetened with honey. Men would bare an arm or a leg to show him that a skin ulcer he had treated had disappeared. Joseph chose not to scrutinise their smiles, their awkward speech, their faces, to avoid identifying those who would have denounced him to the secular authorities had they known he was a Jew.

He walked over to the large lectern where Clément, his mouth gaping in astonishment, was in the process of devouring a Latin translation.

'What is it you are reading that so surprises you?'

'The treatise on fraudulent pharmaceutical practices, master.'

'Oh yes, the one by Al-Chayzarî that dates back two centuries.'

'It says here that in order to increase their earnings pharmacists were in the habit of cutting Egyptian opium with *Chelidonium* or wild lettuce sap or even gum arabic to make it go further. The deception can be detected by mixing the powdered form with water. *Chelidonium* gives off a smell of saffron, lettuce a slightly sickly odour and gum arabic makes the liquid taste bitter.'

'Fraudulent practice has existed since time immemorial, and I suspect it always will – there is much money to be made from being dishonest. A good physician, or pharmacist, should know how to detect it in order to be sure of the effectiveness of the medicine he prescribes to his patients.'

Clément looked up and, unable to contain himself any longer, asked him the question he had been burning to put to him since their first meeting:

'Master . . . Your knowledge is so vast and so varied . . . Have you ever heard of a scholar by the name of Vallombroso?'

Joseph knitted his bushy grey eyebrows and replied:

'Vallombroso is not a man but a monastery in Italy. I am told they have carried out some astonishing mathematical and astronomical studies there, and that the friars are excellent at medicine.'

'Oh . . .'

Disappointment was written all over the child's face. Now he would never be able to understand the scribbled notes in the big red journal.

'Why do you ask?'

'I . . .' Clément stammered.

'Is it as bad as all that?' Joseph coaxed him gently.

'I read somewhere that . . . but please do not imagine for a moment that I give any credence to such nonsense, I read that Vallombroso was the name quoted in a theory according to which the Earth is not fixed in the heavens . . .'

The colour drained from the physician's face and he ordered sharply:

'Be quiet! No one must ever hear you speak of such things.'

Joseph glanced around nervously. The large, bright room, freezing cold in winter, which they were using as a study, was empty.

He moved closer to the child and bent down to whisper in his ear:

'The time is not yet ripe. Mankind is not ready to hear and accept the truth . . . The Earth is not fixed. It spins on its own axis – thus explaining the existence of day and night – and moreover it rotates around the sun, always following the same course, which is what produces the seasons.'

Clément was stunned by the perfect logic of it.

'Do you understand, Clément, that this is a secret? If anyone were to find out that we share this knowledge, it could cost us our lives.'

The child nodded his agreement then spoke in a hushed voice:

'But does this mean that the astrologers are all mistaken?'

'All of them are. What is more, it seems logical to assume that other planets exist which we do not yet know about. And this is why you should not put your faith in astrological medicine's current teachings.' Joseph paused briefly before continuing: 'It is now my turn to ask you to let me into a secret . . . young woman.'

Clément's cry of astonishment rang out in the soundless room.

'For you are indeed a girl, are you not?' Joseph continued in a whisper.

Clément, still speechless, was only able to nod.

'And you will soon be eleven . . . Has anybody ever explained to you the . . . physiological peculiarity characterising the fair sex?'

'I don't know. I know I'll never grow a beard and that there exists a fundamental physical difference between boys and girls,' the child ventured.

'I thought as much. Well now, let us start with that – cosmogony can wait!'

Clément's shock quickly gave way to panic, and in an almost inaudible voice he tearfully implored:

'No one must know about it, master. No one.'

'I realise that. Do not fear. We are joined together by dangerous secrets now, as well as by our thirst for knowledge.'

They turned as one towards the door as it creaked open. Ronan ventured a few steps into the room before offering an apology:

'I trust I have not interrupted you in mid-experiment, revered doctor.'

'No, indeed. We had just finished a demonstration.'

'My Lord Artus has asked to see young Clément.'

'Well, run along, my boy. The Comte wishes to see you. You mustn't keep him waiting.'

'Thank you, master.'

'Come straight back whenever it pleases His Lordship. We have not finished for today.'

'Very good, master.'

The Comte was working in his beloved rotunda. When Clément came in, he looked up from his ledgers and nodded gratefully to Ronan.

'Zounds! What a thankless task is that of a paymaster. It puts me in a most foul mood,' he muttered. 'And yet I should be 'overjoyed and grateful that we have avoided disaster. The harvests were good and the calving season more encouraging than last year.'

As he finished writing a sentence, Clément could not help noticing the elegance of his cursive script.[5] It was then that he recalled the bold handwriting in the notebook – the *rotunda* lettering reserved for scientific, legal or theological treatises; in brief, for scholarly works in Latin. If, as he had always suspected, it was the knight Rioux's script, could this mean he had been a theologian in the Hospitaller order? And if he had been, how would that knowledge further Clément in his investigation? He did not know, but he felt instinctively that it was important.

The Comte replaced his quill in the beautiful silver inkwell shaped like a ship's hull that was sitting in front of him. His face, already pensive, became tense, and the child was filled with apprehension. Why this hesitation? What news was he holding back? The Comte spoke in a faltering voice which he tried unsuccessfully to control:

'Madame de Souarcy has arrived at the Inquisition headquarters at Alençon where she is being held in *murus strictus*.'

Clément leaned against a bookshelf, trying to catch his breath. His whole body seemed to tremble. A firm hand grasped his tunic just as he felt his legs give way under him. The next thing he knew he was sitting in one of the small armchairs dotted around the circular room.

'Forgive me, my lord,' he stammered as he regained consciousness.

25

'No. It is I who should apologise. I fear that keeping the company of men and farmers has left me wanting in manners and consideration. Stay seated,' he insisted as Clément tried to stand up. 'You are still young, my boy . . . And yet you must be aware that some people are obliged to leave behind childish things sooner than others. I must ask you as a matter of urgency to search your memory. You told me how that rascal Eudes de Larnay and his loyal servant plotted to have Agnès arrested by the Inquisition. It would appear that she unwittingly gave refuge to a heretic, a certain . . .'

'Sybille.'

'Yes.'

Clément bit his lip before blurting out:

'She was my mother.'

The Comte looked at him and murmured:

'Now I understand why Madame Agnès was so keen to send you away from her entourage.'

A curious tenderness welled up in Artus, who for days had been gripped by fear. He had known men, soldiers, who would willingly have denounced a child to the Inquisition in order to spare themselves the threat of a trial. And yet she, a helpless woman, or so she thought, had stood up to them. She must know of the conflict that raged in the minds of certain friars. Torn between their carnal desire and their vow of chastity, they feared or loathed women and their seductive powers, and absolved themselves of the temptation they felt in their presence by holding the devil responsible. However, having met Florin, Artus did not believe he was the sort to be troubled too much by self-denial. Yet, indeed, this loathing of women, this need to exercise a destructive power over them, was itself a form of carnal desire.

The Comte felt sickened and angry by turns. Ever since he had first seen Agnès dressed in peasant's breeches calming the bees as she harvested honey, he had dreamed in the early mornings of that long pale neck, of breathing its scent, of brushing its flesh with his still-slumbering lips. He dreamed of her long, fine hands holding the reins gently but firmly, like a true rider. He dreamed of them holding his belly and his loins. The image had become so vivid, so inappropriate, that he would banish it from his thoughts, knowing that it would creep back the moment he lowered his guard.

'In the letter you brought with you, Madame de Souarcy suggested a hidden influence far greater than that of her scheming half-brother.'

'Indeed, my lord. We came to that conclusion. Eudes de Larnay could pay the inquisitor but not guarantee him any influential backing. His power extends no further than his tiny estate and is far less than your own. It stands to reason that someone intervened to reinforce Florin's position.'

Artus walked over to one of the windows with their tiny asymmetrical leaded panes, unusual for the time. Hands clasped behind his back, he stood gazing out at the gardens ablaze with the russet browns and ochres of autumn. In the distance, a pair of swans floated on the pond, so perfectly elegant in their watery element and yet so ungainly on land. One day he would walk there with her, holding her arm. He would introduce her to the capricious swans, the proud peacocks and the albino deer who would peer at them shyly with their big brown eyes as they approached. One day he would recite to her: 'I love to walk among this fragrance and behold the marvel of these flowers,'[6] and she would reply, imbuing the words of Monsieur Chrétien de Troyes* with all the strength of her feeling: 'I was testing your love. Be sad no more, for I love you even more as I know you love me from the very depths of your heart.'[7] One day. Soon.

Defeat Florin. Kill him if necessary.

He found himself speaking to the child as though he were a man of his own age:

'And yet Florin must be aware of my childhood association and friendship with the King of France. His impudence, his . . . immunity must come from Rome. Remember, though, that the Pope is dead and we do not know who his successor will be. It comes as no surprise, then, that it is not a pontiff, but somebody who wields great influence in the Vatican. The late Benoît* was a merciful man, a reformer. He might have advocated compassion and clemency in our case. They gave him no time. His reign lasted but eight months . . . I am convinced that its brevity was intentional. And . . . I sense that his enemies are also ours.'

'But who?' Clément asked.

'We will find out, my boy, I promise you. Go now.'

Templar commandery at Arville, Perche-Gouet, October 1304

THE Templar commandery at Arville was situated in the middle of what had once been the land of the Carnutes on the pilgrim's way to Santiago de Compostela, and was one of the first of its kind to be established, thanks to the generous donation of almost two and a half acres of woodland by Geoffroy III, a noble from Mondoubleau. A small band of knights, together with a few equerries and lay brethren[8] – mostly shepherds and herdsmen – had settled there from 1130 onwards.

The commandery served a triple purpose: as a farm estate that provided meat, grain, wood and horses for the crusaders in the Holy Land; as a recruitment centre and training camp for the Templars waiting to leave for the crusades; and finally it re-established the religious life that had vanished from the once-thriving Gallic community formed by the three towns of Arville, Saint-Agil and Oigny after it had been razed by the invading Romans.

Further donations by the Vicomtes de Châteaudun, the Comtes de Chartres, de Blois, and even the Comtes de Nevers, of woodland and arable land, as well as the right to harvest timber, bake their own bread and trade, had transformed the commandery into one of the richest in the kingdom of France.

Notwithstanding past generosity, the lords of Mondoubleau – the Vicomtes de Châteaudun – had begun to resent the Templars' increasing wealth, and in 1205 their growing concern threatened to undermine the order's state of grace. The dispute worsened to the extent that in 1216 Pope Honorius III excommunicated Comte Geoffroy IV, who was intending to prohibit the Templars at Arville from driving their convoys outside the Mondoubleau estate, from owning a bread oven, from selling their merchandise at the marketplace and from harvesting bracken for animal fodder. Geoffroy IV had finally yielded to papal authority, but not before leading a small uprising.

The knights' activities had soon attracted an extended population as, in exchange for a nominal rent and a few services, they offered bread and dwellings with a smallholding.[9] In the year of 1304 seven hundred souls lived outside the commandery's stout ramparts.

The sun was high up in the sky when Francesco de Leone emerged from Mondoubleau Forest, which was adjacent to Montmirail Forest. The old mare he had hired at Ferté-Bernard moved along at a sluggish pace. The poor animal had already walked so far carrying his weight that he hadn't the heart to goad it on to arrive more quickly. His growing stomach pangs were a reminder that he hadn't eaten since the previous morning when he had finished the bag of provisions his aunt, Éleusie de Beaufort, had handed him just before he slipped away unseen from Clairets Abbey. Leone would never have allowed himself to describe what he felt as 'hunger', out of respect for the ravages of true hunger. He knew he would be offered food upon reaching his destination. This was the one Christian act no monk-soldier could disregard, despite the difficult, not to say hostile, relations between the Knights Hospitaller and Templar.*

Of course Leone could not ask the Templars to help him in the quest that had driven him for so long, a quest brought to him from the underground tunnels at Acre moments before the bloody defeat that heralded the end of Christendom in the Orient. Before joining the slaughter raging above their heads, a Knight Templar, sensing his imminent demise, had entrusted Leone's godfather, Eustache de Rioux, with a journal containing a lifetime of research, questions and unsolvable mysteries. He had spoken of a papyrus scroll written in Aramaic – one of the most sacred texts in all civilisation – and indicated that it was safely hidden at one of the Templar commanderies.

Under no circumstances must the commander at Arville suspect Leone's true motives. As for any hospitality he might receive, Leone was certain that it would be minimal and circumspect. Before his journey had even begun, Leone predicted that it would end in failure. Vain hope was not enough to explain his determination to carry on regardless. He wanted to breathe in the atmosphere of the place, and was convinced that once inside the church he would feel the presence of the secret, the key, that was hidden there – perhaps the papyrus.

He walked up the pebble path leading to the towering ramparts encircling the various buildings. The drawbridge was down over the surrounding moat, fed by the nearby river

Coëtron. To the left stood the stables – reportedly large enough to house fifty or more horses, destined to be transported to the Holy Land on special vessels, which they would board via a drop-down door in the transom. Beyond the stables lay the kitchen and physic garden that supplied the Templar community with a few of its vegetables and most of its medicaments. To the right of the gateway, squeezed between the church and the utilitarian buildings, a smallish dwelling with tiny arrow-slit windows was most likely the preceptor's[10] abode. A little further on stood the church's circular watchtower, built of dark chalkstone – a mixture of flint, quartz, clay and iron ore. This Temple of Our Lady, whose name invoked the Templars' cult of the Virgin, had been set apart from the ramparts, allowing the villagers to attend services without entering the commandery, thus respecting the Templar monks' cloister. In turn, another, smaller door permitted the monks to enter without ever leaving the enclosure. The two-tiered bell tower was supported by a pointed arch with its three rounded arches symbolising the Trinity. At the centre of the enclosure was the tithe barn, where a tenth of all the local harvests collected as taxes were stored. Behind the barn another stout watchtower stood guard over this amassed wealth. Close by, the bread oven – the focus of so much acrimony – defied the Vicomtes de Châteaudun with its presence.

Leone approached what he took to be the commander's dwelling.

His black surcoat with its eight-pronged white Maltese cross did not go unnoticed. A young equerry glanced up at him and the colour drained from his face. He looked around frantically as though searching for help from some quarter, and Leone half expected him to flee. He smiled sadly: how often they had fought side by side, come to one another's aid, laid down their lives for each other without a thought for which colour cross the other wore. Templars and Hospitallers had died together by the thousands, their mingled blood seeping into the soil of foreign lands. Why in times of peace did they forget their brotherhood during those bloody conflicts?

He called out to the young boy:

'Pray, take me to your commander, Archambaud d'Arville.'

'My lord . . . ?' the young man stammered.

Sensitive to the boy's discomfort, Leone added:

'Tell him that Francesco de Leone, Knight of Grace and Justice of the Order of Saint John of Jerusalem, is here. Hurry. My mount and I are both weary.'

The equerry ran off and Francesco dismounted. Nearly half an hour passed, during which time Leone began to doubt whether the preceptor would in fact receive him. Of course he must. To send him away would be a very unwise move on his part in view of the delicacy of the current political situation.

The man who walked through the gateway had an imposing physique, emphasised by a white mantle adorned with a red cross with four arms of equal length, and a long tunic reaching down to the floor. A sword hanging from a wide leather belt swung against his calf. It was difficult to guess the age of the furrowed face, framed by a thick mane of hair and a grizzled beard; forty, forty-five, older perhaps. The commander smiled politely and Leone thought he saw the man's eyes light up as he made his introductions. Indeed, he enquired:

'Are you the Francesco de Leone who was expected to become one of the pillars of the Italian-speaking world in your order?'

Leone was not overly surprised by a commander knowing of the Hospitallers' internal affairs; both military orders contrived as discreetly as possible to find out what they could about the other. But that he should acknowledge it so openly was perplexing.

'It was an honour and a responsibility of which I considered myself unworthy at the time, and which I consequently declined.'

'Proving that, in addition to your reputation for piety and bravery, you are a wise man. To what do we owe the pleasure of this visit, brother?'

Leone had decided to offer a simple excuse in order not to arouse any suspicion. Since he was unable to request a bed for the night at a Templar commandery he had no other choice but to content himself with a brief visit.

'To the need for prayer, a halt for my weary horse and a rumbling stomach, I confess. I am on my way to Céton and do not expect to be there before nightfall,' he lied.

Leone had no way of telling whether Archambaud d'Arville believed him. Nevertheless, he replied:

'You are a welcome guest. One of our people will attend to your mount. As for you and I, we shall begin by sharing a meal.'

'I must leave soon after none* if I am to find lodgings at Céton. I shall visit the abbey there tomorrow morning.'

'Your visit will be a brief one, then, I fear,' announced the other man in a voice that sounded too cheerful to be true. 'But please follow me – I am failing in all my duties.'

Leone walked with him towards the building to the right of the main gateway. So it was the preceptor's dwelling.

Two equerries were seated at the table in the main hall. They bent over their bowls of soup and busily finished the remainder of their meal, clearly keen to leave the room at the first opportunity.

The Templars' table, though far from lavish, was reputedly less frugal than that of the Hospitallers. For the Templars, unlike the Hospitallers, had always been a military order, and since soldiers must be well nourished if they are to fight like lions, the practice of fasting among its members had always been restricted.

A lay brother soon arrived and placed a goblet of hippocras in front of Leone and a thick slice of poor men's bread[11] made of wheat, rye and coarsely sifted barley in front of Archambaud d'Arville. After tracing a cross on the piece of brown bread with the tip of his knife, the commander sliced it in two and gave half to the Knight Hospitaller. They both thanked God for this blessing.

The lay brother then served a slice of spinach-and-bacon pie on each of these trenchers, followed by ox tongue roasted in verjuice.

The faint feeling of bewilderment the knight had been experiencing since he arrived was gradually turning into one of unease. There was something unnatural about the lack of interest Arville showed in his reasons for being there and in his journey in general. Under normal circumstances he would have attempted to glean as much information as possible, knowing that Leone was a prominent figure in the Hospitaller hierarchy.

Their meal took place in awkward silence, punctuated by an occasional comment on the dishes they were eating, or on that year's harvest or the unlikelihood of there being a new crusade.

Arville agreed with Leone's reservations regarding the matter, adding:

'We cannot feed more than fifty animals and are obliged to sell our horses at the market.'

Leone found this idle chitchat disturbing. Something else lurked behind the smug façade of civility. And yet it was unthinkable that the commander knew anything about the reason for his visit, still less about his quest. Had the other man sensed his unease? Whatever the case, his manner changed abruptly to one of forced joviality, adding to Leone's suspicions about his host of a few hours. Archambaud d'Arville began to describe in great detail his own calamitous arrival at Perche-Gouet four years before: his departure from Italy – a country dear to his heart – the neglectful state in which he had found the commandery when he arrived. Indeed, he had been obliged to mete out cautions and minor punishments, alternating bread-and-water penances with two-day fasts – the worst offenders being made to eat their meals on the floor. In this way, the commander explained, he managed to call to order certain monks guilty of committing venial but routine sins. He guffawed as he recalled one greedy Templar sergeant who would sneak out at night and raid the honey, plunging his hands into the barrels. They had discovered him asleep one morning after gorging himself, his body covered in ants. It had taken four days for the swellings from the bites to go down. Another, whose fondness was for the demon drink, would be so inebriated before the first service of the day he had to prop himself up against a pillar in the Temple of Our Lady, and hiccupped after each word as he intoned, '*Salve, Regina, Mater misericordiae; vita, dulcedo et spes nostra.*'[12] Then there were those who had a tendency to ignore their duties, preferring instead to play court tennis in the spacious loft above the stables that had been converted into an area devoted to leisure. Leone smiled politely as he tried to glimpse the reason behind the preceptor's garrulousness. Something was not right; despite the cool weather the other man was perspiring and had already poured himself a third cup of hippocras.

It was getting late. Leone stopped speculating and politely interrupted Archambaud d'Arville's futile but relentless anecdotes:

'Despite the pleasure it gives me to remain in your company, brother, I must soon take my leave. I have a long journey ahead of me and would like to pray before setting off again.'

'By all means, by all means . . .'

And yet, Archambaud's displeasure was palpable. Was Leone nearing his goal or merely being misled by false impressions?

He thought he saw a sudden look of real grief darken the commander's forced cheer as he proposed:

'I cannot allow you to leave without tasting our cider. It is legendary throughout the region.'

Leone accepted with good grace.

Shortly afterwards, they left the tiny building for the temple.

They entered through the pointed archway, reinforced by four salient buttresses. The church had been inspired by the austerity of Cistercian buildings and consisted of a nave made up of four spans, ending in a semicircular apse. Light flooded in through the high round-arched windows. There was only an altar, no benches even. And yet as Leone walked between its pillars he knew that he had arrived. He felt a strange and wonderful light-headedness, and let out a sigh of relief. The commander apparently misconstrued the gesture and held on to his arm to steady him.

'You are weak from exhaustion, brother.'

'Indeed,' he lied. 'Might your generosity extend to granting me one last favour? I would like to spend a few moments alone before thanking you one last time and continuing my journey.'

The Templar walked out into the afternoon sunlight shrugging his shoulders and said:

'I shall go and see to it that your mount is ready. Meet me in front of the stables.'

A sea. A warm, tranquil sea. A cradle of light, welcoming, calming. He had waited so long to run his hand over those vast black and brown stones that he was almost afraid to touch them now. He would not begin searching or lose himself in pointless speculation. Not today. The time had not yet arrived. He was tempted by a sudden feeling of sluggishness to lie down on the broad, dark flagstones and sleep. Today he would allow himself to be bathed, lulled. Today he would reflect upon how privileged he was to be there in the presence of the key. Like Eustache de Rioux before him, Leone was unsure of its exact nature. Could it, as he had sometimes imagined, be a doorway to a labyrinth traced in the stones, visible only from a precise angle? Or was it a manuscript pillaged from some library and brought there by a monk or soldier? Was it the papyrus in Aramaic purchased from a Bedouin in the souks of Jerusalem, as described by the Knight Templar in the tunnels below Acre? Was it a cross or a statue covered with secret symbols? Was it a simple object?

Not today. Archambaud d'Arville would come back to look for him if he tarried. And yet Leone had found what he had been searching for: the certainty that his quest would begin again in that place.

Tomorrow he would think of a way to return and remain there.

As he walked out to join the commander, the light from the sun made him wince. He had an unpleasant hollow feeling in his chest and imagined that the unbearable separation from his quest was once again weakening him.

Archambaud d'Arville was waiting for him in front of the stables. A young lay brother held his mare's reins. Leone sensed from the commander's sudden restlessness that the man was in a hurry to see him leave. He thanked him once again and climbed into the saddle.

Vicinity of the Templar commandery at Arville, Mondoubleau Forest, October 1304

FRANCESCO de Leone was not unduly disturbed by his encounter with the commander, the prospect of which he had found daunting from the outset. Admittedly, the man's strange behaviour had puzzled him, and he had not been taken in for a moment by his garrulous sociability. But then Leone had not expected any generous cooperation from the Templar order and, besides, Archambaud d'Arville could not possibly be aware of the presence of any key – under whatever guise – or he would never have allowed Leone to remain in the Temple of Our Lady alone.

Leone needed to think up a way of gaining free and unlimited access to the commandery in order to achieve his aim of unearthing the secret.

He patted the neck of the hired nag that was carrying him. The animal, unused to such gestures of affection, whinnied and jerked its head nervously.

'Steady, old girl. We are not in any hurry now.'

Could the pretence he'd been obliged to keep up have wearied him to such an extent? He was finding it increasingly difficult to remain upright in the saddle. The horse responded to the slight pressure of his leg and lengthened its stride.

Francesco de Leone was under the impression that he had only just left the commandery enclosure and yet the forest and the night were already beginning to close in on him. He was dripping with sweat and shivering. An unpleasant dryness made his tongue stick to the roof of his mouth and occasional giddy spells caused him to sway in his saddle. Above his head the sky and the treetops turned in circles. He tried to summon up his strength, clutching the reins, and as his body slipped from the saddle he realised that he had been drugged: the fraternal bowl of cider. He wondered whether the drug would kill him or merely render him unconscious and smiled at the thought before collapsing onto the blanket of dead leaves covering the forest floor.

A few dozen yards away, Archambaud d'Arville dismounted. He felt a mixture of disgust and terror. To kill a brother, a man of God who had willingly risked his life to defend their faith, seemed to him an unpardonable sin, and yet he had no choice. The future of the commandery, perhaps even the existence of their order in France, depended on this crime for which he would never be able to forgive himself. The ghoulish figure who had visited him two days before had been unequivocal: Leone must die and his death be made to look like the work of brigands. Arville was unaware of the reasons for this killing, but the missive containing the order to carry it out, which the apparition had handed to him, bore the seal of the halved bulla, which legitimised acts and letters in the interim preceding the election of a new pope. The Templar had already killed, but honourably, as a soldier face to face with his enemy, sometimes taking on five men single-handed. Even as his flesh had been torn and seared, his soul had remained unscathed. To have drugged this formidable swordsman in order to be sure of overpowering him was abhorrent to him, and for the first time in his life he despised himself. He had become a vile executioner, and the knowledge that he was acting on the orders of the papacy did nothing to diminish his guilt.

He drew his dagger and approached his brother's inert body.

Horrifying memories of throngs of men, hideous images of battlegrounds transformed into mass graves came back to him. He heard for the thousandth time the screams of the dying, the ferocious cries of the victors, intoxicated by the smell of blood, crazed by the kill. So many dead. So many dead in the name of eternal love. Would their souls be enriched as a result as they had been led to believe? Was there no other way than slaughter? And yet if he began to doubt now, hell would open at his feet.

The movement behind him was so swift and soundless that he did not notice it. An explosion of pain in his chest. He raised his hand and snagged it on the tip of a short sword. He could feel the metal sliding out of his flesh, only to be plunged in a second time.

He slumped to his knees, vomiting blood. A youthful voice clear as a mountain spring, the voice of a young girl, spoke to him, imploring:

'Forgive me, knight. Forgive me out of the goodness of your heart. It was my duty to save him. His life is so precious, so much more precious than yours or mine. I could not challenge you directly for I was unsure of being any match for you. But I promise you, knight, that I have saved your soul. Grant me forgiveness, I beg of you.'

Archambaud d'Arville had no doubt that the girl was speaking the truth, that she had saved him from the torment of eternal guilt. She had chosen in his place, freeing him from the need to disobey the apparition and the missive from Rome, freeing him from the need to obey.

'I . . . pardon you . . . sister . . . Thank you.'

Esquive d'Estouville remained with the dying man until his last gasp, the tears from her amber eyes dropping onto his surcoat. She knelt down beside him in order to stretch out his body and place his hands upon his bloodstained chest, and gazed at the handsome supine figure. She did not know how long she prayed through her tears for the Templar's soul and for her own.

When she finally rose to her feet, the moon was full. She walked over to Leone's sleeping body and lay down beside him. She embraced him and kissed his brow. She drew her cape over him to protect him from the damp night chill, and spoke in a whisper:

'Sleep, my sweet archangel. Sleep for I am keeping watch. And then I shall vanish once more.'

Esquive d'Estouville closed her eyes, trembling with emotion as she lay next to the big slumbering body that was oblivious to her presence. Was she sinning? Undoubtedly, and yet her sin was a reward for the long years of waiting, for the unbidden, disturbing dreams that she no longer even tried to resist now that they had permeated her waking hours. Ever since she had appeared to him in Cyprus in the guise of a grubby beggar girl capable of deciphering the runic prophecy, her only thoughts were of him. She had devoted her body and soul to

43

their quest but her heart belonged to this man who was near to being an angel. He was ignorant of her feelings, and it was better that way. The mere suggestion of any love that was not motherly, sisterly or born of friendship would have saddened him, for he did not want it and could not return it. But what did it matter? She loved him more than her own life, and this love that she had discovered thanks to him filled her with joy and strength.

Dawn was breaking when Leone came round. His head was gripped by a vicelike pain and his mouth filled with an acid saliva. He managed to sit up. He felt dizzy and tried to suppress a growing sense of panic as his mind drew a complete blank. Where was he? Why was he lying in the middle of the forest in the early morning? He struggled with his hazy recollection of the previous day, forcing himself to retrace his steps. Gradually, faces and words began to emerge from the fog of his thoughts. He had gone to the Templar commandery to meet Archambaud d'Arville, whose garrulousness and false bonhomie had made his head spin. And yet behind all that fraternal cheer Leone had momentarily sensed the man's anguish and despair. The commander had offered him a bowl of cider before he went on his way.

Upon entering the nave of the Temple of Our Lady, Leone had been seized by the wild hope that he would receive a sign proving that the secret he had been pursuing all these years lay within those walls, among those flagstones and pillars. Was the sudden giddiness and the incredible calm he had felt in the temple confirmation of such a sign or simply the first effects of the drug?

Where was his worn-out mare? He rose to his feet, staggering slightly, and looked around. The mare was staring at him a few yards away, tethered to the trunk of a silver birch, refreshed after her night's unencumbered rest. He had collapsed, fallen to the ground. But who had tethered the mare? It was then he noticed the brownish-red patch seeping from beneath a small pile of leaves. He drew his sword from its scabbard as he approached it. He flicked the leaves aside with the blade, already knowing what he would find there. He dropped his sword and fell to his knees beside Archambaud d'Arville's body, then swept away with his hands the flimsy remains of his leafy tomb. Leone was able to deduce what had happened from the two identical stab wounds in the commander's chest, the bloodstains on his white mantle and the compassion and respect with which the killer had treated the corpse. The Knight Templar had trailed him with the clear intention of killing him as soon as the drug had taken effect. But why? Somebody had been there and had shown no compunction in killing a Templar commander in order to defend Leone's life – a protector, then, rather than a rascal or evil brigand. But who and why? Had his champion then fled on the commander's mount? Leone had a vague recollection, but the image escaped him. He tried in vain to summon it back, slowly stroking his finger across his brow.

He was stirred by the thought of the torment this man of God, this warrior, must have endured: to poison a brother and then like an abject executioner to slay him. Who had the authority to compel a Templar commander to perpetrate such villainy?

Assuming Arville's orders had come from his Grand-Master or his chapter, they would still have required the Pope's approval. But the Pope was dead, and Benoît would never have endorsed such a dishonourable act: Leone had known, respected and loved him well enough to stake his life on it.

In the absence of a pope, who possessed sufficient authority to arrange the murder of a Knight Hospitaller? The answer was so glaringly obvious that it struck him with the full force of its monstrosity.

Louvre Palace, Paris, October 1304

THE King's counsellor and confidant Guillaume de Nogaret's* initial surprise at Francesco Capella's absence had turned to concern and then quickly to anger. What had become of this young man in whom he had begun to place his trust? The day after his new secretary's unexplained disappearance, Nogaret had dispatched a messenger to his uncle, Giotto Capella, carrying a missive whose unequivocal content bristled with threats. Had a sudden illness confined Francesco to his bed? To Nogaret's mind there could be no other acceptable explanation for his absence, and he would hate to have to hold Giotto Capella responsible for misleading him by extolling the virtues of a nephew whose behaviour had turned out to be so rude and unreliable.

The letter had thrown Giotto Capella into a panic, and his first impulse had been to leave France without further ado. Then he had taken to his bed, curling up under a pile of counterpanes as he envisaged his life hanging by a thread were the King's counsellor ever to discover his role in this deception. He had spent hours snivelling and trembling as he sweated under the heavy coverlets, justifying his actions with any excuse he could find. What else could he have done faced with Francesco de Leone's blackmail threat? Leone and the other Knights

Hospitaller knew that he was responsible for the Mamelukes breaking through the last defences of the Saint-Jean-d'Acre stronghold. What other choice did he have but to obey Leone by passing him off as his nephew and providing him with the false identity he needed in order for Seigneur de Nogaret to engage him? Naturally, the moneylender had suspected that the knight's intention was to spy on the King's counsellor. But what good would it have done to admit it? None at all. At least not as far as he was concerned. Weary of his own despair, Capella had decided to crawl out of bed and compose a blustering reply. In it he related his nephew's sudden interest in a young lady and his equally unexpected departure from Paris in order to follow her to Italy. He portrayed himself as the despairing uncle, fearful of having offended Monsieur de Nogaret, and ended with a bitter diatribe against the recklessness of youth. Monsieur de Nogaret had been unconvinced, regarding his reply as no more than a feeble excuse.

The King's counsellor felt a cold rage welling up inside him as he put down the page of spidery scrawl. In fact, he could not forgive himself for having allowed a fellow feeling to develop between him and this Francesco Capella, for having deemed him intelligent and possibly divulged too many secrets. He had reflected long and hard on the information he had shared with him and felt reassured when he recalled nothing of any importance. Nevertheless, he would give that weasel Giotto cause to regret recommending his relative. Nogaret would see to it personally that the scoundrel never obtained the post of Captain General of the Lombards of France that he had so long coveted.

That morning Guillaume de Nogaret was still in a bad mood: he had lost a diligent secretary as well as an agreeable companion. He immersed himself in his accounts. His thin lips became twisted in a grimace of displeasure as he drew up the inventory of the King's brother's most recent expenditure of treasury money. How could he put a stop to Charles de Valois's* extravagance without angering the monarch? Valois dreamed of war, of reconquering lost territories; in brief, of raising and commanding armies. Francesco Capella was right to have expressed concern. Just as he was recalling his vanished secretary, he heard a loud bark coming from the royal quarters. One of Philip's lurchers. Nogaret swung round to face the tapestry on the wall behind him and the red stitching of the dogs' mouths on the blue background. He rose to his feet and lifted the hanging. What if Francesco Capella had been sent to spy on him? But by whom? Certainly not by Giotto Capella. He examined the padlock on the safe built into the wall and could see nothing suspicious. Still, he was assailed by doubt. He seized the key hanging on the chain he kept around his neck at all times, and placed it in the small opening. The lock seemed stiff, though he could have been imagining it. He opened the safe and rifled through its contents. Nothing was missing. But why was the black calfskin notebook on top of the pile of letters? Surely he had written or received these since he had last consulted the notebook. Logically it should have been somewhere underneath or in the middle of the pile. Could he be sure of this? After all, the lock had not been forced. The habit of power had made him more mistrustful. Francesco's sudden departure and his uncle's clumsy explanation had heightened his suspicions. Since he could no longer question the nephew he would force the uncle to talk. Nogaret walked over to the door of his office with the intention of calling an usher, but changed his mind as he clasped his fingers round the handle. Would it not be a mistake in these dark and troubled times to admit to a possible lapse in judgement, a mistake for which he might pay heavily? Enguerran de Marigny, who was already the King's chamberlain, was manoeuvring himself into the monarch's good graces with the help of the King's beloved wife, Queen Jeanne of Navarre, to whom he was both confidante and trusted ally. Nogaret, the fearful, timid worrier, envied his rival's self-assurance. Marigny possessed the ability to converse, argue and theorise with such poignancy or passion that his audience took his every word to be gospel. Guillaume de Nogaret knew he was incapable of matching the man's eloquence and manner. If he admitted to the King that he had been spied upon by a man whom he himself had engaged, Marigny would be sure to use this blunder to undermine his reputation. He might feel avenged by delivering Giotto Capella into the hands of the executioners, but it would only weaken his position at court.

After all, nothing in the safe had gone missing. No doubt he was scaring himself unnecessarily.

And yet how on earth did that notebook come to be on top of a bundle of confidential letters he had only recently placed in the safe?

Nogaret sat down at his desk again and studied the nib of his quill pen. No, the shadowy figure whose services he employed was not resourceful enough to be of any use to him in this matter. The King's counsellor detested that cowled sycophant who had admittedly served him well hitherto. And yet the henchman's palpable loathing, bitterness and thirst for revenge made his blood run cold. Hurting others appeared to relieve his tormented soul. Nogaret was no villain. If he were guilty of scheming or worse, his motivation, and perhaps his justification, was always to serve the greatness of the monarchy.

No. He could not use the cowled figure to dig out the truth about Francesco Capella. As for the usual spies, they were all in the employ of the King and most of them also reported to Marigny for a fee. Any inquiry undertaken by Nogaret was in danger of being brought to the attention of his main rival, who would not hesitate to use it against him at the first opportunity.

For the moment his best course of action was to pretend that nothing had happened.

Nogaret sighed with exasperation. He needed a spy, one not driven by envy or fanaticism, an intelligent spy. His isolation at the Louvre was weakening his position. He had gained the King's respect, possibly even his gratitude, but had failed to win his friendship. Nogaret, who found emotions deeply puzzling, had nonetheless learned something important from observing them: however foolish or misguided, emotions were what dictated people's actions. Intelligence only came into play after the fact, to justify or absolve. He need look no further than the King's own weakness on the subject of his warmongering brother, Monsieur de Valois.

A spy. He must find a clever spy who would answer only to him. How would he go about it, knowing that his enemies were watching his every move?

Clairets Abbey, Perche, October 1304

ÉLEUSIE de Beaufort, the Abbess of Clairets, shivered despite the heat given off by the fire in the hearth in her study. She had been chilled to the bone ever since first setting eyes on that inquisitor Nicolas Florin. The old nightmarish visions had found their way back into her waking thoughts, and assailed her to the point where she feared those moments of semi-consciousness that precede sleep.

If the Abbess had ever entertained any doubts as to the purity of the quest that bound her, her nephew Francesco and the late and good Benoît XI together, the arrival of that evil creature had silenced them for ever. But would the light they were striving to restore to the world be enough to defeat the Nicolas Florins who had darkened the centuries since the dawn of time? Francesco, whom she had brought up as her own son, was convinced that it would. And yet he had so little in common with other mortals; he was so much more like an angel who had come down from another world. And what did angels know of rage, terror and physical suffering?

Her eyes grew misty with tears.

Claire, my dear sister, your son is so like you. And yet he is so otherworldly. We are groping blindly through an endless labyrinth. We turn in circles, searching for the guiding thread.

I am plagued by questions to which I can as yet find no answers. Why did you die at Saint-Jean-d'Acre? Why did you not foresee the massacre and flee? What did you know that I did not?

My nights have become a graveyard where I meet you all, my beloved ghosts: Henri, my sweet love, my husband; Philippine, whose precious blood runs through our veins; Benoît, my dear Benoît; Clémence, Claire, my sisters, my warriors.

And she who is one of us. What does she really know of her true destiny?

I am tormented by anguish, Claire, by the thought that we might be mistaken, that it is all an illusion. What if there is no key, no door?

We are like that game of tarot the Bohemians have recently brought back from Egypt, or China. We play our cards without knowing their real significance. For who can truly claim to know?

I am afraid, Claire, and yet I cannot name my fears. There is a danger emanating from these stout walls, these sombre archways where I believed I would find peace. I sense it in every passageway, on every stair. An evil beast inhabits these places now. No one can see or hear him and few of us are aware of his presence. It would take Clémence's courage or your foresight to defeat him. Or Philippine's triumphant resolve. I am merely a frightened old woman, who has convinced herself she is erudite and therefore knows all there is to know about the human soul. And look at me now, alone, my limbs crippled with pain, plagued by visions I am powerless to comprehend, terrified by the depth of the abyss into which I find myself staring. I shiver with an inner cold that tells me evil is among us. It escorted Florin through these doors. It crept into our midst and has been spying upon us ever since, infiltrating our conversations, even our prayers. It is biding its time. Why, I do not know.

Do you remember the small town in Tuscany our parents took us to when we were young? Do you remember the peasant children brandishing a devil made of brightly coloured cloth and how it petrified me? I screamed and sobbed and refused to move. You rushed over and snatched it from them, and they looked on in anger as you hurled it to the ground and trampled on it. Then you walked towards me smiling and said: you give him strength by believing in him. The devil is generous. He is the scapegoat for all our sins and accepts the blame at no great cost to us.

You were right, dear sister, and I would be excommunicated if anyone were ever to find out what I believe. That there is no devil. That the eternal battle between good and evil exists in man alone. I have met one of evil's willing adepts; I have touched him. He smiled at me and he was beautiful.

I am afraid, dear Claire.

Adélaïde Condeau, the sister in charge of the kitchens and meals at Clairets Abbey, scoured the contents of one of the cabinets in the herbarium, which was crammed with phials, sachets made of jute, earthenware flasks and a host of other receptacles. She almost felt guilty for being there without first asking permission from the Abbess or the apothecary nun, Annelette Beaupré, who treated the herbarium as if it belonged to her. She defended it jealously and at times with surprising vehemence. It was rumoured that Annelette, whose father and grandfather had both been physicians, had never accepted not being allowed in turn to practise their art and had joined the abbey because it was the only community that permitted her to do so. Adélaïde could not swear to the truth of these statements, though they might explain in part the apothecary nun's arrogance and bitterness. Whatever the case, Adélaïde was in need of some sage with which to season the magnificent hares sent by a haberdasher[13] from Nogent-le-Rotrou the previous day, and which she was planning to liven up with a purée made from plums picked after an early frost.

Sage was a common remedy used in the treatment of headaches, stomach pains, paralysis, epilepsy, jaundice, swellings, aching legs, fainting fits and a host of other ailments. The apothecary nun must have stocked up on it during the summer months, especially since this medicinal herb also made a delicious sauce when mixed with white wine, cloves, ginger and black pepper. Adélaïde searched in vain for a large bag embroidered with the words *Salvia officinalis*. She found *Pulicaria dysenterica*, *Salicaria*, *Iris foetida*, nettle, borage and betony, but no sage. Exasperated, she wondered whether the apothecary nun had placed the bag on one of the top shelves. After all, she was as tall and robustly built as any man. The young nun dragged over a stool and clambered onto it. She saw no sign of any sage. Groping with her fingers behind the first row of sachets and phials, she discovered a jute bag that had fallen down the back. She pulled it from its hiding place.

Adélaïde jumped off her perch and emptied the contents of the little bag onto the table used for weighing and making up preparations. The sour-smelling yellow-brown flour had to be rye, but what were those little black flecks? She leaned over to smell it and the pungent odour made her recoil.

'Sister Adélaïde!' a voice rang out behind her.

The young nun almost leapt into the air and clasped her hand to her chest. She turned to face the apothecary nun, whose vast medicinal knowledge was no excuse for her tetchiness, not in Adélaïde's eyes anyway.

'What are you doing here?' the other woman continued in an accusatory tone.

'I just . . . I just . . .'

'You just what, pray?'

The young girl in charge of meals finally managed to stammer out an explanation as to what she was doing in Sister Annelette's jealously guarded sanctuary.

'In short, I was looking for some sage for my sauce.'

'You could have asked me.'

'I know, I know. Only I couldn't find you anywhere so I decided to look for it myself. I even stood on a stool and . . .'

'If you had a modicum of good sense, dear sister,' remarked the other woman disdainfully, 'you would know that I am hardly likely to keep a remedy I use so frequently in such an inaccessible place. Sage is . . .'

Annelette paused in mid-sentence. Her eye had alighted on the mound of flour on the table top. She walked over to it, frowning, and demanded:

'What is this?'

'Well, I confess I don't know,' said Adélaïde. 'I found that bag on the top shelf. It had fallen behind the others.'

Incensed, Annelette sharply corrected the girl:

'My bags and phials do not fall; they are arranged in perfect rows after being weighed and listed in my inventory. You must be aware that some of these preparations are highly toxic and I need to be able to identify their content and usage at a glance.'

It was the apothecary nun's turn now to lean over the small mound of powder. She pushed aside the blackish clusters with the tip of her forefinger. When she raised her head again, her face had turned deathly pale. Her voice betrayed none of its usual arrogance as she stammered:

'D-dear God!'

'What!'

'This is ergot.'

'Ergot?'

'Ergot is a fungus that grows on rye - small kernels form on the ears. Ancient texts claim that it causes gangrene, giving the limbs the blackened and withered aspect of charred skin. The corpses look as though they have been burnt. Some scholars attribute "St Anthony's fire"[14] to it – the violent delirium accompanied by hallucinations[15] we hear so much about, which some fools take to be visitations or possession. This powerful poison is probably responsible for wiping out entire villages.'[16]

'But what do you use it for?' asked the increasingly anxious Adélaïde.

'Have you taken leave of your senses, Sister Adélaïde! Do you really imagine that I would prepare such quantities of a harmful substance like this? Admittedly, I always keep a small sachet of it – for it possesses excellent properties. It relieves headaches,[17] incontinence and haemorrhages[18] in older women. But never as much as this.'

'How should I know . . . Please don't be angry with me,' spluttered the young girl, on the brink of tears.

'Oh, pull yourself together! Spare me your floods of tears. This is a serious matter and I'm in no mood to have to comfort you.'

At this, Adélaïde went running into the garden where she burst out crying.

Annelette's eyes were riveted on the contaminated rye so she scarcely heard the young nun's sobs. Who had prepared this flour and to what end? Who had hidden it in the herbarium and why? In order to incriminate her should it be discovered? More importantly, who but she was well versed enough in poisons to know about ergot's horrific properties?

Should she inform the Abbess? She was in no doubt. Éleusie de Beaufort was one of the few women at the abbey whom Annelette considered truly intelligent and for whom she consequently felt a combination of affection and respect. For this reason she was reluctant to upset her. The past few months had been a trying time for the Abbess, and the inquisitor's arrival appeared to have sapped her usual strength.

First of all she must think. What better place than a medicine cabinet to conceal poison. Moreover, it was conceivable that an intruder had managed to enter the abbey enclosure and slip into the herbarium. On the other hand, the idea of someone returning regularly to fetch the hidden substance was absurd. The poisoner must be attached to the abbey. The chaplain who took the services was an improbable candidate owing to his age, his near-blindness and his increasing tendency to fall asleep. This meant that the poisoner had to be a woman.

During the next half-hour, Annelette went through a mental list of all the sisters. She began by eliminating the lay servants who had been dedicated to God. Not one of them could read or would be capable of preparing a poison whose existence was known only to a handful of scientists. She forced herself to ignore personal likes and dislikes, limiting herself to complete impartiality and objectivity – no small achievement for someone who tended to judge her fellow human beings harshly.

Nonetheless, she immediately struck Éleusie de Beaufort off her mental list. Éleusie was a learned woman but her total lack of interest in the sciences made her a poor candidate. And Éleusie's faith was so exacting that it would not tolerate any imperfection. She ruled out Jeanne d'Amblin on the same grounds, despite the antipathy she felt towards the woman – an antipathy she was honest enough to admit sprang from her envy of the extern sister's freedom from the cloister. She doubted Jeanne even knew ergot existed. As for that sweet but silly girl Adélaïde, whom if anything she found exasperating, she was at a loss in any situation that did not involve plucking a bird, skinning a hare or scalding the bristles off a baby pig. And Blanche de Blinot, the senior member of the abbey who was Éleusie's second in command, as well as the prioress, was so ancient that she looked as though she might crumple up at any moment. Her deafness, a source of occasional mirth to the younger sisters, infuriated Annelette to the point where she avoided talking to her for fear of being obliged to repeat the same sentence five times over. In contrast, the cellarer nun, Berthe de Marchiennes, with her permanent expression of devoutness, was a more than likely suspect. She was educated, the youngest member of a large but impoverished family that had looked upon her – the eleventh child and a female into the bargain – as superfluous. Berthe was one of those women who grow more graceful with age but who when young are extremely plain. Lacking both a dowry and good looks, the monastic life had offered itself as a last resort. Annelette froze. Couldn't this be a description of her own life? The abbey had been the only place where she could exercise her talents. Another face replaced that of the perpetually pained cellarer nun: Yolande de Fleury – the sister in charge of the granary. Who was better placed than she, whose task it was to oversee the sowing of the crops, to have knowledge of crop disease and access to the contaminated rye? By the same token, Adèle de Vigneux, the granary keeper, must be considered a prime suspect. Likewise the treasurer nun, the infirmary nun and the sister in charge of the fishponds and henhouses, and so on . . . And yet, opportunity alone could not explain such a heinous crime as poisoning. The culprit needed a motive, but above all a killer's instinct. Despite the low esteem in which she held her fellow human beings, Annelette was forced to admit that the majority of the other sisters possessed no such instinct.

Night was falling when she left the herbarium, after removing the troublesome flour from the table top. She had whittled her list down to a few names, faces, possibilities. Still, Annelette Beaupré was clever enough to realise that she had very little evidence to back up her suspicions. She had simply used a process of elimination to exclude those she considered unlikely killers.

After she had recovered from her fright and stopped crying, Adélaïde Condeau made what she considered an important decision: she would do without the sage and therefore avoid any further confrontation with that shrew Annelette. How unpleasant she was when she set her mind to it, that overgrown creature! Adélaïde immediately reproached herself for having such uncharitable thoughts. She screwed up her face as she finished the cup of lavender and cinnamon tea sweetened with honey that Blanche de Blinot, the senior nun, had kindly brought her. She had put too much honey in and it tasted sickly, especially taken cold. Her face broke into a smile: Blanche was very old, and it was well known that old people developed a taste for the only sweetness they had left in life.

Rosemary was a perfect herb, and went well with game. Moreover, she had enough of it stored in the kitchens to make another visit to the herbarium unnecessary. Three novices had spent the morning gutting and quartering the hares that now lay in a macabre heap on one of the trestle tables. This was Adélaïde's favourite time of day; vespers* was about to begin and the novices, who, like her, were excused from attending the service in order to prepare supper, were busy laying the table in the great hall under the watchful eye of the refectory nun. A moment of calm descended upon the enormous vaulted kitchen, broken only by the roar of the fire in the great hearth, the occasional patter of a sister's feet hurrying to the scriptorium, the crackle of the stove or the gurgle of pipes.

Adélaïde had been daunted at first by her promotion to head of kitchens and meals; it seemed to be more about accounts and inventories than pots and pans. Sensing her hesitation, the Abbess and Berthe de Marchiennes – the cellarer nun to whom she reported directly – hastened to assure her that her primary duty would continue to be that of providing them with food. For Adélaïde loved to chop, mix, prepare, purée, simmer, braise, thicken and season. She loved preparing food for people, nourishing them. No earthly pleasure could compare in her eyes with trying to invent new recipes for soup or crystallised fruit, as she frequently did. Perhaps the root cause was her precarious start in life; she had been close to starvation when a cooper discovered her at the edge of Condeau Forest.

The long wooden spoon she was holding made a hollow sound as it slipped from her hand and bounced off the tiled floor. The bread. The rye bread she had secretly given the Pope's emissary to nourish him on his journey. She had not ordered any that week from Sylvine Taulier, the sister in charge of the bread oven. So where had the little loaf come from? A sudden giddy spell nearly caused her to lose her balance and she clutched the edge of the table just in time. What was happening to her? She felt as though thousands of pins and needles were pricking her hands and feet, jabbing at her face and mouth. She tried to make a fist with her hand, but her limbs felt numb. Her stomach was on fire and a cold sweat poured from her brow, drenching the collar of her robe. She was finding it difficult to breathe. Still holding on to the edge of the trestle table, she attempted to move towards the door, towards the others. She wanted to cry for help but no sound came out of her mouth.

She felt herself slump to the floor and she put her hand on her chest. She couldn't feel her heart. Was it even beating? She opened her mouth and tried to breathe, but the air refused to flow into her lungs.

Why had she been saved by that man, only to be poisoned a few years later? What sense was there in that?

A last prayer. May death take her quickly. Her prayer would not be granted.

For more than half an hour Adélaïde veered between pain and incomprehension. Fully conscious, the sweat running down her face, she could make out the other sisters flooding into the cavernous kitchen, frightened, shouting, weeping. She saw Hedwige du Thilay cross herself and close her eyes as she held her crucifix up to her lips. She recognised Jeanne d'Amblin's distraught face, and saw her press her hand to her mouth to stifle a cry. She saw Annelette leaning over her to sniff her mouth and smell her breath. She felt Éleusie's soft lips brushing her forehead and her tears dropping onto her hand. Annelette lifted a finger moist with saliva to her mouth and tasted it.

The tall woman rose to her feet, and for the first time the young girl in charge of the kitchens thought that underneath her sister's gruff exterior was an inner warmth. She heard her murmur:

'My poor child.'

The apothecary took the Abbess aside and Adélaïde could no longer hear what they were saying:

'Reverend Mother, our sister has been poisoned with

aconite. She is suffocating to death. Unfortunately, she will remain conscious throughout. There is nothing we can do except to gather round and pray for her.'

Adélaïde Condeau struggled in vain against the creeping paralysis that was slowly immobilising her whole body, up to her cheeks, trapping her voice in her throat. She tried with all her might to utter a single word: bread.

As the nuns knelt around her and she was given absolution, the single, precious syllable echoed in her head: bread.

When she could no longer draw breath, when she opened her mouth wide to suck in the air that was denied to her, she imagined that she had finally managed to utter the word.

Her head flopped to one side, cradled in Éleusie's arms.

Château de Larnay, Perche, October 1304

D RESSED in a sumptuous sapphire-blue robe adorned with a
fur trim and embroidery as fine as that of any princess,
Mathilde de Souarcy strutted up and down in front of the ladies
and gentlemen of her imaginary court, alternately curtseying
and putting on a coquettish air.

As she now considered herself a grown woman, she had
instructed her servant to braid her hair into coils around her
head.

She clucked with delight. How boring it had been stuck inside
that bleak abbey where her mother had thought fit to send her
after the Grand Inquisitor from Alençon had come to inform
her that the time of grace had begun. How tedious to have to get
up so early and go to church, and be forced to help make beds
and fold linen for love of thy neighbour! And yet, there were
plenty of lay servants to relieve well-born girls like her of those
duties. During what she considered a scandalous imprisonment,
which had lasted less than a week, Mathilde's biggest fear had
been that she might end her days amid the dreary, bustling
activity of Clairets. However, she had not counted on the
devotion of her dashing uncle Eudes. God only knows how
relieved she had felt when she learned of his arrival at the abbey.
He had immediately demanded that the Abbess hand over his

niece, and Éleusie de Beaufort had been unable to resist the order for very long. Eudes was Mathilde's uncle by blood and in the absence of her mother became her official guardian. Indeed, owing to her uncle's generosity she had lived like a princess for the past few weeks. The bed chamber he had provided for her had been that of the late Madame Apolline. It was spacious and well heated thanks to the large hearth, which was the height of modernity, possessing as it did two small shutters, one on either side, allowing the heat to circulate more efficiently. On the bare stone walls, brightly coloured hangings depicting ladies taking their bath kept out the damp. She slept every night in the vast bed, and felt a little uneasy when she tried to imagine the activity that must have taken place there – for she could only assume that it was here Madame Apolline had received her husband. What had gone on between those sheets? She had attempted to find out by occasionally probing Adeline or Mabile. The two fools had burst into fits of giggles and told her nothing. A mirror stood on a dainty jewellery dresser with sculpted legs. Her miserable rags had been stored in two large chests flanking the hearth until, one day, her uncle had angrily demanded that they be burnt and his niece dressed in keeping with someone of her status. True, some of the finery he had given her had belonged to her late aunt Apolline. But she did not resent her uncle for having the dresses altered to fit her. What a deplorable waste it would have been to throw them away, especially since poor Apolline, who was naturally ungainly, had done them little justice. Multiple pregnancies had only increased her agonising clumsiness. She had always given the impression of being trussed up in her robes and veils, and would stand like a peasant woman with her hands supporting her back, weakened by so many swollen bellies. In contrast, when worn by Mathilde, the linen and silk fabrics floated like delightful clouds.

An unpleasant thought blighted her good mood. Her mother was now in the hands of the Inquisition, and although Mathilde was unaware of the precise nature of the task of these friars, she knew them to be unforgiving and that anyone unfortunate enough to enter their headquarters was unlikely ever to emerge again. However, they were men of God and the Pope's emissaries. If her mother had incurred their wrath, then it must be seen as punishment for a grave sin she had committed. Indeed, now she came to think of it, Mathilde was indulging her mother by not resenting her even more than she already did, for if Agnès de Souarcy was found guilty, the scandal threatened to taint her by association and thus jeopardise her future.

At least she was free of that good-for-nothing Clément. Mathilde had often felt sickened by her mother's weakness for that common farm hand, son of a lady's maid. How arrogant he had been towards her, though she was the sole heir to the family name! And he was mistaken if he thought she hadn't noticed the expression of pained sympathy on his face when she spoke to him sometimes. The fool! Now she was enjoying her sweet revenge! He had fled the manor like a thief, proving in Mathilde's view that his conscience was not clear. She had gleaned from Adeline that, besides the draught horse his mistress had supplied him with, he had taken only some food and a blanket. He must have left his crossbow, for serfs were not permitted to carry weapons. Yet another of her mother's stupid ideas! A gleeful thought crossed the young girl's mind. The forest was an unsafe place full of two- and four-legged predators. What if the ugly brat had been ripped to shreds?

This happy thought was interrupted by the cautious entrance of the servant Barbe, provided for her by her uncle.

'Well, what do you want?' Mathilde snapped.

'Seigneur Eudes requests the honour of being permitted to visit you in your chamber, Mademoiselle.'

Mathilde's face lit up at the mention of her beloved uncle.

'The honour is mine. Well, don't stand there – go and tell him!'

No sooner had the girl left the room than Mathilde rushed over to the mirror to check her hair and the fall of her dress.

Eudes chuckled as she lifted her arms and twirled around to let him see how his gift showed off her pretty figure to advantage.

'You are a vision of loveliness, dear niece, and your presence here brightens up my household,' he declared, forcing a note of concern into his voice.

The young girl was flattered by the compliment and fell straight into the crude trap he had laid for her.

'And yet you seem so serious, uncle.'

Eudes was delighted to have so easily got her right where he wanted her.

'It concerns your mother, my little princess, whom, as you know, I love as a sister. You see, her impending trial will have unfortunate repercussions for us all. If, as I fear, Madame Agnès is found guilty of heresy, it will bring shame upon us both. I know you are a clever child. You will therefore understand that a verdict such as this would not favour our dealings with the

King of France – not to mention the disgrace that would tarnish the family name for ever. My life is done, but yours is only just beginning, and it would be a terrible injustice if . . .' He ended with a sigh of despair.

Mathilde lowered her head in dismay. So, her uncle was confirming her own fears of the past few weeks. On the verge of tears, she murmured:

'How unfair it would be indeed for us to be associated with my mother's sins. Is there nothing we can do, uncle . . .?'

'I have mulled over the alternatives during the last few nights when I was unable to sleep. It seems to me there is only one sure way . . . but it pains me to tell you what it is.'

'Pray do, dearest uncle, I entreat you. The situation is serious.'

'It is . . . Oh, the suffering I am about to cause you, you whose happiness is closest to my heart . . .'

Mathilde did not doubt his words. Far away from Manoir de Souarcy's cold, gloomy interior, she was at last living the life she had always longed for: fine clothes, a servant to do her hair each morning, twice-weekly baths in milk and water scented with rosemary and violets, greeted like a young lady wherever she went. No! She had been deprived of it for long enough by her mother's stubbornness and she refused to allow what was rightfully hers to be taken away from her! Moreover, she had an equal duty to protect her uncle, her benefactor.

'I implore you . . . Nothing could be more terrible in my eyes than to see you publicly disgraced as a result of my mother's mistakes – especially after you have been so good to her – too good.'

Magnificent! The pretty little fool had fallen straight into his lap!

'You are so good, my radiant princess. What a comfort you are to me in my hour of torment. This painful solution would seem, then, to be the only one left to us. An accusation.'

Mathilde showed no surprise, for she had already thought of it herself. Had not Pope Honorius III advised in one of his encyclicals: 'Let each draw his sword and spare neither his fellow man nor even his closest relative'? She saw nothing wrong in obeying the orders of God's representative on earth.

'As you know, niece, in the eyes of the Inquisition, failure to denounce a heretic is tantamount to complicity . . . It pains me to torment your sweet soul with such a decision.'

'No, uncle. If my mother had not foolishly given refuge to that . . . that traitor Sybille, who was pregnant to boot, then you and I would not be in this situation. And after all . . . perhaps that devilish fiend, that succubus, did sow the seeds of heresy in my mother's soul, condemning her to eternal damnation, which is far more terrible than any trial. I shudder at the thought.'

Inquisition headquarters, Alençon, Perche, November 1304

T HE first few days of the month had been warm and exceptionally wet. The slightest shower of rain would send evil-smelling torrents of mud hurtling through the streets, and yet Nicolas Florin did not yearn for Carcassonne's sunnier climes. He had, as he liked to think of it, 'sown the seeds' of some very lucrative affairs, whose crop he would harvest once Agnès de Souarcy's trial was over. Indeed, he was at any moment expecting a visit from one of his future guarantors of wealth.

Nicolas Florin had given instructions for Agnès de Souarcy to be left alone for a week in her cell in the dungeon underneath the Inquisition headquarters. She was not permitted to wash herself, and her chamber pot was to be cleaned out only every three days. Besides water, her diet would consist of three bowlfuls of milk soup made with root vegetables,[19] and a quarter portion of famine bread, which Agnan, his secretary, had ordered especially from the baker. The man, surprised by such an odd request in a year when harvests were good, had assumed it was part of a penance.

Florin had been a little disappointed for he was sure that she would refuse such lowly nourishment. And yet she had dutifully finished every last crumb. He knew why: Agnès de Souarcy was preparing to hold out for as long as she could. Good . . . It would only make his game more enjoyable. A week. It was a long time to spend alone in the dank gloom with only one's own thoughts for company, thoughts that turn in circles and always end up imagining the worst. Nicolas's plan was a simple one, and had until then proved effective. Keep the accused in wretched isolation, terrify them for a few days, interrogate them and then allow a few visitors to bring them an agonising taste of what they were missing: freedom, their loved ones' faces, the realisation that life outside, however hard, was sweet by comparison. In fact, this strategy was aimed at breaking down the most stubborn resistance in order to obtain a confession and he did not expect a confession from the beautiful Agnès, who was guilty of nothing more than refusing to yield to her half-brother's lust. However, these bullying tactics would give the affair the appearance of an authentic trial, and he had spent hours relishing the thought of his victim's face already twisted with fear.

He gave a sigh of contentment as he cast his eye over the narrow room that served as his office. His small desk, made of a second-rate wood that had begun to split, was almost buried under a pile of casebooks. These were indispensable to the inquisitor, who was obliged to record in them every last action, meeting, witness accusation, punishment meted out or torture employed. The aim was not so much to ensure the thoroughness of the procedure as to make sure that no case would ever be lost. If the accused were eventually found innocent, who was to say that he might not be tried again for some other crime?

*

His secretary, Agnan, entered silently, his head bowed, and waited for Florin's permission to speak.

'Well, Agnan. What is it?'

'Seigneur Inquisitor, your visitor has arrived.'

'Bring her in.'

The other man slipped soundlessly out of the room.

Marguerite Galée belonged to a wealthy family of burghers from Nogent; shipbuilders who no doubt had taken their name from the vessels they constructed.[20] Nicolas had carefully researched the state of their finances.

The lady cut a fine figure in her fur-trimmed coat, too warm for the time of year. She could not have been more than twenty-two. Twenty-four at the most. The perfect oval of her face was framed by the sheerest of veils. A hint of vulgarity in her eyes belied the unassuming elegance of her posture, her upper body leaning backwards slightly so as to avoid stepping on the narrow train attached to the front of her dress, as worn by ladies of the nobility. The tiny silk slippers covered in mud that peeped out at every step were additional proof of her wealth, for by evening the sludge in the streets would have irrevocably ruined them.

Nicolas stood up to greet her and, holding out his hand, guided her to the chair on the other side of his desk. She sighed and gave a pretty shrug of her shoulders as she spoke hesitantly:

'A distant relative, Baron de Larnay, heartily recommended you to me, Seigneur Inquisitor. I find myself in a very delicate situation from which I know not how to extricate myself. I have come to you . . . for advice, Seigneur Inquisitor. Your wisdom, which is equalled only by your indulgence, has been remarked upon among a . . . discreet circle.'

How exhilarating life was becoming: this ravishing, exceedingly rich young woman lowering her gaze before him and addressing him by his title 'Seigneur Inquisitor' at the end of every sentence; and as for the Baron de Larnay, well, he was turning out to be more interesting than he had first thought.

'You flatter me, Madame.'

'No, Seigneur Inquisitor. On the contrary, I . . . This is such a delicate matter . . .'

He paused. Marguerite Galée had been testing the water ever since she arrived and caution told him that he should continue feigning an inquisitor's disinterested observation. However, he was afraid the lady might take fright and renounce her plan, in which case he risked seeing the generous compensation he was hoping for go up in smoke. The predatory look in her eye when she first arrived encouraged him to throw caution to the wind:

'Madame, pray look upon this office as a confessional. I have listened to many stories in here, few of which have surprised me. It is not always easy to bring about justice. Is it not my role to remedy such matters . . . and my reward to receive the gratitude of such pure souls as yours?'

She raised her head and a knowing smile played across her lips, as alluring as an exotic fruit.

'What a relief, Seigneur Inquisitor . . . The first of my worries is that, unhappily, I have as yet been unable to conceive. The second is that my husband is very ill . . . the doctors fear that the pain in his chest, which has left him breathless for weeks, will grow worse . . .'

She paused and bit her lip. Florin encouraged her to go on with an affectionate gesture.

'Despite his advanced age, my husband's father enjoys such perfect health that I am beginning to find it suspicious.'

So, this was the reason for the lady's visit. Her father-in-law must be extremely wealthy. If her husband were to die before his own father without leaving an heir, this avaricious beauty wouldn't see a penny of the old man's money. Florin felt a nagging doubt. There were plenty of poisons available with which to rid oneself of an old man who clung stubbornly to life, which a woman such as she would have no difficulty in procuring. On the other hand, he had witnessed it many times: it was much easier to arrange for someone else to carry out a murder than to perpetrate it oneself. Even so, he was a little disappointed in her. Admittedly, though, an inquisitorial procedure was above suspicion, whereas a case of poisoning might incriminate the beneficiary.

'Suspicious, you say?'

'Indeed, as is my inexplicable sterility. You see, my father-in-law . . . Well, I would be putting it mildly if I said that he is not overly fond of me.'

'Do you suspect him of improper practices?'

'Most emphatically.'

'Of practising magic? I am referring to black magic, the use of incantations and the invocation of evil spirits. Is this what you mean?'

'Just so. I even suspect him of having a hand in my poor dear husband's illness.'

Whom you will dispatch the moment the old man has given

up the ghost, thought Nicolas, affecting an air of deep disquiet.

'This is a most serious accusation, Madame. Indeed, a witch resembles a heretic in his worship of demonic idols. Have you any proof?'

'Well, he . . .' She appeared to hesitate, but went on: 'He eats meat on fasting days . . .'

A sensible man, for fasting days are a most tiresome invention, Nicolas thought to himself. He was going to have to help the beautiful Marguerite, for she had clearly not thought out this stage of her offensive.

'A most valuable piece of evidence. There exist others even more damning. For example, do you suspect that your father-in-law undermined your husband's health and prevented you from conceiving with wax figurines?' he suggested.

She nodded.

'Good. In your opinion, does he summon demons in a cellar or a burnt-out chapel?'

'There is one not far from where he lives.'

'It is common in these places to find evidence of black masses, such as inverted crucifixes and candles blackened with soot. You will need to verify this in the presence of a notary. Do you suspect him of taking part in sexual acts of a depraved and unnatural nature?'

'I am convinced of it . . . with me he tried to . . .'

And a man of good taste into the bargain, Florin reflected approvingly, if indeed there was any truth in the accusation.

'Why, the scoundrel! However, I had more repulsive, bestial acts in mind.'

She raised her eyebrows questioningly.

'For example, involving animals such as goats . . .'

During the next half-hour, Nicolas Florin listed every piece of evidence Marguerite needed to plant so that the men-at-arms and the notary, whose testimony was crucial to the inquisitors, could find it without any difficulty.

She was beaming as she stood up to leave. She approached his desk, her hands outstretched in a gesture of gratitude. He grasped them, raised one to his lips and ran his tongue over her palm. She closed her eyes in ecstasy and murmured:

'This affair promises to be most intoxicating, Seigneur.'

'I am ready to intercede at a moment's notice, Madame.'

She threw him a beguiling look as she left the room, and he unfolded the note she had slipped into his hand. Printed on it was a sum: five hundred pounds. There was no need for any contract. Who would be foolish enough to default on a debt to an inquisitor – pecuniary or otherwise?

The would-be Marguerite Galée walked along sedately until she turned the corner of the Inquisition headquarters, when she felt her legs give way beneath her. She leaned against the enclosure wall for a moment and took a deep breath. She heard a low voice like an instantly soothing balm, a voice she associated with a past miracle.

'Come, there's a tavern nearby. You look pale. Come and rest awhile, my friend.'

The tall cowled figure put his arm around the waist of the false Marguerite Galée and helped her along the few remaining streets. The young woman could not stop shaking and was unable to speak until they had sat down at a corner table of the establishment, which was almost deserted at that time of day. She nearly spilled the wine she was sipping from a goblet down her beautiful hired coat. The alcohol helped rid her of her feeling of nausea. Francesco de Leone removed his heavy cloak and asked:

'How do you feel, Hermine?'

'I was so afraid.'

'You're a brave woman. Drink some more and catch your breath.'

Hermine obeyed. How strange that this magnificent man, the only man ever to have refused her when all she had to offer by way of gratitude was her body, could calm her with a look or one of his inscrutable smiles. How strange that he alone had helped her feel at peace with her own soul – and even with those of others.

She was able to summon up that afternoon of pure terror as vividly, painfully and perfectly as if it had taken place only yesterday.

He had not judged her, the beautiful archangel; he had barely spoken. He had stood between this woman whom he did not know and an angry volley of stones. The blood had trickled down his forehead and onto his cheek. He had not protested or backed away or drawn his sword from the scabbard swinging against his calf. He had simply looked at them, and his piercing blue gaze and the cross above his heart had made even the most vehement of her tormentors bow their heads.

Stoned. They wanted to stone her to death. Hermine had belonged to a Cypriot lord – bought and paid for like a bolt of silk, a pack of hunting dogs or a censer. When he died, his frantic widow claimed that Hermine had bewitched him, had stolen him from her bed and killed him with her caresses and love potions. The ludicrous nature of these accusations had deterred no one: they were reason enough for an execution. A horde of men, women and even a few children had chased her for hours along the cliffs, shouting and jeering merrily as they passed each other bottles of wine. Finally they had cornered her in a cove. Exhausted, Hermine had curled up like a terrified animal, shielding her head with her arms. She had recognised the excitement in their eyes. The thrill of sanctioned murder. A shower of stones rained down on her. Then all of a sudden he had appeared and thrust her behind his back and they had scuttled away like crabs, those evildoers turned executioners, intoxicated by a taste of power.

It was strange. She would have travelled to the ends of the earth for her knight and yet he had only wanted her to go to the end of the street, as far as the Inquisition headquarters.

Hermine held out her hand and Francesco clasped it between his. This simple contact made the young woman close her eyes. He released his grip, and she murmured:

'Forgive me.'

'It is I who must ask your forgiveness for placing you in a dangerous situation.'

'You warned me. Pleasing you is so sweet to me.' She smiled apologetically before continuing: 'I enjoy being eternally indebted to you. I owe you my life and you can never forget me – for the lives of those we save belong to us. We cannot change this however much we may wish to.'

It was his turn to smile now. Like Éleusie, and his mother and sister before her, Hermine unknowingly reawakened his compassion, allowed him to lower his guard, to fall asleep without clasping the hilt of his sword. Hermine and the other women who lived in his memory had the power to wash away for a moment the Giotto Capellas of this world and all the baseness he encountered.

'What is your opinion of him?'

'It is not a question of opinion, dear knight, but of fact. He is the worst kind of vermin. No. Vermin is not the right word. He is vile, corrupt, beyond redemption.'

'I understand. Things have been made even easier for the likes of him since the Pope granted inquisitors the right to absolve each other of any blunders or transgressions[21]. And this generosity has been extended to allow them to preside over torture sessions, which was previously forbidden. I'll wager Florin could not have wished for a more appetising gift.'

'They frighten me,' murmured Hermine.

'They frighten everybody and the fear they inspire is their main weapon. Tell me about the meeting.'

She recounted every detail of her encounter with Florin, including the moist caress he had left on the palm of her hand. He listened, nodding occasionally.

'There is something I don't quite understand, Francesco,' she continued. 'You must have already guessed all this from what your aunt told you about Florin's dealings with Larnay.'

'Of course, and . . .' He paused, then changed his mind: 'You see, my dear Hermine, a man is being condemned and I must know whether his cruelty is the result of a sickness of the soul or of the mind. Thanks to you, I am now certain that there is nothing wrong with his reason since he sells trials for personal gain. I shall make one more appeal to him . . . and if he fails to respond his time of grace will be up.'

She paused before asking the dreadful question:

'Is he to die?'

'I do not know. I . . . do not plan an enemy's death. It either happens or it does not.' He grew silent for a moment before continuing: 'The landlord has agreed to let you change upstairs. My dear friend, it is time for you to return to Chartres. I have hired a horse-drawn carriage for you. I do not know how to thank you enough.'

'By not thanking me at all. As I have already said, we are responsible for our debts whether we are lenders or borrowers. You will never be rid of me or of the memory of me, my handsome knight.'

He studied her in silence for a moment and then closed his eyes and smiled:

'I have no wish to be, Hermine. Until we meet again, my fearless one.'

Her eyes brimming with tears, she tried to disguise her emotion, declaring in a sharp voice:

'Don't forget to return the fur-trim coat to the draper's and above all to get back the outrageously high deposit. These people would suck us dry if they could! On the other hand, the shoes are in a pitiful state and they are sure to demand compensation.'

'I knew Florin would notice them.'

T HE grime sticking to her hands and legs disgusted her. Her scalp itched and the stench of her dress, soiled with sweat and sour milk from the soup she ate each evening with a spoon she could not see, sickened her. She had removed her veil, dipped a corner of it in the ewer of water and tried to wash herself as best she could. How long had she been there? She had lost all sense of time. Three, five, eight, ten days? She had no idea and clung to the thought that sooner or later the inquisitor would have to interrogate her. And then . . . No. She must avoid thinking about what would happen then. Florin was counting on using fear to break her and make his task easier. There is nothing more destructive than despair – except perhaps hope.

Had it been night or day when she slept? The nightmares had kept coming, but she had discovered a way of keeping her waking fears at bay by reliving the most precious moments in her life. They were few and far between and she was obliged to conjure up the same ones over and over again: gathering flowers, harvesting honey, the birth of a foal, Clément's knowing smile. She had spent hours reciting the ballads of Madame Marie de France, starting again from the beginning when she forgot the words. She had recreated entire conversations of no import: stories Madame Clémence had told her, instructions she would give for a dinner, soothing words she used with Mathilde, a discussion on theology with the chaplain. Nothing of any import. Her life amounted to nothing of any import.

Agnès jumped. The sound of heavy footsteps on the stone stairs that she had descended she could not remember when, followed by Florin who was eager to show her her cell. She stiffened, listening hard, trying to interpret every sound. Was he coming to interrogate her?

The steps ended long before they reached her door. The sound of something sliding and the shuffle of feet. A heavy object being dragged. She rushed over and pressed her ear to the wooden panel and waited, straining to hear through the silence.

A shriek followed by a wail. Who was it? The man who had begged her to die quickly?

The shrieking began again and continued for what seemed to her like an eternity of pain.

The torture chamber was right next to the cells.

Her mind became awash with dark, screaming, bloody images.

Agnès slumped to her knees in the mud and wept. She wept as though the world were about to end. She wept for that man, or another, for the weak and innocent – she wept because of the power of brutes.

She did not pray. She would have needed to invoke death for her prayer to have any meaning at all.

*

83

Was it morning when she awoke on her pallet with no memory of having dragged her body there? Had the endless torment just finished? Had she fainted? Had her mind mercifully allowed her a moment's oblivion?

So, the torture chamber was right next to the cells. In this way the torments of other prisoners fed the fear of those still waiting in the evil-smelling darkness of their cells.

She felt a slight sense of relief in that place that tolerated none. There would be the weeks of questioning first. The intrinsic obscenity of the thought shocked her: those others she had seen crouched on the floor were being tortured, not her, not yet. The intention of Florin and the other inquisitors became clear. They wanted to break them, to reduce them to pitiful, terrified, tormented souls in order to convince them that salvation lay in siding with their executioners, in confessing to sins they had never committed, in denouncing others, in destroying their innocence.

Break. Break their limbs, their bones, their consciences, their souls.

Someone was approaching. Her heart missed a beat as the footsteps paused in front of her cell. A wave of nausea made her throat tighten as the bolt grated. She stood facing the door. Florin stooped to enter the tiny space, a sconce torch in his hand.

The inquisitor enquired directly in a soft voice:

'Have you made peace with your soul, Madame?'

The frightened words 'Indeed, my Lord Inquisitor' echoed in Agnès's head and yet she heard herself reply calmly and unfalteringly:

'My soul was never in turmoil, Monsieur.'

'It is my job to find that out. I consider the interrogation room more suitable for the initial cross-examination of a lady than this cell which' – he sniffed the lingering odour of excrement and stale food in the air and screwed up his face – 'which smells like a sewer.'

'I have become habituated to it, as you assured me I would when I arrived. However, the other room would allow you to sit down and me to stand up straight.'

'Do you give me your word, Madame, that you do not need shackles or a guard?'

'I doubt that it is possible to escape from the Inquisition headquarters. Besides, I am weak from these few days of semi-fasting.'

Florin nodded then turned to leave. Agnès followed him. A fair-haired youth was waiting a few feet away, carefully holding an escritoire upon which stood an ink-horn and a small oil lamp. He was the scribe charged with recording her declarations.

As they passed the barred cells, Agnès searched in vain for the man who had grasped her ankle. Her eyes closed in a gesture of quiet relief as she realised that he must be dead. He was free of them.

The nearer they came to the low-ceilinged room, the more Agnès felt as if the air were coming alive. It felt lighter, more vibrant. They crossed the enormous room to the hallway. She felt curiously elated at the sight of a patch of sky heavy with rain clouds, seen through the tiny windows looking out onto the courtyard. They turned right and walked up another staircase made of dark wood. When they reached the landing, Florin turned to her. The effort of climbing fourteen steps had left Agnès breathless. Florin observed:

'Fasting allows the mind to soar free.'

'You are living proof of it.'

She bit her lip in fright. Had she taken leave of her senses? What did she think she was saying? Surely if she angered him he would wreak his revenge. He had all the means at his disposal.

Florin lost his composure for an instant. This was the other woman speaking, the one he had already glimpsed behind Agnès's pretty face. He could have sworn that she was completely oblivious to the transformation. He was mistaken. An inexorable calm washed over Agnès, flushing away the seeds of terror Florin was attempting to sow; the powerful shades whose presence she had felt during her first encounter with the inquisitor had returned.

They stopped before a high door, which the young scribe hurriedly opened. Agnès walked through, looking around her as though she were a curious visitor. For the past few moments, she had been overwhelmed by an odd sense of unreality, as though her mind were floating outside her body.

Agnès stood in the middle of the freezing, cavernous room, her mind a complete blank. Strangely, the exhaustion she had felt when she left her cell had given way to a pleasant languor.

Four men sat waiting impassively at a long table: a notary and his clerk, as required by the procedure, and two Dominicans, besides the inquisitor. The mendicant friars sat staring down at their clasped hands resting on the table, and Agnès thought to herself that despite the difference in age they could almost be twins. It was in Florin's power to call upon two 'lay persons of excellent repute', but such people were less well versed in theology and so less intimidating to the would-be heretic. Four austere-looking men dressed in black robes sitting together formed a threatening wall.

Monge de Brineux, Comte Artus d'Authon's bailiff, would not be present at the interrogation as Florin had neglected to invite him.

The inquisitor sat down in the imposing, ornately sculpted armchair at one end of the table, while the young scribe settled himself on the bench.

She listened through a fog to Florin's booming voice:

'State your Christian names, surname and status, Madame.'

'Agnès Philippine Claire de Larnay, Dame de Souarcy.'

At this point the notary rose to his feet and read out:

'*In nomine Domini, amen.* On this the fifth day of November in the year of Our Lord 1304, in the presence of the undersigned Gauthier Richer, notary at Alençon, and in the company of one of his clerks and two appointed witnesses, Brother Jean and Brother Anselme, both Dominicans of the diocese of Alençon, born respectively in Rioux and Hurepal, Agnès Philippine Claire de Larnay does appear before the venerable Brother Nicolas Florin, Dominican, Doctor in Theology and Grand Inquisitor appointed to the region of Alençon.'

The notary sat down again without glancing at Agnès. Florin continued:

'Madame, you are accused of having given refuge to a heretic by the name of Sybille Chalis, your lady's maid, of having helped her escape our justice and of having allowed yourself to be seduced by heretical ideas. Further accusations have been made against you which we consider it preferable not to discuss here today.'

The procedure allowed him to keep that trump card in case she managed miraculously to clear herself of the charge of heresy.

'Do you admit to these facts, Madame?'

'I admit to having employed in my service one Sybille Chalis, who died in childbirth during the winter of 1294. I swear on my soul that I never had the slightest suspicion of her heresy. As for the seductive power of such heretical abominations, I know nothing of it.'

'We will be the judge of that,' Florin retorted, suppressing a smile. 'Do you confess to having kept the son of this heretic, a certain Clément, who in turn entered your service?'

'As I have already stated, I did not suspect his mother's heresy, and saw in the gesture an act of Christian charity. The child has been brought up to love and respect the Church.'

'Indeed . . . and what of your own love of the Holy Church?'

'It is absolute.'

'Is it indeed?'

'It is.'

'In that case why not prove it here and now? Do you swear on your soul and on the death and resurrection of Christ to tell the whole truth? Do you swear that you will conceal nothing and omit nothing?'

'I swear.'

'Take heed, young woman. The seriousness of this oath far outweighs any you have sworn thus far.'

'I am aware of that.'

'Very well. Since it is my job to try by every means possible to clear you of the charges, I must ask you before we begin to tell me whether you know of any persons who might seek to harm you?'

She stared at him, feigning puzzlement through her exhaustion. Brother Anselme, the younger of the two Dominicans, believing the point needed explaining to her, cast a searching glance at the other friar before venturing:

'Sister, do you believe anyone capable of gravely perjuring themselves in order to harm you, out of hatred, envy or sheer wickedness?'

A second trap. Clément had warned her. It was better to supply a long list of potential informers than to absolve out of hand a close friend or relative who might turn out to be her fiercest accuser.

'I do. And for reasons so disgraceful that I am ashamed to mention them.'

'Pray give us their names, Madame,' the Dominican demanded.

'My half-brother, Baron Eudes de Larnay, who has hounded me with his incestuous desires since I was eight. His servant Mabile, whose surname I do not know and whom he introduced into my household in order to spy on me. Finding nothing to satisfy her master, she invented tales of heresy and shameful carnal relations in order to tarnish my name.'

Agnès went quiet as she tried to think who else might wish her harm. She hoped that her chaplain, Brother Bernard, had spared her, but after all she did not know him well. How could she be sure?

'Who else?' Brother Anselme insisted.

'My new chaplain, who does not know me well, might have misjudged me. Perhaps one of my serfs or peasants resents paying me tithes. My servant girl Adeline. I cannot imagine what possible grudge she could hold against me, but I have reached the point where I trust no one. Perhaps she took offence when I told her off one day.'

'Oh, we know that sort with their vipers' tongues. They turn up at every trial and their accusations are treated with caution. In contrast, a man of the cloth . . . However, we shall see. Anybody else?'

'I am not guilty of any discrimination.'

'If this is the truth, then God's acknowledgement will enlighten us accordingly. Anybody else, Madame?' Brother Anselme insisted, glancing again at the other Dominican, who remained impassive.

Agnès thought quickly: Clément, Gilbert the simpleton, Artus d'Authon, Monge de Brineux, Éleusie de Beaufort, Jeanne d'Amblin and many others occurred to her, but no one who was capable of perjuring themselves out of sheer spite. Gilbert, perhaps. He was a gentle soul but weak and malleable enough for an inquisitor easily to put words in his mouth. She added regretfully:

'Gilbert, one of my farm hands. He is a simpleton and understands very little of anything. He lives in a world of his own.' Suddenly fearful of endangering him, she corrected herself: 'But his soul has always remained faithful to Our Lord, who loves the pure and innocent . . .'

She weighed her words. She must avoid implying that Florin

was assembling false accusations or biased testimonies. She was still unsure whether the two friars Anselme and Jean were Florin's henchmen, but she did not want to risk vexing them by incriminating a representative of their order, a doctor in theology moreover.

'. . . He is dull-witted and slow of speech and it would be easy to draw stories out of him that might appear strange or even suspicious.'

'Madame . . .' the Dominican chided her softly in a sad voice. 'Do you truly believe that we would consider the accusations of a simpleton?'

She was sure they would not, but this way the notary was obliged to record that Gilbert was a simpleton. Any accusation forced out of him, then twisted to show his lady in a bad light, would be considered suspect.

'Is that all, Madame?' Anselme insisted again, turning quickly to look at Friar Jean. 'Think hard. It is not the aim of this court to entrap the accused by deceitful means.'

She bit her lip, narrowly avoiding blurting out the words that were on the tip of her tongue:

'God will recognise his true people, and you are not among them.'

Instead she affirmed:

'I can think of no other informant.'

Florin was ecstatic. Even before Agnès entered the interrogation chamber he knew it would never occur to her that her own daughter might be her most vehement accuser. The young girl, pampered by her uncle, had filled a page with well-turned phrases written in appallingly bad script containing enough

poison to deal her mother a deathly blow. The girl's accusations –
a mishmash of heresy, sorcery and immoral behaviour – smacked
of Eudes de Larnay's scheming and Florin had not been taken in
for a moment. On the contrary, he was certain of Agnès's
innocence. It was a source of comfort to him that such a pretty
exterior could conceal so much malice, resentment and jealousy,
for the flawed natures of the majority of his fellow creatures
guaranteed him a long and fruitful career. He was already
savouring the thought of Agnès's devastation upon reading this
ignoble calumny. Her own daughter, whom she had made every
effort to protect, was prepared to send her to the stake without the
slightest hesitation. What a delightfully amusing thought.

He approached Agnès and handed her the Gospels. She
placed her hand on the enormous black book bound in leather.

'Madame, do you solemnly swear before God and upon your
soul to tell the truth?'

'I do.' She recalled the words Clément had taught her, and
added: 'May God come to my aid if I keep this vow and may He
condemn me if I perjure myself.'

Florin gave a little nod to the notary, who rose to his feet and
declared:

'Agnès, Dame de Souarcy and resident of Manoir de
Souarcy, having been read the accusation and having placed her
right hand upon the Gospels and sworn to tell the whole truth
concerning herself and others, will now proceed to be cross-
examined.'

Florin thanked the notary with a polite gesture and studied
Agnès at length, half closing his eyes, as though in prayer,
before enquiring in a soft voice:

'Madame de Souarcy, dear child, dear sister . . . Do you believe that Christ was born of a virgin?'

The cross-examination had begun with all its ruses and pitfalls; if she replied 'I believe he was' it could be interpreted as a sign that she was unsure. Clément had read her a list of all the trick questions. She replied in a steady voice:

'I am certain that Christ was born of a virgin.'

A flicker of annoyance showed on Florin's face. He continued:

'Do you believe in the one Holy Catholic Church?'

Again, it was necessary to rephrase the sentence in order to prevent any unfavourable interpretation:

'There exists no other church than the Holy Catholic Church.'

'Do you believe that the Holy Ghost proceeds from the Father and the Son as we believe?'

She remembered Clément reading her the exact same sentence as though it were yesterday. Most of the accused responded in good faith, 'I do.' The Grand Inquisitor then pointed out that they were skilfully twisting the words in the manner of heretics and that by 'yes, I do' they really meant 'yes, I believe that you believe it' when in fact they believed the contrary.

'It is clear that the Holy Ghost proceeds from the Father and the Son.'

Florin continued in this vein for a few minutes before realising that he would not catch her out. He declared in a loud voice for all to hear:

'I see that Madame de Souarcy has learned her lesson well.'

Before he could interrupt her, she retorted:

'To what lesson are you referring, Seigneur Inquisitor? Are you suggesting that faith in Jesus Christ is learned by rote like the alphabet? Surely we are born with it, of it. It is what we are. It illuminates and pervades us. Might you have learned it as another learns a meat recipe? I shudder to think.'

The colour drained from the inquisitor's face and he clenched his jaw. He stared at her darkly through his soft eyes. It flashed through her mind that he would have hit her if there had been no witnesses.

The Dominican friar who had questioned her cleared his throat awkwardly. She had scored a victory over Florin and he would be merciless. But she had also gained some time and, without knowing why, the need to hold out as long as she could seemed imperative.

Florin, struggling to regain his composure, ordered her to be taken back to her cell. As she descended into her daily hell, she kept repeating to herself:

'Knowledge is power. The most invincible weapon, dear sweet Clément.'

The moment the guard had pushed her into her cell and slammed the heavy door behind her, she fell to her knees, clasped her hands together and tried to comprehend where the strength to hold her head up high and stand firm had come from.

'Clémence . . . My sweet angel . . . Thank you.'

Back in the interrogation room, Florin was seething. He could not understand how the week of fasting and solitary confinement he had inflicted on his prey had not worn down her last resistance. This female had questioned him, ridiculed him in front of two of his brothers. He reviled her and – why not admit it? – he was beginning to fear her.

After she had gone he tried to manoeuvre himself back into a position of strength by declaring in a passionate voice filled with regret:

'Such a clever tongue is a sure sign of a perverse and devious mind, and points more clearly to heresy than any accusation. We have seen how these lost souls defend themselves thanks to the deviant teachings they receive, and how they try to confuse us with their antics. Women, who by their very nature are treacherous and scheming, are even more expert at it.'

Maître Gauthier Richer, the notary, gave a little nod of approval. In his view, the cunning, calculating nature of women made them prime recruits for the devil. However, Nicolas Florin sensed that his little speech had not entirely convinced the two Dominican friars who had been summoned as witnesses. In particular Brother Jean, who had not yet spoken and refused to catch the inquisitor's eye.

Brother Anselme spoke again in a soft voice:

'Let us reconsider, brother, my Lord Inquisitor, young Mathilde de Souarcy's damning testimony.'

'Damning indeed,' Florin repeated, pleased by the choice of adjective. 'In it Mademoiselle Mathilde . . .'

'A direct reading of it might prove more enlightening, brother,' interrupted Jean de Rioux, speaking for the first time.

Florin searched for a hint of suspicion, hesitation or even complicity, in the man's voice, but found nothing to betray his witness's attitude. A fresh concern was added to the rage the inquisitor had felt during Agnès's declaration. The presence of religious witnesses belonging to the same order as the inquisitor made a mockery of justice. Indeed, Florin could not recall a single occasion during any trial where the former had contradicted the latter. This was the real reason why he had chosen not to summon lay witnesses. Even so, everything about Brother Jean de Rioux worried him: his thoughtful silence, his composure, his unwillingness to look Florin in the eye, even his hands, which were oddly robust for a man of letters approaching fifty. Moreover, Anselme de Hurepal appeared to seek his approval before each of his interventions. He chided himself: he was behaving like a frightened child again. It was only natural for these two fools to take their role seriously, but he would give them short shrift as he had the others.

He approached the table and plucked Mathilde de Souarcy's statement from under a small pile of papers. He began reading aloud:

'I, Mathilde Clémence Marie de Souarcy, only child of Madame Agnès de Souarcy . . .'

He did not see Jean glance at Anselme. The younger man interrupted on cue:

'Pray, Brother Inquisitor . . . We are able to read. I believe that it would be most helpful if we acquainted ourselves with Mademoiselle de Souarcy's words in quiet contemplation, the better to consider their significance.'

Florin almost uttered a curse. What! Did these two fools dare to cast doubt on his word? Brother Anselme insisted:

'Are we to understand that this young girl is not yet of age?'

'She will be soon – in a year's time. Besides, the accusations of children against their parents are not only admitted but strongly encouraged regardless of their age. Indeed, who is better placed to judge corruption than those who live with it, who put up with it day in, day out?'

'Indeed,' the Dominican conceded, stretching out his hand.

Florin reluctantly passed him the statement.

Brother Anselme read it first and then handed it over to Brother Jean. The Dominican's impassive expression and his slowness in reading exasperated Florin. Finally, Brother Jean looked up and remarked:

'These words are enough to condemn her without further ado.'

The inquisitor felt as though a weight had been lifted off his shoulders and said, smiling:

'Did I not tell you? She is guilty and although it pains me greatly to say it I hold out little hope of her salvation.'

His relief was short-lived.

'Even so . . . Is it not extraordinary that this young girl who barely knows how to hold a quill and whose script is so clumsily executed expresses herself with such consummate skill? Let us see . . . "My soul suffers at the thought of the constant abominations committed by Madame de Souarcy, my mother, and her persistent sinfulness and deviance make me fear for her soul" or "The young chaplain, so devout the day he arrived, oblivious to this shadow of evil hanging over us . . ." or "God granted me the strength to resist living with evil despite my mother's constant example . . ." Gracious me! What convincing rhetoric.'

Brother Jean raised his head and for the first time Florin's eyes met his. The man's gaze was infinite and he had the dizzying sensation of walking through a never-ending archway. Florin blinked involuntarily. Jean declared in a firm voice:

'May I share our concern with you, Brother Inquisitor? Although we are only present in an . . . advisory capacity, we would find it very distressing if your purity and ardent faith were manipulated by false witnesses. We therefore strongly recommend that Mademoiselle de Souarcy be brought here to the Inquisition headquarters to be questioned before this assembly without her uncle being present.'

Florin hesitated for a fraction of a second. It was in his power to refuse this precautionary measure, but such a refusal would come back to haunt him. An unpleasant thought occurred to him. What if these two monks had been secretly placed as witnesses by Camerlingo Benedetti, to whom he owed his departure from Carcassonne and his new post at Alençon? What if they were in fact papal inspectors, like the ones sent by the Holy See to settle internal disputes in the monasteries or to ensure the smooth running of trials? Nicolas's career was too promising for him to take any unnecessary risks. He was in no doubt that the wretched little Mathilde would stand by her testimony and that Eudes could be counted upon to help her. However, the Dominican's request would mean a delay in proceedings. Still, the cloaked figure who had insisted Agnès de Souarcy must die had not specified any precise date.

The most prudent course of action would be to comply.

'I am grateful to you, brother, for your concern. The knowledge that others are at hand to ensure the purity and integrity of the inquisitorial tribunal is invaluable to one such as I who presides in solitary judgement. Scribe . . . record the summoning of the witness and send for Mademoiselle de Souarcy.'

Another thought cheered him.

Once Mathilde had arrived he could arrange a confrontation between mother and daughter. What a delightful spectacle that promised to be.

Clairets Abbey, Perche, November 1304

ÉLEUSIE de Beaufort closed her eyes. A warm tear trickled down her face into the corner of her mouth. Blanche de Blinot, the senior nun, clenched her fist spasmodically and repeated as though she were reciting a litany:

'What is happening, what is happening? She is dead, isn't she? . . . How could she be dead? She was still so young!'

Gentle Adélaïde's corpse lay in its coffin, which was resting on a pair of trestles in the middle of the registry, waiting to be taken to the abbey's Church of Notre-Dame. Annelette Beaupré had struggled with the dead girl's stubborn tongue, which protruded gruesomely, and had finally resorted to gagging the dead girl with a strip of linen in order to keep the thing inside her mouth. Consequently the dignity refused to her in death was restored.

They had all paid their respects, tearfully, silently or in prayer, to the young woman who had been in charge of the kitchens and their meals. Annelette had studied their different demeanours, the uneasy, distant or forlorn expressions on their faces, determined to discover the culprit among them, for she was convinced that her theory was correct and had shared her thoughts with the Abbess.

Éleusie had protested at first, but had soon yielded to the

apothecary's implacable logic and accepted the unacceptable: they were rubbing shoulders every day with the goodly Adélaïde's killer. Her fear had given way to painful despair. Evil had slipped in with that creature of darkness Nicolas Florin. She had felt it.

The Abbess had remained at her desk for many hours, unable to move, unsure of how to act, of where to start. She had learned that no amount of prayer or lighting of candles could drive out evil. Evil would only recoil in the face of pure unflinching souls who were prepared to fight to the death. The titanic battle had no end; it had existed since the beginning of time and would go on raging until the end. Unless . . .

The time for peace had not yet come. Éleusie was going to fight because Clémence, Philippine and Claire would have taken up arms without a second thought. Why was she still alive when the others would have been so much better equipped for battle?

Early that morning, Jeanne d'Amblin had left on her rounds to visit the abbey's regular benefactors and new alms givers.[22] The extern sister had been reluctant to leave the Mother Abbess alone to face whatever came next. Éleusie had used all her authority to persuade Jeanne to go. Now she regretted her decision. Jeanne's competence, her energy, her firm but gentle resolve were a comfort to her. She raised her eyes and glanced at Annelette, who was shaking her head.

She walked over to the apothecary, pulling Blanche behind her, and said in a hushed voice:

'I want everybody, without exception, in the scriptorium in half an hour.'

'That might prove dangerous,' replied the tall woman.

'Might we not do better to lead a more . . . discreet investigation?'

'There is no greater danger than refusing to see, daughter. I want everyone to be there except for the lay women. I will see them later.'

'The murderess might lash out if she feels cornered. If she fears discovery, she might attack another sister, perhaps even you.'

'That is precisely what I'm hoping, to make her panic.'

'It is too risky. Poisoning is such a subtle art that even I am powerless to prevent it. Could we not . . .'

'That is an order, Annelette.'

'I . . . Very well, Reverend Mother.'

A wall of still white robes ruffled only by a slight draught. Éleusie made out the tiny faces, brows, eyes and lips of the fifty-odd women, half of them novices, who were waiting, wondering why they had been summoned. And yet Éleusie was sure that no one but the murderess had suspected the true magnitude of the tidal wave that was about to engulf the scriptorium. Seated at one of the writing desks, Annelette lowered her head, fiddling absent-mindedly with a small knife used for sharpening quill pens. One question had been nagging at her since the evening before. Why would anyone find it necessary to kill poor Adélaïde? Had she uncovered the identity of the poisoner? Had she seen or heard something that implicated her killer? For the cup of herbal tea, which the apothecary had discovered, had been given to the sister in charge of meals at a time in the evening when she was alone in the kitchens. The murderess must have taken advantage of this fact to bring her the fatal beverage. In addition to these questions another worry was plaguing Annelette: what if the poisoner had taken the drug from her medicine cabinet in the herbarium? The apothecary nun was in the habit of treating pain, facial neuralgia and fever[23] with dilutions of aconite.

'Daughters . . . Sister Adélaïde is with Our Lord. Her soul, I know, rests in peace.' Éleusie de Beaufort breathed in sharply before continuing in a strident voice: 'However, the suffering endured by whoever has usurped the will of God will be eternal. Her punishment in this world will be terrible and the ensuing torment inflicted upon her by the Almighty unimaginable.'

Some of the sisters glanced at one another, unable to grasp the meaning of this judgement. Others stared at their Abbess with a mixture of amazement and alarm. The morbid silence that had descended was broken by a flurry of voices, feet scraping the floor and stifled exclamations.

'Silence!' thundered Éleusie. 'Silence, I have not finished yet.'

The astonished nervous whispers instantly came to a stop.

'Our sweet sister Adélaïde was poisoned with a cup of honey and lavender tea that contained aconite.'

Fifty gasps rose as one and reverberated against the ceiling of the enormous scriptorium. Éleusie took advantage of the ensuing hubbub to examine the faces, searching in vain for any sign that might reveal the culprit.

'Silence!' Éleusie exclaimed. 'Silence this instant! As you would expect, I do not intend to ask which of you brewed the tea as I doubt I would receive an answer.' She paused and looked again at the fifty faces staring back at her, her gaze lingering on Berthe de Marchiennes, Yolande de Fleury, Hedwige du Thilay, but most of all on Thibaude de Gartempe. 'However, you – and by you I mean the person responsible for this unforgivable crime – have underestimated me. I may not know your name yet, but I shall find it out before long.'

A tremulous voice broke the profound silence following this promise:

'I don't understand what's going on. Will somebody please tell me what our Reverend Mother is saying?'

Blanche de Blinot was fidgeting on her bench, turning first to one sister then another. A novice leaned over and explained to her in a whisper.

'But . . . I took her the tea!' Thrown into a sudden panic, the old woman groaned: 'You say she died from a cup of poisoned honey and lavender tea? How could that be?'

Éleusie looked at her as though a chasm were opening at her feet.

'What are you saying, Blanche dear? That it was you who brewed the tea for Adélaïde?'

'Yes. Well . . . No, it didn't happen quite like that. I found the cup on my desk when I was preparing to go to vespers. I sniffed it . . . and well, I have never really cared much for lavender tea, it is too fragrant for me,' she said in a hushed voice, as though confessing to some terrible sin. 'Although I am partial to verbena, especially when it is flavoured with mint . . .'

'Blanche . . . The facts, please,' Éleusie interrupted.

'Forgive me, Reverend Mother . . . I digress . . . I am getting so old . . . Well, I assumed Adélaïde had prepared it for me and so I took the cup back to the kitchen. She is . . . was such a considerate girl. She said it was a shame to waste it and that she would drink it herself.'

Éleusie caught the astonished eye of the apothecary nun. Who else besides the two of them had understood the significance of this exchange? Certainly not Blanche, the intended victim, who was agonising over having handed the poisoned tea to her cherished sister. Somebody had wanted to get rid of Blanche. But why? Why kill a half-deaf old woman who spent most of her time snoozing? Éleusie could feel a pair of hate-filled eyes boring into her from she did not know where. She made a monumental effort to carry on:

'I am now in possession of the evidence I needed in order to follow up my suspicions. My theory of how to unmask the culprit is based upon the identity of the victim. Adélaïde's death, however terrible, was a mistake. It is all becoming clear. You may go now, daughters. I shall write directly to Monsieur Monge de Brineux, Seigneur d'Authon's chief bailiff, informing him of this murder and providing him with the names of two likely suspects. I shall demand that the culprit be given a public beating before being executed. May God's will be done.'

No sooner had she closed the door of her apartments than her show of authority, her bravado, crumbled. She sat on the edge of her bed, incapable of moving or even thinking. She waited, waited for the hand that would administer the poison, for the face filled with bottomless loathing or fear. She heard a sound in the adjoining study, the faint rustle of a robe. Death was approaching in a white robe, a wooden crucifix round its neck.

Annelette stood in the doorway to her bed chamber. Visibly upset, she stammered:

'You . . .'

'I what?' murmured Éleusie, her weary voice barely audible.

Trembling with rage, the tall woman roared at her:

'Why did you make such a claim? You have no more idea who is responsible for this horrific act than I. Why make believe that you do? Have you taken leave of your senses? She will kill you now to avoid being unmasked. You have left her no other option.'

'That was my intention.'

'I am helpless to protect you. There exist so many poisons and so few antidotes.'

'Why did she try to poison Blanche de Blinot? The question haunts me, yet I can think up no answer. Do you think that Blanche . . .'

'No. She still hasn't realised that she was the intended victim. She is too upset by Adélaïde's death. I have taken her back to her beloved steam room.'

'And what about the others?'

'The few who possess a modicum of intelligence suspect the truth.'

'Who would do this?'

'Don't you mean why?' corrected Annelette. 'We are all in danger until we unravel this deadly plot. We must stop looking at the problem from the wrong angle. I, too, confess to concentrating on scrutinising the other sisters, but it is not the right approach. If we discover the motive, we will have the culprit.'

'Do you think you will succeed?' asked Éleusie, feeling

reassured for the first time by the imposing woman's forbidding presence.

'I shall do my utmost. Your meals will no longer be served separately. You will help yourself from the communal pot. You will neither eat nor drink anything that is brought or offered to you. What were you thinking! If the murderess gives any credence to your declarations and thinks she's been unmasked she'll . . .'

Éleusie's exhaustion gave way to a strange calm. She declared resolutely:

'I have cut off her retreat. Now she is forced to advance.'

'By killing you?'

'God is my judge. I am ready to meet Him and have no fear.'

'You seem to place very little importance on your own life,' said Annelette disdainfully. 'Death is a trifling matter, indeed . . . It comes to us all and I wonder why we fear it so. Life is a far more uncertain and difficult undertaking. Have you decided to renounce it out of convenience or cowardice? I confess I am disappointed in you, Reverend Mother.'

'I will not permit you to . . .'

Annelette interrupted her sharply:

'I don't give a fig for your permission! Have you forgotten that when you accepted your post you vowed to watch over your daughters? Now is not the time to go back on that vow. What were you expecting? That your time here at Clairets would pass by like a pleasant stroll in the country? It might have but it didn't. Until we discover the intentions of this monster we will all be in danger.'

'I thought death was a matter of indifference to you?'

'It is. However, I confess that I place great value on my life and I haven't the slightest intention of giving it away to the first killer who comes along.'

Éleusie was preparing a sharp rejoinder but was deterred by the sombre look in Annelette's usually clear eyes. Annelette continued in a low voice:

'You surprise me, Madame. Have you already forgotten all those who went before us? Have you forgotten that our quest outweighs any one of us and that our lives and deaths are no longer our own? Would you yield so easily when Claire chose to perish on the steps at Acre rather than surrender?'

'What are you talking about?' whispered Éleusie, taken aback by this unexpected declaration. 'Who are you?'

'I am Annelette Beaupré, your apothecary nun.'

'What do you know about the quest?'

'Like you, Madame, I am a link in the chain. But a link that will never yield.'

'What are you talking about? A link in what chain?'

'In a thousand-year-old chain that is timeless. Did you really believe that you, Francesco and Benoît were alone in your search?'

Éleusie was dumbfounded.

'I . . .'

'I believe Benoît was aware of every link down to the last rivet.'

'Who are you?' the Abbess repeated.

'My mission is to watch over you. I do not know why and I do not ask. It is enough for me to know that my life will not have been in vain, that it will have been one of many fragments joining together to form the foundation of the purest and most noble sanctuary.'

A silence descended on the two women at the end of the confession. The Abbess's incredulity was swept away by the sudden revelation. So, others besides Francesco, Benoît and her were working in the shadows and fearful of being discovered. Annelette's chain conjured up a more far-reaching enterprise than Éleusie had ever imagined. How blind she had been never to have suspected. She wondered whether her nephew had been more perceptive. No. He would never have left his beloved aunt in the dark. This explained the frequent coincidences that had guided Éleusie's life all these years, as well as Francesco's sometimes inexplicable discoveries and Benoît's help, even her appointment at Clairets. Éleusie had never requested the post, and yet it was here that the secret library was located. And Manoir de Souarcy was a stone's throw from the abbey.

Agnès.

'Annelette . . . Tell me more about this . . . this chain.'

The large woman sighed before confessing:

'I have told you most of what I know, Reverend Mother. For a time, I believed that our dear departed Benoît was in charge of its organisation. I was mistaken. Indeed, I am not even sure how apt the idea of a chain is.'

'In that case who ordered you to watch over me?' Éleusie was growing exasperated.

'Benoît, of course.'

'Our Pope, Nicolas Boccasini?'

'Yes.'

'How could that be? Did you know him?'

'I belonged to his entourage when he was Bishop of Ostia.'

'But he knew nothing about me . . . I was a mere intermediary.'

'Perhaps.'

Éleusie's annoyance was gradually giving way to alarm. She was beginning to feel that they were all unknowingly caught up in an enormous spider's web. She stammered:

'Are we not unwitting pawns on a chessboard we cannot even perceive?'

'What does it matter if the chessboard is glorious? That is not the question. I am convinced that the person bringing death to our abbey is also responsible for the demise of the papal emissary whose apparently charred corpse was found in the forest with no signs of any fire nearby . . . Ergot of rye.' Annelette appeared to reflect for a moment before adding: 'Did you feed that messenger, the one who came here to see you?'

The Abbess understood instantly what the apothecary nun was driving at, and her heart sank at the thought that she might have unconsciously aided the poisoner. She exclaimed:

'Dear God . . . you don't suppose the bread I gave him . . . Could the oats, barley and spelt wheat used to make our daily bread have been contaminated?'

'Ergot can infect other plants, though it is rare. And the flour Adélaïde found in the herbarium was unquestionably rye. It remains to be seen who gave the man the poisoned bread.'

Éleusie chided herself for feeling selfishly relieved.

'It seems likely that the monster also killed the emissaries that were sent before and after the one you received here,' Annelette continued.

Éleusie stared at her in silence. It was clear to her, too, and she could have kicked herself for not seeing it sooner. Tears of deep despair welled up in her eyes. Clémence, Claire, Philippine . . . You who have carried me all these years would be so disappointed by my weakness now.

'Do you think there may also be a connection with Madame Agnès's arrest and the arrival of that inquisitor?' she heard herself ask in a muffled voice she barely recognised as her own.

'It would not surprise me at all, Reverend Mother. However, I must know more before I can decide. Who is Madame de Souarcy really? And why is she so important to you? The secrecy we swore for our own protection complicates matters. You know that my task is to protect you and yet I know nothing of yours. Now that Benoît is dead, I think we must change the rules of the game.'

Éleusie paused:

'What do you know about . . . What did Benoît tell you about . . .'

The apothecary smiled sadly and declared:

'It is a difficult subject to broach, is it not? You cannot be sure how much I know, and I have no notion of the extent of what has been revealed to you. We observe one another, both reluctant to break our vow of absolute silence. I, too, have been hesitating for a long moment, Madame. I veer between the certainty that in the face of this partially glimpsed danger we must inevitably confide in one another, and the fear of making a disastrous error of judgement by unreservedly giving you my trust.'

Annelette's words perfectly captured Éleusie de Beaufort's own thoughts.

'Then we must be brave, daughter, for it takes courage to trust others. What did Benoît tell you about the quest?'

The apothecary's gaze strayed towards the window:

'In truth, not a great deal. Benoît was afraid that too much knowledge might endanger the brothers and sisters who had joined his cause. No doubt he was right. His death is painful evidence of it. He revealed a few of the facts to me, but in such a disjointed way that I cannot be sure of having grasped everything. I can only relate them to you as they were related to me, over time. He spoke of a thousand-year-old struggle between two powers. Since the discovery of a birth chart, or rather two birth charts that are now in our possession, this secret but bloody war has been moving steadily towards its climax. One of the two planetary alignments concerns a woman whose whereabouts will become known during a lunar eclipse. Up until now the estimation of these two birth dates has been hindered by an erroneous astrological calculation. This woman must be protected, even at the cost of our lives. You play a key role in her protection, and I in turn am your guardian. That is all I know.' Annelette turned her gaze from the gardens and studied Éleusie before concluding: 'Why did I not think of it before? The woman is Agnès de Souarcy, isn't she?'

'We think so . . . but we are not entirely sure. All of Francesco's research and calculations point to it being her.'

'Why is her life so precious?'

'We still do not know despite our endless speculations. Madame de Souarcy has no link with the Holy Land . . . Therefore she does not belong to the holy lineage as we had first supposed. Come and sit down here next to me, Annelette.'

The towering woman moved a few paces from the door with what seemed a heavier step than usual. Éleusie enquired:

'Are you afraid?'

'Of course I am, Reverend Mother. And yet doesn't human greatness lie in the ability to conquer that inborn fear which makes us want to hide in a hole and never come out, and carry on fighting?'

Éleusie gave a wistful smile.

'You might be describing my life. I have always been afraid. I have tried hard to be brave and have failed more often than I have succeeded. I increasingly regret that death spared me and not one of my sisters. Any one of them would have been so much stronger and more resolute than I.'

Annelette sat down beside her on the edge of the bed and said softly:

'How can you be sure of that? Who knows where or to what end we are being moved on the chessboard of which you spoke?'

The apothecary nun let out a sigh. The two women sat in silence for a moment. Éleusie was the first to speak:

'I feel as if I am surrounded by an impenetrable fog. I have no idea what to do or which way to turn.'

Annelette sat up straight, declaring in her usual commanding tone:

'We are not alone now. There are two of us, and I have no intention of allowing that evil snake to strike again with impunity. No! She will have me to contend with, us, and we will show her no mercy!'

The Abbess felt some of the same self-assurance – the same

anger even – that she detected in Annelette. She too sat up straight and asked:

'What can we do?'

'Firstly, we must increase our vigilance in order to guarantee our own safety. As I told you, Abbess, our lives are no longer ours to do with as we please, and certainly not to make a gift of to any murderess. Secondly, we shall conduct an investigation. Benoît is dead. We are therefore on our own and can expect no more timely help from him. The criminal is cunning. I suspect that she pilfers my remedies from the cupboard in the herbarium, which proves that she is well versed in the art of poison. I plan to remove the contents of certain bags and phials. We will need to store them in a safe place . . .'

Éleusie immediately thought of the library. No, she would keep the knowledge of that secret place even from Annelette.

'Then I will lay a little trap of my own for that snake.'

'What trap is that?'

'I prefer it to remain a surprise, Reverend Mother.'

Annelette's caution reassured Éleusie: the apothecary nun would not be taken in by anybody. So she did not insist upon being told her plan and simply nodded.

'And now,' her daughter continued, 'we must turn our thoughts to Blanche de Blinot. Why would anyone want to murder a senile old woman who is going deaf and forgets everything she says or does from one moment to the next?'

The portrait was scarcely a charitable one, but Éleusie was beyond the customary petty reproofs it had been her task to mete out before.

'Blanche is our most senior nun,' the apothecary continued,

'and your second in command, as well as acting prioress during her moments of lucidity, which are becoming few and far between.'

Annelette jumped up. A sudden thought had occurred to her. She pointed an accusatory finger at the Abbess and all but shouted:

'And she is guardian of the seal!'

'My seal!' Éleusie cried out in horror, also jumping up. 'Do you think somebody might have taken it? A seal breaker![24] My seal can be used to send secret messages to Rome, to the King, to sign deeds, even death sentences . . . and any number of other things . . .'

'When Blanche is not using the seal to authenticate minor documents in your name in order to lighten your chores, where is it kept?'

'In my safe with my private papers.'

No sooner had she spoken than it dawned on her. Annelette appeared not to notice her unease for she insisted:

'And is it there now?'

'No . . . I mean, yes, I am certain it is,' confirmed the Abbess, touching her chest to make sure that the key she always wore on its heavy chain was still there.

The sudden change in her voice alerted Annelette, who studied her attentively and waited for her to continue.

'As an extra precaution, every abbey safe has three keys. The lock will not open without the combination of all three. It is the custom for the Abbess to have custody of one, the guardian of the seal another and the prioress the third.'

'Am I to understand that as guardian of the seal and prioress Blanche keeps two keys?'

'No. Our senior nun's waning faculties induced me to take one back and entrust it to the cellarer nun, who answers directly to me and whose position in the abbey hierarchy makes her the obvious next choice.'

'That spiteful creature Berthe de Marchiennes! I wouldn't trust her with my life.'

'You go too far, my child,' Éleusie chided half-heartedly.

'And what of it? Have we not gone beyond polite pleasantries? I don't trust the woman.'

'Nor do I,' the Abbess confessed, 'and she is not the only one.'

Éleusie paused for a moment before recounting the curious scene she had stumbled upon some weeks before: the exchange between the schoolmistress, Emma de Pathus, and Nicolas Florin, whom she had been obliged to lodge at the abbey.

'Emma de Pathus actually spoke to the inquisitor whose presence we were forced to endure?' echoed Annelette Beaupré, stunned. 'The man is evil. He is one of our enemies. What could they have been talking about? Where might she know him from?'

'I have no idea.'

'We must keep a close watch on her, then. But firstly we must ensure that nobody has stolen the key from Blanche.'

'The safe cannot be opened without my key.'

She could read in her daughter's strained expression the thoughts that she was keeping to herself. Éleusie voiced them for her:

'Indeed . . . If Berthe de Marchiennes . . . I mean, if the murderess is already in possession of the other two keys, then I am the last remaining obstacle,' she concluded. 'Let us go and question Blanche . . . Dear God, poor Blanche . . . what easy prey.'

They found the old woman in the steam room as they had expected. Blanche de Blinot sought relief for her aching bones in the only room that was heated at that time of year. She had made a little niche for herself in the corner where, with the aid of a lectern, she was able to sit and read the Gospels instead of standing up on painful limbs. The senior nun looked up at them, her eyes red from crying, and stammered:

'I would never have believed that I might one day live through such a terrible thing, Reverend Mother. Poor little Adélaïde, a poisoner in our midst, and one of our own. Has the world come to an end?'

'No, dear Blanche,' Éleusie tried to comfort her.

'Everybody is convinced that I am gradually losing my faculties and no doubt they are right. But my mind hasn't stopped working entirely. That tea was meant for me, wasn't it?'

The Abbess paused for a moment before admitting:

'Yes, dear Blanche.'

'But why? What have I done to make anyone wish to kill me? I, who have never offended nor harmed even the smallest of creatures?'

'We know, sister. Annelette and I have considered this atrocity from every angle and have gradually come to the conclusion that it wasn't a personal attack on you. Do you still have the key I gave you? The key to the safe.'

'The key? So this is about the key?'

'We think it might be.'

Blanche sat up straight on her lectern, trying not to wince with pain.

'What do you take me for!' she exclaimed in a voice that

brought back to Éleusie some of the woman's former determination. 'My mind might wander sometimes, but I am not senile yet, contrary to what some say.' She shot Annelette a withering glance. 'Of course I still have it. I can feel it all the time.'

She pulled a leg out from under the lectern and thrust an ungainly leather shoe at the apothecary nun.

'Come on. Since you're still young, take off my shoe for me and roll down my stocking.'

The other woman obeyed. She discovered the tiny key under the sole of Blanche's foot. The metal had left its indentation in the pale flesh.

'This can only add to your aches and pains,' Annelette remarked.

Intent upon scoring a victory, Blanche retorted:

'That may be so, but I can be sure I'll never mislay it. Do you really think you are the only one in this abbey with an ounce of common sense?'

The apothecary nun stifled a smile she deemed incongruous in these perilous circumstances, and confessed:

'If indeed I did entertain such thoughts, you have proved me wrong.'

Blanche acknowledged her sister's rejoinder with a nod of satisfaction and declared:

'Your honesty does you credit.' A sudden sadness extinguished the old woman's fleeting contentment. 'You are right about one thing, though. I am very old and prone to falling asleep. No. I do not resent any remarks you might have made about my enfeebled state.' Turning to the Abbess, she concluded: 'Reverend Mother, you are aware of the friendship, esteem and affection I feel for you. Pray relieve me of the burden of this key. If I found this painful hiding place, it was because there were times when during my too frequent naps I felt something brush against my neck or waist. Perhaps it was merely an impression, as in a dream. But I took it seriously enough to choose . . . my shoe.'

'And it was very wise of you, Blanche,' Éleusie praised her. 'Let us entrust the key to our apothecary. We will publicly announce that you have been disencumbered of it at your own request without revealing who its new keeper is and in this way . . .'

'No one will try to kill me in order to steal it,' the old woman finished the sentence for her.

'What a shrewd idea of yours, sister, to keep it in your shoe. I shall do the same,' Annelette lied.

She had already decided upon a hiding place. She regretted lying to poor Blanche but continued to believe that the old sister's advanced age had weakened her faculties and was concerned lest she give herself over to idle and dangerous chatter. Only she and the Abbess would know where she planned to keep the key.

They left Blanche de Blinot, safe in the knowledge that she would sleep more easily.

Back in her study, the Abbess said:

'Lend me your key for a few moments. I am going to ask the cellarer nun for hers, too. I want to make sure that my seal is safe. I shall see you afterwards, Annelette.'

The other woman understood that she was being dismissed and did not take offence. No doubt the safe contained private documents. Moreover, she had to prepare her little trap, as she had chosen to refer to it.

Éleusie de Beaufort found Berthe de Marchiennes, the cellarer nun, by the hay barn. She was overseeing the counting of the hay bales being stacked in a pile by four serfs. Éleusie was instantly puzzled by Berthe's expression. She could detect no hint of sorrow on her face, or indeed any emotion whatsoever. Éleusie stifled a growing feeling of hostility. Berthe had not been close to Adélaïde, nor was she to any of the sisters. The cellarer nun was muttering under her breath:

'For goodness' sake! What idlers! At this rate we'll still be here at nightfall.'

'The bales are heavy.'

'You are too charitable, Reverend Mother. The men are slothful, that's all. All they think of is eating their fill at our expense. My father was right to . . .'

Berthe stopped in mid-sentence. Her father had beaten the living daylights out of his serfs, blaming them for all his own mistakes. He had starved them and left them to die like animals and the Abbess knew it. Just as she knew that the late Monsieur de Marchiennes had taken one look at his newborn baby girl before declaring her ugly as sin, without prospects, and never giving her another thought. Berthe clung to a dream she knew to be impossible. She still aspired to the life she felt she had been deprived of, a life in which she would have been beautiful, the life her name predisposed her to, had it not been for her father's indifference and stubborn foolhardiness, which had been the ruin of the family.

'My dear Berthe, would you please lend me the key to the safe which I put in your charge.'

Éleusie thought she saw a flicker of hesitation on the cellarer's face, and was surprised by the woman's sudden awkwardness as she stammered:

'Why, naturally . . . I . . . I always keep it with me. Why . . . Of course it is not for me to question your reasons for opening the safe, but . . .'

'Quite so,' interrupted Éleusie sharply. 'The key, if you please.'

The Abbess was becoming uneasy, on edge. Was Berthe going to tell her she had lost it? Had her silent reservations about the cellarer nun been justified? She held out her hand.

The other woman's crumpled, embittered little face creased up even more. She unbuttoned her robe, pulled out a long leather thong and lifted it over her veil. On the end of it hung the key.

'Thank you, daughter. I shall return it to you the moment I have finished with it.'

A quarter of an hour later Éleusie was shaking so much as she jiggled the three keys into position in the lock that it took her two attempts. She scarcely glanced at the seal, but let out a loud sigh of relief as her hand alighted on the *pergamêné*[25] containing the plans of the abbey. It was the only record of the existence and location of the library, and the Abbess was no longer in any doubt that this was what the murderess was looking for.

Château de Larnay, Perche, November 1304

Eudes de Larnay reread for the fifth time the brief summons signed by the inquisitor, Nicolas Florin.

What was the meaning of this new development? When Florin had advised him to produce a written statement from Mathilde de Souarcy, he had understood that the young girl would not be required to appear before her mother's judges. It was not so much that the baron wished to protect his niece, but that he was afraid that the tissue of lies he had filled her with might begin to unravel during a cross-examination.

And what of it! Florin had enough evidence to keep Agnès rotting in prison for a few months and to dispossess her of her dower! Since he was now Mathilde's legal guardian, her inheritance belonged to him for the time being. Time enough for him to achieve his aim. That flighty little madam wouldn't have a penny left to her name once he had finished with it. And when her uncle had tired of her youthful charms he would send her to a nunnery whether she liked it or not. After all, girls there were fed and clothed and at least no one could hear them lamenting their fate.

He felt that the inquisitor was treating him very lightly. He even appeared to make barely veiled threats. Eudes reread the note aloud:

'. . . You will bring your niece to the Inquisition headquarters at Alençon without further ado and leave her alone in our company so that we may determine the reliability of her suspicions and grievances regarding Madame her mother . . .'

There was no entreaty, no polite phrasing.

Eudes was seething. It meant taking Mathilde all the way to Alençon. No doubt they would have to arrange a wagon since the foolish girl was terrified of horses and slumped over the neck of her mount like a straw doll hanging on to the reins. Agnès was like a centaur in comparison, undaunted even by the perilous ladies' side-saddles. The fastest, most spirited destriers responded to the pressure of her calf as though they had at last found their true master. It was Eudes, no one else, who had taught her to sit in a saddle from the age of five. She had shrieked with laughter, ducking to avoid low branches, fearlessly fording river beds, clearing hedges and was often the victor when they raced each other.

Suddenly, he felt aghast at the stupidity of his plan. What had he been thinking! Besides money and the power it brings, all that had ever mattered to him was Agnès. How had it come to this? What did he care for that foolish, heartless girl strutting about in cast-offs while her aunt, who had died giving birth, was barely cold in the ground? Agnès would rather have put on the clothes of a beggar than accept such unseemly gifts. She would have held her head up high, a queen among queens clothed in rags, and all would have bowed before her. She would have slept on bare boards like a dog rather than occupy the deserted conjugal bed. Dear God, how had it come to this?

Was it him or their blood ties that repulsed her so? It must be their blood ties. If he believed otherwise, it would drive him mad. Yet what did she really know of her true origins? Agnès's mother might have lied in order to force the late Baron Robert to recognise her child. In any case, his father Robert, his grandfather, and now Eudes himself, the last in the male line of the de Larnay family, had sired so many bastards that he sometimes wondered whether he might not be bedding his sisters, nieces, cousins, aunts, even his own daughters. And what of it? In the end were they not all descended from Adam and Eve? Had not Adam and Eve borne two sons, one of whom had killed the other? They all shared the same blood.

A thought was slowly forming through his rage and jealousy, through the pain of his unrequited love and frustrated desire. Until then he had believed he was the sole originator of his plan, but had he not in fact been manipulated? True, he had for years dreamed of wreaking his revenge on Agnès, of making her pay for her arranged marriage to Hugues de Souarcy by robbing her of her dower. But never of handing her over to the Inquisition. He trawled his memory.

Incapable of admitting that he was an animal driven by his passions and brutalised by his lack of intelligence, Eudes discovered the one person he could blame: Mabile.

He raced up to the servants' quarters, where his mistress and accomplice had been holding court since her return to the château. She had cleverly insinuated to the other servants that not only did she serve her master in his kitchen but also in his bed, thus making them respect her more, since none could be sure of the true extent of her influence.

Eudes found her sprawled on her bed, dipping her finger in

a pot of honey and licking it. She greeted his arrival with a suggestive smile and opened her legs beneath her dress. Under other circumstances such an invitation would have produced an immediate effect. Not today. He seized the girl by the scruff of her neck and slapped her with such force that she moaned:

'What . . .?'

'You lied to me! You've been lying to me from the start,' he exploded.

Bewildered, Mabile snapped back:

'Well, that makes two of us.'

Another blow, this time from his fist, sent her hurtling to the floor.

The servant understood that her master's anger was real and that he was quite capable of giving her a thrashing. Dragging herself up onto all fours, she cried:

'My lord . . . what is it?'

'The truth. I want the truth this instant. If you lie to me again I'll kill you.'

The girl's fear gave way to rage. That loathsome Agnès. She should have known. She sat back, her legs folded under her, and hissed:

'Is my lord feeling pricked by remorse? Well, it's a little late for that.'

Eudes walked over to the crouching girl and kicked her in the chest, eliciting a cry of pain. She fell forward, and even as she gasped for breath her body shook with malicious glee as she spluttered:

'I'll wager the lovely Agnès isn't quite so full of herself these days. And, if you don't mind me saying so, I wouldn't bother trying to save her. The punishment reserved for perjurers is scarcely better. And the same goes for that haughty little madam you treat as though she were the lady of the house. It's too late, I tell you! That lynx Agnès de Souarcy is going to die and it serves her right.'

'Who told you that?'

'I found your mysterious visitor's suggestion most appealing, a real ghoul he was . . . Though not unreasonable. He spoke of such punishments and abuse as I could never have dreamed of inflicting upon the lovely Agnès, and then gave me the name of the Grand Inquisitor you were to see.'

Eudes realised that Mabile's hatred would only end when her rival was dead. He understood that he had been used, that he had fallen headlong into a trap he had wrongly believed was of his own making.

'Why . . . Why do you hate her so much?'

'Why?' she hissed venomously. 'Why? Because without even having to ask she received everything I begged to be given. Because she grudgingly deigned to accept what I wanted so desperately I was prepared to kill for it. Because when you bed me you want me to be her. Need I go on?' She let out a spiteful laugh before concluding: 'I'm not without brains . . . It was I who stole her pretty little handkerchief and planted it a few yards from where the bailiff's men found that corpse. The fools . . . They didn't even realise that if they didn't find it the first time they looked, it was because somebody had hung it on a low branch after the murder. If the bastard manages to escape the clutches of the Inquisition, which I doubt, she will fall directly into the hands of secular judges.'

Eudes felt as though a huge abyss were opening up in front of him. He enquired in a trembling voice:

'She never really lay with her chaplain, did she?'

'What of it? Provided people believe she did, that's good enough for me. As for that pest Clément's mother being a heretic, it is more than likely, but I couldn't give a fig either.'

Eudes felt an icy chill descend on his thoughts and declared blankly:

'You have half an hour in which to leave the château. You will take with you only enough food for a day's consumption. You will be searched before you go. Should you dare to return here or communicate any of our shameful secrets you will meet a slow and painful end.'

With these words he left the room. Mabile remained motionless for a few moments, unsure whether to cry tears of rage or sorrow. Rage prevailed for she had learned long ago that tears offered no protection.

She rose to her feet, vowing through clenched teeth:

'You'll pay for this a hundredfold, my master!'

Fortunately, the money she had been squirrelling away for years was hidden in a safe place at Clairets. Together with what she knew about Eudes, from whom she intended to exact a high price in exchange for her silence, it would enable her to start a new life elsewhere on a good footing. Pleased at her own foresight, she prepared to leave, putting on several layers of clothing.

'You'll pay for this, I swear upon my soul.'

*

Eudes lay slumped over the table in the main hall, his head resting in a red pool that was too watery to occasion any alarm on the part of Monsieur Manusser, Madame Apolline's former apothecary. Furthermore, the empty pitcher lying beside him suggested that his master's sleep was not due to tiredness. He tapped Eudes on the shoulder then quickly stepped back. Eudes groaned in his drunken stupor then sat up, his eyes half closed.

'What is it?' he roared.

'Mabile left an hour ago, my lord; she took the road north. You instructed me to inform you.'

'Is it dark yet?'

'Almost.'

'Was the hussy searched before she left?'

'Your orders were carried out to the letter. Barbe searched her thoroughly, including her private parts. Mabile could not have concealed anything of value or any document about her person. We provided her with an oil lamp, as you requested, and with enough food for a day.'

'Good. Is my horse saddled?'

'Just as you instructed, my lord.'

Eudes stood up, a little unsteady on his feet, and said:

'I need to clear my head. Have a bucket of cold water sent to me at once. I must . . . visit my mine.'

Sceptical but eager not to provoke his master's rage, the apothecary bowed and left.

Eudes's fist came crashing down on the table.

'Ugly whore! Your evil scheming is over! Prepare to commend your soul to God – if indeed he does not reject it in disgust, for it must be putrid.'

He had given her an hour's start to enable her to put a good distance between herself and Château de Larnay. The light from the oil lamp would help him find her.

Eudes rode through the forest. The sky was clear and the night air fresh and invigorating. A fine evening for an execution. Mabile had become too dangerous. Even so, he would follow her advice. It was impossible for him to retract his accusations, still less those he had put into his silly little niece's mouth. He soon spotted her. She was following the road, keeping close to the edge of the forest, ready to sneak into the undergrowth at the slightest sound. She swung round to face the thunder of hooves, and Eudes raised his arm to put her at ease. He slowed his mount, stopping a few paces from her.

'I let my temper get the better of me,' he conceded gruffly.

Mabile raised her lamp so that she could see her master's face. Reassured, she gave a grin of triumph.

'Let us return,' Eudes ordered.

He dismounted and walked towards her. She wriggled coquettishly and pressed her body up against his. Two hands gripped her throat. She gasped and tried to struggle, scratching at his eyes, her legs thrashing about helplessly. He pressed as hard as he could, grunting with the effort. He felt something give in the girl's throat. Mabile kicked one last time then went limp. He released his grip and her lifeless body slumped to his feet like a bundle of rags.

He dragged her into the bushes. Looking back one last time without a trace of sorrow or remorse on his face, he left her lying a few yards from the road with her skirts hitched up. If anybody found her before the animals got to her, they would conclude that she had been raped and left for dead by some vagabond. Her peasant's dress would rule out any thorough investigation.

Eudes felt relieved as he climbed back into his saddle. After all, she was just a servant, a strumpet who had turned out to be a little cleverer than the others. What's more, she had been presumptuous and, above all, foolish enough to have lied to him about the chaplain. He should have got rid of her sooner. He had been far too indulgent. They were all the same, these harlots. Give them an inch and they take a mile!

Clairets Abbey, Perche, November 1304

NIGHT was falling. A sharp wind had risen and was rattling the wooden shutters on the herbarium door. A pensive Annelette examined the contents of her tall medicine cabinet. She enjoyed these peaceful moments of solitude, this feeling of using her intelligence to rule over a domain that might be limited to the stout walls of the tiny building, but was hers.

Her fear had abated, as had her concern for the Abbess's life. They had discussed the threat; now it was time to act. She was faced with a cunning enemy, clever as well as crafty – in short a worthy adversary. What had begun as a mission to protect the Abbess had turned into a personal challenge, a sort of wager with herself. Would she turn out to be the stronger, wilier opponent? Annelette's foe, unbeknownst to her, had provided her with the chance to prove her ability. Annelette had waited all these years for an occasion to test the extent of her superiority, but had lacked any objective yardstick. Deep down, she was convinced that she was confronted with a creature whose brain worked exactly like hers, with the enormous difference that her opponent had chosen to serve evil. The apothecary nun had submitted fairly easily to the monastic rules of this community of women whom she mostly despised – just as she would a community of men. For her it was the lesser of two evils. And yet the thought of doing battle with another mind thrilled her. She would leave the prayers and supplications to others and make use of the intelligence God had given her. This was the most glorious mark of appreciation, the most complete form of allegiance she could show Him.

Annelette let out a sigh of contentment: the battle was about to begin and she would show no mercy. She would bring to bear all her scientific knowledge, her intellect and her loathing of superstition in the bid to combat her enemy's cunning wickedness. She experienced a frisson of elation: when had she ever felt this free, this strong? Probably never.

She began by taking down all the bags of dried, powdered plants, the phials and jars containing the solutions, decoctions, spirits and extracts she had prepared during the spring and summer seasons. On the edge of the stone slab she set aside for later use a small ampoule with a brown wax seal and then sorted the other remedies into two separate piles on the larger table. On the left she placed those preparations which could not prove fatal in the tiny quantities a poisoner would use if adding them to food or drink: dried sage, thyme, rosemary, artichoke, mint, lemon balm and a host of others used to flavour food, as well as for treating minor ailments. On the right, she put the toxic substances that she would give to Éleusie to put in a safe place. Curiously, the phial of distilled *Aconitum napellus* root, which she used to treat congestive inflammations, general aches and pains and gout, did not appear to have been tampered with. Where, then, had the murderess procured the aconite that had killed poor Adélaïde? Unless she had been planning this for some time and had stolen the liquor the year before. Annelette then carefully examined the embroidered red lettering on the bags whose contents were toxic, and wondered which of them she might have chosen had she harboured evil intentions. Her gaze lingered on the crushed *Digitalis purpurea*[26] leaves she used for treating dropsy and heart murmurs, the *Conium maculatum*[27] she prescribed for neuralgia and painful menses, and the powdered *Taxus baccata*[28] she mixed with handfuls of wheat in order to exterminate the field mice that attacked their granary. She was startled by how light the last bag felt. She hurried to the lectern where she kept her bulky register. In it she recorded the details of every prescription and what each bag weighed at the end of the week. She should have ten ounces of *Taxus baccata*. She rushed over to the scales. The bag weighed just over nine ounces. Nearly an ounce of yew was missing – enough to kill a horse, and therefore a man or a nun. Who would be the next victim? She scolded herself. She was looking at the problem from the wrong angle again. There were two possibilities. One was that their enemy was allied to the forces of darkness struggling to put an end to their quest. If this were the case, the poisoner would run into two obstacles in the form of her and Éleusie de Beaufort. The other possibility was more mundane but no less lethal. The poisoner was motivated by hatred or jealousy, in which case the next victim's identity would be far more difficult to predict. Another thought occurred to her and she checked her register again for the date when she had last weighed the bag. She could now completely rule out one of her least likely suspects: Jeanne d'Amblin. The powdered yew could only have been stolen during the two days preceding Adélaïde's murder – that is to say during one of the extern sister's rounds. In any event it was a clever choice for there was no antidote. The symptoms of yew poisoning were nausea and vomiting followed by shaking and dizziness. The victim would quickly plunge into a coma before dying. The discovery confirmed Annelette's suspicions: the murderess was knowledgeable about poisons . . . Or else she had been advised by someone who was, but who?

She must reflect, find a method of counterattack. The bitter taste of yew could only be disguised in something very sweet and heavily spiced. In a cake. Or – and this would be the height of criminal ingenuity – in another bitter-tasting medicinal potion. Thus whoever drank the nasty-tasting brew would not suspect that it contained poison.

It took Annelette a good hour to finish stacking the lethal substances in a big basket and replacing their phials and bags with harmless ones. She swapped aconite for sage, digitalis for milk thistle and filled with verbena the bag marked *Daphne mezereum*,[29] that beautiful red-flowering plant, three berries of which were enough to kill a wild boar. The murderess could pride herself on having alleviated her next victim's cough, colic or cramp if she decided to use it.

A smile spread across Annelette's lips. She had come to the final stage of her plan. She removed the piece of cloth covering the crate of eggs she had filched from under the nose of the sister in charge of the fishponds and the henhouses. Poor Geneviève Fournier would probably have a fit when she discovered that fifteen of her beloved hens had not laid. She saw in the number of eggs she collected each morning proof of her good ministering to her birds and of the Lord's munificence in her regard. The more eggs they laid the more puffed up with pride she became, until she took on the appearance of a plump, contented mother hen. Annelette frowned at herself for thinking such uncharitable thoughts. Geneviève Fournier was a charming sister, but her harping upon the necessity of singing canticles to her hens, geese and turkeys in order to fatten them up for eating bored the apothecary sister as rigid as the necks of the ducks Geneviève crammed with grain.

She looked up as she heard a muffled sound coming from outside. It was well after compline.* Who was up at this time of night? She lowered the covers of the two lighted sconce torches and walked towards the herbarium door. The sound started up again: cautious footsteps on the pebble paths that formed a cross separating the herb beds. She pulled open the shutter and found herself face to face with Yolande de Fleury, the sister in charge of the granary and one of her prime suspects, for who could obtain contaminated rye more easily than she? The plump woman turned white with fright and clasped her hand to her chest. Annelette demanded in an intimidating voice:

'What are you doing here at this time of night, sister, when all the others are in bed?'

'I . . .' the other woman stammered, her cheeks turning red.

'You what?'

Yolande de Fleury gulped and seemed to spend a long time searching for an explanation as to why she was there:

'I . . . I felt an attack of acid stomach coming on just after supper . . . and I . . .'

'And you thought you might find the right remedy yourself.'

'Blackthorn usually . . .'

'Blackthorn can be used for a range of ailments. It possesses diuretic, laxative and depurative qualities, as well as being very good for curing boils. You aren't suffering from boils or acne by any chance, are you, sister? As for acid stomach . . . Milk thistle, centaury and wormwood are preferable. In short, any number of medicinal herbs other than blackthorn. I will therefore ask you again: what are you doing here?'

'I confess that my excuse was a clumsy one. The truth is that I am upset about what has been happening, about poor Adélaïde's terrible death, and I needed to take the air, to think . . .'

'I see. And despite the hundreds of acres of land around our abbey you felt it necessary to "take the air" outside the herbarium?'

The other woman appeared even more distraught, and Annelette thought she might burst into tears. And yet something in her manner, although secretive, convinced Annelette that Yolande de Fleury was not prowling around in the hope of stealing poison from her medicine cabinet. Moreover, the murderess must already be in possession of the powdered yew.

'That's enough, sister! Go back to your dormitory this instant.'

Yolande then astonished the apothecary by clutching the sleeve of her robe and whispering nervously:

'Will you report my presence here to the Abbess?'

Annelette pulled her arm free and, stepping back, retorted:

'Naturally.' She felt suddenly angry and scolded the other woman sharply: 'Have you forgotten, sister, that there's a monster in our midst? Don't you realise that the murderess may have procured the poison from my cabinet, the poison that caused the horrific death of the sister in charge of the kitchens and meals? Or are you simply hare-brained?'

'But . . .'

'No buts, sister. Go back to the dormitory straight away. The Abbess will be duly informed.'

Annelette watched the young woman's hunched, weeping figure vanish into the darkness. What had the foolish woman really been doing there? Her inept excuses had made Annelette frankly doubt that she could be the poisoner. And yet . . . What if her clumsiness were a clever façade?

She went back into the herbarium to finish preparing her masterstroke. She replaced the bags containing the switched contents in the cabinet, and pulled a face as she picked up the tiny ampoule with the wax seal that she had set aside earlier. Cracking the eggs one by one, she separated the slippery whites into an earthenware bowl before adding a few drops of the almond oil which she had had sent from Ostia and used for treating chilblains and cold sores. She stirred the mixture vigorously then sighed as she held her breath and opened the phial. The foul stench of rotten teeth or stagnant marshes filled her nostrils instantly. The substance was essence of *Ruta graveolens* – commonly known as fetid rue or herb of grace. Annelette suspected that the plant's alleged effectiveness as an antidote to bites from poisonous snakes or rabid dogs[30] did not explain the appellation herb of grace, choosing to give credence to a more mundane explanation: despite the Church's condemnation, humble folk for whom another mouth to feed would spell disaster used fetid rue as an abortifacient. In a more concentrated or wrongly administered dose it could prove fatal.

She quickly emptied the contents into the foamy egg whites and stirred the mixture vigorously again with her spatula, trying hard not to retch. Finally, when she was satisfied, she spread a layer of the mixture on the floor directly in front of her medicine cabinet. The oil would prevent it from drying too quickly and make it stick better to leather or wooden soles. She then heaved the big basketful of lethal substances onto her hip and left without locking the door behind her.

The Abbess was expecting her. Annelette Beaupré listened attentively as she walked through the darkness, guided only by the feeble light of a sconce torch. In fact, she did not really feel afraid. The murderess was almost certainly not endowed with the kind of physical strength that would enable her to carry out a direct attack, certainly not on somebody her size.

MATHILDE de Souarcy had arrived an hour earlier escorted by Baron de Larnay, who Nicolas Florin thought was in a lamentable state. His purple-streaked face suggested he had been drinking. The inquisitor was delighted. The signs of human weakness always put him in a good mood. The young girl's sumptuous fur-lined coat, more suitable for a married woman, was evidence that her uncle treated her like an elegant kept woman. Agnan had left them waiting in a tiny, freezing-cold room.

Eudes de Larnay was growing increasingly uneasy, despite the outward display of calm he had affected in order not to scare his niece. He had gone out of his way to be charming to her during the long journey to Alençon, complimenting her on her figure, her appearance, her melodious voice. He had gone through her accusation with her and done his best to point out any possible pitfalls it contained. Finally, he had reminded her that at the slightest sign of any retraction the inquisitorial tribunal had the power to declare her a false witness, which would have dire consequences for them both.

The repulsively hideous young clerk who had shown them into the room reappeared. Eudes stood up as though to accompany his niece, knowing full well that she had been summoned alone. Agnan blushed and stammered:

'Pray remain seated, my lord. Mademoiselle de Souarcy has been requested to appear alone before the tribunal.'

Eudes slumped back in his chair and cursed under his breath.

The anxiety he had managed to suppress throughout the voyage was beginning to gain the upper hand. What if Mathilde let herself be intimidated by this Grand Inquisitor? What if he caught her out with clever arguments, on the finer points of doctrine? No. Florin would receive a generous payment once Agnès had been found guilty. The young girl's claims were a godsend and it was not in his interests to cast doubt upon them. But who were these other judges? Had Nicolas Florin guaranteed their complicity out of his own pocket? After all, Mathilde might be desirable but she was a halfwit.

He had no reason to be alarmed. Mathilde was determined not to do anything that might send her back to that pigsty, Souarcy.

How appealing indeed was the pretty young damsel who was feigning coyness for their benefit; quite the little lady in her sumptuous dress of purple silk, set off by a diaphanous veil of shimmering azure. She stood with her head slightly bowed and her graceful hands clasped over her belly in an admirable show of false modesty. Florin silently approved Eudes de Larnay's taste and wondered whether he had bedded her yet.

He walked over to the young girl and declared in a mellifluous voice:

'Mademoiselle . . . Allow me firstly to praise your courage and unwavering faith. We are all able to imagine just how agonising this must be for you. Accusing a mother is a most painful thing, is it not?'

'Less painful than witnessing her transgressions, it must be said.'

'Quite so,' said Florin ruefully. 'I must now ask you to state your Christian name, surname, status and domicile.'

'Mathilde Clémence Marie de Souarcy, daughter of the late Hugues de Souarcy and of Agnès Philippine Claire de Larnay, Dame de Souarcy. My uncle and guardian, Baron Eudes de Larnay, kindly took me in after my mother's arrest.'

At this point the notary stood up to give his little recital:

'*In nomine Domini, amen.* On this the eleventh day of November in the year of Our Lord 1304, in the presence of the undersigned Gauthier Richer, notary at Alençon, and in the company of one of his clerks and two appointed witnesses, Brother Jean and Brother Anselme, both Dominicans of the diocese of Alençon, born respectively in Rioux and Hurepal, Mathilde Clémence Marie de Souarcy does appear before the venerable Brother Nicolas Florin, Dominican, Doctor in Theology and Grand Inquisitor appointed to the region of Alençon.'

The aforementioned inquisitor thanked him with a perfunctory smile and waited for him to sit down again on the bench. He glanced at the two Dominicans. Brother Anselme was staring at the young girl. As for Brother Jean, whose hands rested on the table before him, he appeared lost in the contemplation of his fingernails. Nicolas stifled his amusement: none of them had the slightest idea of the little tragedy he had arranged, which was about to be played out before them.

Nicolas Florin picked up the big black book that lay on the table and walked up to Mathilde until he was almost touching her:

'Do you swear upon the Gospels to tell the whole truth, to conceal nothing from this tribunal and that your testimony is given freely without hatred or hope of recompense? Take heed, young lady, for by swearing this oath you commit your soul for eternity.'

'I swear.'

'Mademoiselle de Souarcy, you declared in a letter written by your own hand and dated the twenty-fifth of October, I quote: "My soul suffers at the thought of the constant abominations committed by Madame de Souarcy, my mother, and her persistent sinfulness and deviance make me fear for her soul," and then, "The young chaplain, so devout the day he arrived, oblivious to this shadow of evil hanging over us, has much changed under her influence." While reassured in your regard, our concern for your mother grows when we read your words: "God granted me the strength to resist living with evil despite my mother's constant example, but my heart bleeds and is in pain." Are these your exact, unaltered words?'

'Indeed, my Lord Inquisitor,' Mathilde acknowledged in an infantile voice.

'Do you wish to retract, tone down or in any other way modify your accusation?'

'It is an exact reflection of the truth. Any change would be mistaken and a terrible sin.'

'Very good. Scribe, have you recorded the witness's consistency?'

The young man nodded timidly.

'You are still so young, but I implore you to try your best to help us by remembering. When did you first notice that Madame de Souarcy's soul was being contaminated by evil, and what were the signs?'

'I cannot give a precise date . . . I must have been six, possibly seven. I . . .' Mathilde lowered her voice to a whisper as though the enormity of the words she was about to pronounce made her breathless: 'On several occasions I saw her spit the host into her handkerchief during Mass.'

A horrified murmur rose from the men seated around the table. Florin secretly praised Eudes de Larnay. He could hardly have thought up a better idea himself.

'Are you certain your eyes were not playing tricks on you? It is so . . . monstrous.'

'I am certain.'

The grate of a bolt, less rasping than usual. Agnès, exhausted and trembling from lack of food, mustered all her strength and stood up. The slightest effort left her breathless. She had spent the past few nights in a fever and the rancid smell of sweat, mixed with the stench of excrement from the latrine, made her feel sick. Fits of coughing had left her throat raw and she shivered uncontrollably. Her scalp itched so much that she could no longer tell whether it was simple dirt or if her head was crawling with lice. Her dress hung loosely from her body and, despite the coat Florin had given her in a show of kindness, the icy cold pierced her to the bone.

She immediately recognised the gaunt, unsightly face of Florin's clerk, but could not recall the name Florin had used to address him on the evening they had arrived at the Inquisition headquarters – an eternity ago.

'What . . .'

Her teeth were chattering feverishly and she was unable to end her sentence. The words seemed to elude her, like faint sparks flickering in her mind.

'Hush, Madame. I am not supposed to be here. If he ever found out ... I have been going over the evidence for your trial . . . It is a stain on our Holy Church, Madame, a parody, worse still, a wicked deception; every witness statement in your favour, including that of the Abbess of Clairets, my lord the Comte d'Authon, your chaplain Brother Bernard and many more, has gone missing. To begin with I thought they must have been mislaid, and I duly informed the Grand Inquisitor, only to be rewarded with his anger and contempt. He insisted that he had no recollection of them and made it clear that if any evidence had gone missing I was to blame . . .'

A remote feeling of relief. Agnès swayed; her head was spinning. It took all her strength of mind to comprehend what the young man with the weaselly face was telling her. And yet she had not forgotten the flicker of compassion that had rendered him almost beautiful.

'He cleverly insinuated that if I mentioned this loss to anyone, I would be held accountable and punished for my incompetence, adding that out of his compassion and affection for me he would say nothing. I do not fear punishment. My soul is free from sin. Do you know that I was afraid when this beautiful man chose me to be his clerk? I believed . . . I believed him to be an angel come down to earth. I believed that behind the repulsive façade others see he had sensed my purity and devotion. I believed that he had seen my soul as only angels can. Poor fool that I was. He delights in my ugliness for it makes him appear even more beautiful. He has a wicked soul, Madame. He threw out the testimony in your favour. Your trial is a tragic farce.'

'I don't . . . What is your name?' she asked in a dry, hoarse voice.

'Agnan, Madame.'

She cleared her throat:

'Agnan. I am so weak that I can barely stand. He is . . . He is more than just a wicked soul. He is an incarnation of evil. He has no soul.'

She felt herself topple forward and just managed to steady herself by holding onto one of the wall rings used to chain the prisoners' arms above their heads.

Agnan retrieved a lump of bacon and two eggs from his sleeveless cassock and handed them to her.

'Eat these, Madame, I implore you. Gather your strength . . . And clean your face. What you are about to endure is . . . villainous.'

'What . . .'

'I can tell you no more. Farewell, Madame. My thoughts are with you.'

All of a sudden he had gone and the door was bolted so quickly after him that Agnès was unsure of having even seen him leave the cell. She stood trembling, clutching the precious bacon and eggs to her chest, unable to make any sense of his parting advice. Why should she wash her face? What did it matter if she appeared dirty and stinking before her judges, before Florin's paid puppets?

The cross-examination had been going on for over an hour. Florin and Brother Anselme had alternated points of doctrine with questions of a more personal nature in an improvised duet.

'And so,' Florin insisted, 'Madame de Souarcy your mother considered that Noah's inebriation after the flood was sinful, even though he was pardoned for not having known of the effects of wine upon the mind, having never tasted it before?'

'My mother thought him guilty anyway and managed to convince Brother Bernard.'

'Did Madame de Souarcy believe the wisdom of her judgement to be above that of God? That constitutes blasphemy,' the inquisitor concluded.

'Yes,' Mathilde acknowledged, adding ruefully, 'but there is so much more, my Lord Inquisitor.'

Brother Anselme glanced at his fellow Dominican, who had raised his head for the first time since the beginning of the cross-examination and now prompted Anselme to speak with a blink of his eyes:

'Mademoiselle de Souarcy, you write, and I quote: "The young chaplain, so devout the day he arrived, oblivious to this shadow of evil hanging over us, has much changed under her influence. During Mass he utters strange words in a language I cannot understand but which I know is not Latin." Do you recognise these words as your own?'

'I do. They are an exact description of the truth.'

'You are aware that those who have turned from God and gone the way of the devil are sometimes rewarded with the power to speak in strange tongues in order to assist them in their dealings with the devil,' Florin emphasised.

'I did not know,' Mathilde lied convincingly, her uncle having already stressed its importance.

'It is a significant point, which may result in the arrest of Brother Bernard. In your opinion did the two accomplices engage in sinful invocations?' the inquisitor insisted.

Mathilde pretended to hesitate before confessing in a tremulous voice:

'I fear they did.'

'Pray, be more precise, Mademoiselle. Your testimony must help us to shed light upon the true extent of their corruption. We will then be in a position to determine whether your mother is guilty of latria[31] or of dulia,[32] for we do not consider these two heresies in the same light, a further example of our extreme tolerance.'

Mathilde stifled a sigh of relief; two days ago she had no idea what these terms meant and would have been at a loss for words. Her uncle, fearing she might be questioned on this point, had explained them to her, emphasising the extreme seriousness of the crime of latria and insisting that her mother must be accused of it along with the other charges laid against her.

'It pains me greatly to have to tell you. They invoked devils during Mass and recited loathsome prayers in a sinful language, as I wrote in my accusation, then they knelt and sang their praises.'

'In front of you?'

The young girl trembled, seemingly on the brink of tears, as she stammered:

'I believe my mother wished to lead me down the path to hell.'

More shocked gasps rose from the men seated on the bench.

Mathilde heaved a sorrowful sigh before adding:

'One day . . . the servant whom my uncle had been kind enough to give us came to find me. She was so upset she could barely speak. I followed her to the little sacristy in the chapel. A pile of chickens lay there with their throats cut.'

'So, they offered sacrificed animals!' exclaimed Florin, who had been enjoying himself immensely since the cross-examination had begun.

This young girl was a sensation. Her uncle could turn her into a sideshow.

Mathilde nodded and continued:

'In that case they are guilty of latria and this is no doubt the most painful confession I shall ever make.'

Brother Anselme studied her for a few moments before asking:

'Do you believe that Sybille Chalis is to blame for Madame de Souarcy's crimes against the faith?'

'My mother repeatedly told me of her attachment to the girl and of the sorrow she had suffered at her death. Indeed, she always showed an exaggerated fondness for Sybille's posthumous son, Clément.'

Florin chimed in:

'The boy fled even before Madame de Souarcy's time of

grace was up, a clear sign of his overwhelming guilt. Pray continue, Mademoiselle.'

'It is my belief that Sybille sowed the seeds of heresy in my mother, for which she will be damned, and that her son continued her work using all his guile.'

Just then, the door to the vast room opened and Agnan slipped in, hugging the walls until he reached the Grand Inquisitor's armchair. He leaned over and whispered to him that Madame de Souarcy was on her way up the stairs to the interrogation room. Nicolas nodded and rose to his feet:

'Mademoiselle, your bravery is equalled only by your purity. For this reason I do not hesitate to put you face to face with the enemy of your soul. I feel certain that the ensuing exchange will greatly enlighten the noble members of this tribunal, if indeed there is still any need.'

Mathilde stared at him, trying to grasp the meaning of what he had just said. Her puzzlement was fleeting. Her mother walked slowly into the room. No one else present noticed the deep sorrow in the looks exchanged by Brother Anselme and Brother Jean.

Agnès had heeded Agnan's baffling advice after gobbling up the only proper food she had received since her imprisonment. The bacon and eggs had given her a feeling of inner warmth she had not had for days, and her shivering had subsided. She had then managed to give her face a cursory wash and to braid her tangled hair, sticky with grime.

When she saw Mathilde, her pale face brightened and she smiled for the first time since her arrival. She rushed towards her daughter, arms outstretched. The young girl recoiled and turned away. Confused, Agnès came to a halt. She felt a shudder of panic. Had they arrested her daughter, too? Had Eudes perpetrated a second and no less heinous crime? She would kill him, even if it meant eternal damnation.

Suddenly she became aware of a pair of eyes boring into her, and she turned to face them. Brother Jean, the one she had never heard speak, was staring at her. It puzzled her when he shook his head slightly, but she would soon understand.

Florin walked towards her nimbly and gracefully, as though he were gliding over the flagstones.

'Madame de Souarcy. Your dishonesty and the cunning eloquence you have displayed here will be of no use to you now. An angel has guided us to this pure young girl,' he concluded, gesturing towards Mathilde.

Agnès looked at the inquisitor and then at her daughter. What was he saying? She would hold the girl in her arms. Everything would be all right then, she was sure. Life would return to normal then. She would protect her, she would do battle with them all, and the young girl would emerge triumphant. Agnès would not tolerate her being imprisoned, forced to endure the same suffering as her mother. It was only then that she noticed Mathilde's clothes: the sumptuous dress of heavy silk, the veil so sheer she could not recall having seen one finer, her fingers laden with rings. Madame Apolline's magnificent square turquoise, the Bohemian garnets she had worn on her index finger, her thumb ring studded with grey pearls.

She did her best to ignore the voices clamouring inside her head and the truth they were trying to foist upon her. One voice broke through her stubborn refusal to hear – that of Clémence – and said in a whisper: 'Do you see the magnificent amethyst crucifix draped around her neck, my dear? It was left to Madame Apolline by her mother. She wanted to be buried with it. Why do you think Eudes has given it to your daughter? Those pretty wine-coloured beads bought her betrayal.'

The crucifix. Poor sweet Apolline. She would often kiss it while she prayed, as though somehow it restored some of the love of her mother, snatched from life so young.

A sigh in her head. Not hers. The voice's.

Her own sigh rising up her throat. Agnès felt the floor give way beneath her feet. A cold, dark shadow descended over her thoughts. A stony silence filled her head. She collapsed. During the infinite moment when she saw the flagstones flying towards her, during the infinite moment it took for her to hit the ground, she repeated to herself: what have they done to you, my child? Damned. They are damned and will pay a hundredfold for what they have turned you into.

When she came to, she was in a tiny room heated by an ember pot. Agnan handed her an earthenware bowl whose contents she swallowed without saying a word. The fiery alcohol made her cough and suffused her chilled body with warmth.

'The cider is strong but you will find it invigorating.'

'How long . . .'

'Nearly half an hour. You are not with child, are you, Madame?'

Agnès shook her head and murmured:

'You offend me, Monsieur, I am a widow.'

'Upon my soul, I beg your pardon. Madame . . . Mademoiselle your daughter has gone to take lunch with Baron de Larnay. The hearing will resume upon their return.'

She said in a voice she scarcely recognised, a calm, strangely resolute voice:

'So, she was not arrested.'

'No indeed, dear lady, she is your most fearsome accuser . . . I read her letter to Florin. It is pure poison, so sulphurous that it burns the eyes and fingers. I could not . . .'

'I understand,' she interrupted, 'and I am grateful to you for your brave and daring attempt to warn me.'

She reached out and touched his hand. The young man blushed and grasped her fingers which he held to his lips. Choked with tears, he stammered:

'I thank you, Madame, from the depths of my soul.'

'But . . . it is I who am indebted to you. Why do you . . .'

'No. You are living proof that my life has not been in vain, and for this I can never thank you enough. As God's weak creature, I will have found greatness if my miserable efforts help to save innocent souls such as yours, for you are innocent, of that there is no doubt. One as ugly as I could hope for nothing more.'

Suddenly his expression changed. The emotion that had made his voice catch gave way to an unbending resolve:

'Mademoiselle de Souarcy has learned her lesson well, but she is as foolish as she is wicked. This is your only weapon against her.'

'I . . .' Agnès tried to reply but Agnan cut her short:

'There is no time, Madame. They will be sending for you shortly.'

He related her daughter's damning testimony. She was choked with sobs at first. Then she tried to think who could have so thoroughly corrupted her daughter, and felt overcome by a murderous desire to kill the demon, to cleave his heart in two with her short sword, a gift from Clémence that had remained sheathed since her marriage. She envisaged him falling at her feet, a pool of blood spreading underneath him. That demon Eudes. That demon Florin. And then the truth she had been trying to avoid from the moment she first saw Mathilde in the interrogation room thrust itself upon her. Mathilde had joined the forces of evil, bartering her soul for a few colourful trinkets. As her mother she was at least partially to blame. Undoubtedly she had not prepared her daughter well enough, had not provided her with the means to resist the frivolous yet powerful allure of such trivial things. Perhaps she had lavished too much care and attention on Clément's education.

I love you so dearly, Clément. Live, Clément. Live for me.

We are so alike, Clément. Why are you the only light that enters my cell, the one I cling to in order to stay sane? Live, I beg you. Live for my life's sake.

'It appals me to be the bearer of this cruel blow, Madame,' Agnan apologised.

'No, Monsieur. On the contrary, you have made me feel that I am not alone in this hateful place, and whatever becomes of me I cannot thank you enough for that. You have helped me prepare for an event I would never have dared envisage. Thank you, Agnan.'

He lowered his eyes, profoundly grateful that such a beautiful lady would call him by his Christian name.

When Agnès came face to face with Mathilde she was immediately struck by the change in her. Where was the little girl she had brought into the world, had brought up – admittedly fickle and given to tantrums and yet so gay? Before her stood a little woman – a little woman who was no longer her daughter, who was intent upon sending her to the stake. The hatred and resentment she felt for her mother boiled down to a few bits of finery, a few glistening trinkets on her fingers. Agnès had hoped the young girl might try to avoid her gaze. She would have seen in it evidence of some lingering affection or regret, perhaps. Instead Mathilde stared brazenly at her mother with her light-brown eyes, raised her head and pursed her lips.

What followed had been a nightmare skilfully staged by Florin. The horrors, the absurdities Mathilde had uttered in order to seal her mother's fate had left Agnès speechless, unable to respond. Thus, if the flesh of her flesh were to be believed, in addition to heresy she was guilty of sorcery and lechery. A strange torpor had overtaken Agnès. She had refused to fight back or even to defend herself. When, after each new lethal outburst from her daughter, Florin had asked her triumphantly: 'What have you to say to that, Madame?' she had limited herself to replying repetitively: 'Nothing.'

What did the euphoria she sensed in Nicolas Florin matter? Or the brief smiles of encouragement he gave to Mathilde? Nothing. Nothing now.

'If we have understood correctly, you claim that Brother Bernard sprinkled his prayers and sermons with words from a strange, demonic tongue?' the Grand Inquisitor insisted.

'Yes. It certainly wasn't Latin, still less French.'

'Did your mother also speak in this evil tongue?'

'I heard her use it, though not as often as the chaplain.'

'It is common knowledge that women have less of an aptitude for languages than men.'

Maître Richer nodded as he did whenever Florin made a spiteful remark about the fair sex. His ill-tempered little face contorted with petty satisfaction.

'Mademoiselle de Souarcy, I should like to refer back to Clément, who has so . . . opportunely disappeared,' the Grand Inquisitor continued. 'Do you think that he too was seduced by evil?'

Mathilde, weary after two hours of cross-examination, felt a renewed vitality. She made a supreme effort to hide the instinctive hatred she felt for that loathsome wart of a boy. In a voice filled with sorrow, she declared:

'I am sure of it. After all, he could have been contaminated in his mother's womb.'

Why hadn't her uncle Eudes anticipated her being questioned about that vile brat? She paused for a moment before elaborating:

'He, too, spoke in that sacrilegious tongue, and with consummate ease. Indeed, now I come to think of it I am convinced he was the sly but determined architect of my mother's downfall.'

Agnès felt a pain, like a knife striking her chest. She began to stir as though from a long sleep. Clément. Mathilde was attacking Clément. A sudden rush of energy caused the Dame de Souarcy to stand bolt upright. Never!

'Ah! The undeniable proof!' Florin boomed. 'A trio of devil worshippers. I thank eternal Providence for having allowed us to discover them before they were able to poison innocent souls. The boy must be found, arrested and brought before us.'

All of a sudden, the vicelike grip that had been choking Agnès dissolved. Her body forgot the weeks of imprisonment and starvation, the feverish nights. Mathilde, her daughter, her own flesh and blood, not content to manoeuvre her into the merciless clutches of the Inquisition, was throwing Clément into the jaws of those ruthless beasts. Never!

She raised her head and stared coldly at her daughter. Pronouncing each syllable crisply, she retorted:

'My daughter scarcely knows how to spell in French. She has such difficulty reading her prayers that I have been forced to make her learn them by heart. As for the letter she supposedly wrote, there is no doubt in my mind that it was dictated to her or that she copied it out. Since she does not understand a word of Latin, not even dog Latin, how could she be fit to judge the strangeness of any language, whether profane or sacred?'

Florin tried desperately to counterattack, but could only hiss:

'A feeble defence, Madame!'

'It's a foul lie!' Mathilde screeched.

A slow, deep voice boomed through the room. The others all turned to face Brother Jean, who had risen to his feet and was speaking for the second time during the hearing:

'*Te deprecamur supplices nostris ut addas sensibus nescire prorsus omnia corruptionis vulnenera.* How would you render this, Mademoiselle?'

Mathilde decided that this was the moment to burst into tears. She stammered:

'I am . . . exhausted. I can't go on . . .'

'What has become of your recently renewed vigour? How would you render this very simple phrase, Mademoiselle? Did you at least recognise it as Latin and not a profane language?'

A silence descended. Florin searched desperately for an argument, cursing himself for getting carried away by his predilection for games. Incapable of remaining annoyed with himself for very long, he quickly turned his rage on Mathilde. What a fool, what an idiot to have mentioned Latin when she couldn't understand a word of it!

'Madame,' said Brother Jean, turning to Agnès, 'how would you render this sentence?'

'We beg of You humbly to endow us with the unwavering ability to shun all that might corrupt the holy purity.'

'Notary, in accordance with the precautions laid down by the inquisitorial procedure, which state that if any part of an accusation is shown to be false the entire accusation must be called into question, I challenge that of Mademoiselle Mathilde Clémence Marie de Souarcy. I have no doubt that our judicious Grand Inquisitor will endorse this precaution.'

Brother Jean waited. Florin clenched his jaw in anger. Finally he spoke:

'Indeed. The accusation of this young woman is called into question.' He struggled with the urge to hurl himself at Mathilde and beat her, adding: 'Scribe, make a record of the fact that this tribunal has expressed grave doubts regarding Mademoiselle de Souarcy's sincerity and is concerned that she may have already perjured herself. Write down also that the same tribunal reserves the right to bring charges against her at a later date.'

Mathilde cried out:

'No . . .!'

She took a few paces towards the inquisitor, her hands outstretched, and stumbled. Agnan rushed to grab her and led her outside to where Eudes was, rashly, savouring his imminent victory.

Brother Jean tried to catch Agnès's eye, but she was far away. She had plunged into a world of unimaginable pain. She had lost Mathilde and doubted she would ever find her again.

She clung to her last source of hope, of strength: Clément was out of harm's way, for now.

'The fool!' Eudes bawled. 'The unbelievable fool! Why didn't he warn me that he intended to put you face to face with Agnès? I would have dissuaded him . . . You are no match for her.'

Jostled by the movement of the wagon rolling down the road alongside Perseigne Forest, which led to the eponymous abbey, Mathilde had not stopped crying and snuffling into her deceased aunt's lace handkerchief, embroidered with the letter *A* in pretty sea-green thread. Her uncle's last remark cut her to the quick and she stared up at him, her face puffy from weeping. How pink and unsightly she looked, he thought, just like a piglet – a shapely piglet, perhaps, but a piglet all the same.

'What was that you said, Uncle? Am I no match for my mother?'

This was not the moment to upset the little woman. After all, until Agnès had been found guilty he remained her provisional guardian.

'What I mean, my dear girl,' he corrected himself, patting her hand, 'is that you are still young and relatively ignorant of the shrewd tactics used by certain people. It is a great credit to you that you still have scruples.'

'How true, Uncle,' agreed Mathilde obsequiously.

'Your mother . . . well, we both know her well . . . She is cunning and manipulative . . . In short, I admire you for having stood up to her. What an ordeal it must have been for a young girl such as you.'

Mathilde was slowly beginning to feel better. Once again she was cast as her mother's victim – a role she liked so much that she believed in it more and more.

'Yes. But . . .'

'I could have shown that clown of an inquisitor which questions would be favourable to us! But no, the fool was intent on playing his own little game,' interrupted Eudes, still annoyed.

'Something the inquisitor said worried me, Uncle. He threatened to charge me with perjury.'

Had it not been for that depleted mine of his, which was

ruining his financial as well as his political prospects, he would have happily left her to her fate.

'What of it? Another two hundred pounds will see to it. Anything to please you, dear niece.'

'Another?'

Eudes attempted to extricate himself:

'Yes. Two hundred pounds here, another two hundred pounds there, a hundred more for the abbey, and so on . . .'

Mathilde realised in a flash that her mother's trial had been arranged from the beginning, paid for by her uncle. The knowledge comforted her, made her feel secure. The power of money was so tremendous that she determined never to be without it again, at whatever cost.

YOLANDE de Fleury, the sister in charge of the granary, stood, pale-faced, holding her tiny frame as upright as possible, before the Abbess's desk. Éleusie de Beaufort turned towards the windows. The fine layer of early-morning frost that covered the gardens had not yet melted. A mysterious silence appeared to have enveloped the abbey. The Abbess strained her ears: no laughter rang out behind the heavy door to her apartments, breaking off as an admonishing finger was raised to a pair of lips. Sweet Adélaïde had taken with her into her icy tomb the gaiety which these austere, unyielding walls had never managed to stifle. Éleusie had not seen fit to do so either, contrary to the recommendation of Berthe de Marchiennes, the cellarer nun, who would no doubt have preferred everybody to wear her own perennially miserable expression. Claire and Philippine had always been so cheerful, Clémence, too – at least before she married that wretched oaf, Robert de Larnay. Each stifled giggle or suppressed smile from her nuns reminded Éleusie of her sisters and their carefree childhood. It was without doubt Adélaïde's cheerfulness, her daily wonderment, her ceaseless chatter even, that had made her one of Éleusie's favourite daughters.

The insistent gaze of the sister in charge of the granary brought her back to her study, back to the present.

'I shall repeat the question, dear Yolande. What were you doing wandering around outside the herbarium at night?'

'What a nasty telltale,' murmured the sister, her little round chin quivering.

'Our apothecary was only doing her duty. It was imperative that I be informed of your nocturnal foray, which is all the more worrying in the light of . . . the present circumstances.'

'Reverend Mother, you don't imagine that I went there with the intention of stealing poison!'

'I didn't imagine that a poisoner would rob us of our dear Adélaïde either,' the Abbess retorted sharply. 'Answer me.'

'I felt dizzy . . . and terribly restless . . . I needed to take the night air.'

Éleusie heaved a deep sigh:

'So you insist upon sticking to that unlikely tale. You are not making it any easier for me, Yolande, but worse still you are making it more difficult for yourself. You may go now, daughter. Return to your barns, but do not imagine that I've finished with you yet.'

Yolande de Fleury left without further ado. A few moments later Annelette Beaupré walked into her study, accompanied by Jeanne d'Amblin. Despite Blanche de Blinot's role as second in command at the abbey, Éleusie had not invited her to this meeting. Poor Blanche had scarcely uttered a word since discovering that someone had tried to poison her.

Éleusie gave them a summary of the short, unsuccessful conversation she had just had with the sister in charge of the granary.

Annelette said sharply:

'Why does she insist upon behaving in a way that can only make us suspicious?'

'I do not believe for a moment that she could be this . . . this monster,' declared Jeanne, shaking her head.

Annelette retorted instantaneously:

'In that case, what was she doing at night outside the herbarium?'

'I don't know . . . Perhaps she really did need some fresh air. It is possible. What do you think, Reverend Mother?' the extern sister asked, turning to Éleusie.

'What should I think . . .? Naturally I do not see Yolande de Fleury as a *toxicatore*.[33] But then I do not see any of my daughters in such a wicked role. As for Yolande, I am beginning to wonder whether her stubbornness might not conceal . . . a . . . how should I say . . . Goodness, how embarrassing . . .'

'Pray explain to us, Reverend Mother,' said Jeanne d'Amblin, trying to make her feel less awkward.

'Well, as we all know in every cloistered community where celibacy is the rule . . . and this applies no less to our brother monks . . . I mean . . .' She adopted a more matter-of-fact tone. 'Rome is aware that in some monasteries, a lack of emotion and physical contact can lead some of us to engage in relationships with . . . a fellow nun or monk of the same sex.'

Jeanne d'Amblin stared at the hem of her dress and Annelette declared:

'Are you suggesting that Yolande might be carrying on an . . . improper relationship in a place of prayer and meditation?'

'I have no idea, daughter. It is simply a thought that occurred to me, if only because I far prefer it to the idea of

Yolande as a poisoner. One is a minor misdemeanour we can only hope is passing, the other a vile murder requiring flagellation and death.'

A brief silence descended. Annelette Beaupré knew all about such practices. A blind eye was turned to them in the hope that they would remain hidden, above all from the outside world. She herself had been the object of furtive glances and smiles that were more than expressions of sisterly warmth. Such infatuations of the heart and the senses baffled her, and reinforced her general lack of respect for her fellow human beings. Why this need for fleshly contact and kisses when there were so many marvels waiting to be studied and understood? If she had managed to avoid being bedded by a man, it was certainly not so as to be bedded by a woman. Jeanne d'Amblin broke the uneasy silence:

'I can make no sense of this dreadful business! Why would anyone want to poison Adélaïde and why try to kill Blanche, if she really was the intended victim? Unless . . . unless this is a case of insanity or' – she paused to cross herself before finishing her sentence – 'demonic possession . . .?'

The apothecary glanced at Éleusie, seeking her consent, which Éleusie gave with a nod. Annelette explained:

'Assuming that madness does not lie at the root of this murderous act, the only motive we can think of, and which bears some weight . . . are the keys to the safe containing our Reverend Mother's seal. It is customary for the guardian of the seal, our senior nun, to be entrusted with one of these keys. A second is kept by Berthe de Marchiennes, and the third, naturally, is in the hands of our Reverend Mother.'

Jeanne d'Amblin's eyes opened wide with astonishment, and she murmured:

'Falsified documents? But that's terrible . . . That seal can send innocent people to the gallows! And . . . And a lot more besides . . .'

'Undeniably,' Éleusie interrupted. 'But rest assured, Jeanne, the seal is safe; it has not been moved.'

'Oh, thank God . . .' she whispered.

Éleusie could not tell whether the momentary relief this piece of news brought her outweighed their common concern.

Annelette intervened impatiently:

'Yes! If indeed we have discovered the murderess's true motive, we are confronted with a difficult choice. If the seal is what she wants, she will try again. As we plan to announce later, I am now in possession of our senior sister's key. Our Reverend Mother will hold on to hers and the third will remain in the keeping of Berthe de Marchiennes.'

A sudden flash of comprehension registered on Jeanne d'Amblin's face and she all but cried out:

'But that means . . . that means . . . she will try to kill all three of you? Oh no . . . oh no, I couldn't bear it!'

'Do you have a better idea?' asked Annelette, who was becoming irritated.

'Well . . . Well, I don't know . . . I'll think of something, be patient! You say that she tried to poison Blanche in order to take her key. I've got it. Why not hide them somewhere instead of keeping them under our robes or around our necks? Let's hide them in a secret place that only one of us will know about, our Reverend Mother, for example. That way we will trounce the monster at her own game. Poisoning our Abbess won't help her discover the hiding place.'

The logic of the idea should have convinced Annelette, and she was surprised when it didn't. Even so she was honest enough to wonder, fleetingly, whether this was not because she resented Jeanne for thinking of it first.

'Your idea is a good one,' she conceded. 'Let us think about it. Before we do, there is another rather more urgent matter that requires our attention.'

Éleusie cast a bemused glance at her apothecary daughter, who continued:

'First of all, Jeanne, I should inform you that almost an ounce of yew powder has gone missing, the powder I use for killing the rats and field mice that attack our granary.'

'Why was I not told about this earlier?'

'It was stolen during your rounds.'

'Sweet Jesus,' murmured Jeanne d'Amblin. 'She could . . .'

'Yes, she could easily kill one of us with it . . . Which makes me think that another murder is imminent.'

'"Urgent" is certainly the right word!' the extern sister remarked.

'Jeanne, there is a favour I should like to ask of you.'

The sudden hesitancy in the apothecary nun's usually forthright voice alerted the other two women. Having not been consulted beforehand about the appropriateness of any request, Éleusie wondered what she could be about to say.

'I trust that our Reverend Mother will not be offended by my asking you this without giving her prior warning. I . . . Let us just say that I have formed my own suspicions regarding some of the other nuns – suspicions which I am aware may be wholly unfounded . . .'

Such circuitous, cautious speech coming from Annelette, who was normally so blunt, made the other two women uneasy.

'. . . Our Reverend Mother has not influenced my suspicions in any way. To cut a long story short,' she continued more boldly, 'I have very little trust in Berthe de Marchiennes.'

'You go too far,' murmured Éleusie, incredulous.

'Well, that is how I see it,' Annelette retorted, not without a hint of resentment. 'In any event I would like you to keep her key, Jeanne.'

The extern sister looked at her as if she had gone raving mad before exploding:

'Have you taken leave of your senses? Absolutely not! And become the murderer's target in Berthe's place? I refuse! If you were to ask me to guard our Reverend Mother's key in order to protect her life, I would accept. Not without trepidation, I confess, but I would accept. But do not imagine for a second that I would do the same for Berthe . . . Never!'

Despite the gravity of the circumstances, Éleusie found herself stifling a smile. This was the first time she had ever seen Jeanne lose her calm. She said reassuringly:

'My dear Jeanne, I am grateful to you for wanting to protect me. I am grateful to you both. It has taken these terrible events to show me who my true friends are. As for my key . . . I will keep it. Nobody else should bear the burden of responsibility I took on when I joined Clairets.'

Jeanne lowered her eyes to hide her sorrow. Éleusie tried to put her mind at rest:

'My dear Jeanne, this is not my funeral oration. I have no intention of being poisoned before this evil has been eradicated.'

A few moments later when they took leave of one another, Éleusie conveyed to the apothecary with a meaningful look that she wished to speak to her alone.

Annelette accompanied Jeanne d'Amblin along the corridor leading to the scriptorium then took leave of her on the pretext of wanting to verify something, and returned via the gardens.

Éleusie de Beaufort was still standing behind her heavy oak table, apparently not having moved.

'And this little trap you are setting, daughter, when will you give me the results? Time is running out. I can sense the beast is about to strike again.'

'Soon . . . I am waiting, watching and waiting.'

Inquisition headquarters, Alençon, Perche, November 1304

NICOLAS Florin studied the Comte Artus d'Authon, seated on the other side of his tiny desk, with an air of bored politeness.

'I regret, Seigneur, that since you are not a direct relative of Madame de Souarcy I cannot allow you to visit her. I assure you that it pains me not to be able to indulge you in this matter, but I am obliged to follow strict rules.'

Florin waited to see the effect of this barely concealed snub. Artus remained calm, contriving not to betray his simmering rage to the inquisitor. The evil rat was revelling in his power.

'I understand that Madame de Souarcy's cross-examination has already begun.'

'Yes.'

'Do you suppose the trial will go on for long?'

'I fear it will, Seigneur Comte. But do not ask me any further details. The inquisitorial procedure, as you know, is shrouded in the utmost secrecy. We are most keen to preserve the honour and dignity of those brought before us until formal proof of their guilt has been established.'

'Oh, I do not doubt for an instant that Madame de Souarcy's honour and dignity are of the utmost concern to you,' retorted Artus d'Authon.

Florin clasped his hands on his black robe and waited to see what the powerful lord would do next. Would he attempt to bribe him as he had during their first meeting? Would he threaten him or beg him? And he, Florin, which would he prefer? A combination of all three, of course.

But instead of this, Artus's fleshy lips parted in a strange smile, a smile that bared his teeth. Suddenly he stood up, much to the surprise of Florin, who automatically followed suit.

'Since, as I anticipated, my request has been in vain, I would not want to waste any more of your time. I therefore bid you goodbye.'

After the Comte had left, Florin sat brooding. What had in fact occurred? Why had the arrogant fool not begged him? Had he not received a stinging insult? He certainly felt the blood rush to his cheeks as if he had just been slapped. Who did that Comte think he was! So, he wanted to see his female, did he? Well, he should come back in a few days' time. Since she had failed to confess under cross-examination her torture would begin the very next day.

Seized by a murderous rage, he sent his desk flying. Stacks of files and notes lay scattered about the office. He shrieked:

'Agnan, come here this instant!'

The young clerk rushed in and gazed incredulously at the disarray. Florin growled ominously:

'Don't just stand there, you fool, pick it up!'

It was almost none when Francesco de Leone, who was standing in a porch, saw Nicolas Florin leave the Inquisition headquarters. The Dominican responded to the polite greetings of a few passers-by with an unassuming smile then turned into Rue de l'Arche. Leone pulled his cowl over his face and straightened the short, waisted peasant's tunic he was wearing underneath the thick leather apron of a smith. He fell in behind the inquisitor, maintaining a few yards' distance between them. A grubby-looking boy passed him by, then slowed down all of a sudden and sauntered along with his arms behind his back, gazing up at the surrounding buildings. Leone wondered for a moment whether he wasn't up to some mischief.

The knight had no real plan – as he had assured Hermine after her performance as the wealthy Marguerite Galée, eager to send her father-in-law to a better world. He was not sure whether he was hoping to discover compromising evidence that would force Florin to back down or waiting for a situation to arise that would require killing him. Leone was aware that he was allowing himself to be guided by the other man's actions, which might or might not lead to his death. This was not a hypocritical attempt to evade responsibility. Leone had been responsible for many deaths, but had never chosen his victims. Florin, however undeserving, would enjoy what he had been unable to offer the others: a private judgement of God. If he were not meant to die, he would be spared. This was what the Hospitaller sincerely believed.

The inquisitor lengthened his stride, as though he were in a hurry to get somewhere. Perhaps, also, now that they were further away from the Inquisition headquarters he was no longer worried lest somebody question his haste. Curiously enough, the little beggar boy had also quickened his pace and was keeping the same distance between himself and Florin. Leone's soldierly instinct alerted him.

Florin turned right and walked up towards Rue des Petites-Poteries. All of a sudden, he slipped into Rue du Croc. Leone hurried after him but by the time he reached the cobbler's shop on the corner, Florin had vanished and he found himself face to face with the little rascal who was looking equally bemused. Just as the boy was about to run off, Leone leapt forward and grabbed him by the tunic.

'Who are you following?'

'Who, me? Nobody, I swear!'

The knight took hold of the boy's ear and, leaning over, whispered:

'You were following the Dominican, weren't you? I'm a man of little patience so don't lie to me. Who sent you?'

The boy panicked. He certainly didn't look very friendly, this smith. He tried unsuccessfully to wriggle free from his grasp.

'Let go of me!' the boy protested, trembling with fear.

Putting on a threatening voice, Leone said:

'If you tell me the truth, I'll give you three silver coins and let you go. However, if you continue lying to me, I'll give you a good thrashing and throw you in the River Sarthe.'

The little urchin's eyes filled with tears at the thought, but he replied astutely:

'And why should I believe a smith when he says he has three silver coins? I've already got one from my client and he promised me another when I tell him what he wants to know, but he looks like a real lord.'

Without letting go of the boy's ear, Leone reached into his purse with his other hand and took out three coins.

'All right,' the child muttered. 'But let go of my ear. You're hurting me, you brute.'

'If you attempt to run off . . .'

The child interrupted him, shrugging his shoulders:

'Why would I choose a dip in the Sarthe when I can earn proper money?'

Leone stifled a grin and released his ear, but remained ready to pounce at the boy's slightest movement.

'Who paid you to spy?' Leone asked him again.

'He offered me two silver coins to follow the Dominican.'

'Do you know his name?'

'No.'

'What did he look like?'

'Very tall. A big man, bigger than you. And dark, with dark eyes, too. He wears his hair shoulder-length and dresses in fine clothes and carries a sword. A powerful man by the looks of him. I'd say he's a baron, possibly even a count.'

'What age?'

'A lot older than you.'

'What exactly did he ask you to do?'

'To follow the inquisitor without being seen and find out where he lives.'

What was Artus d'Authon doing mixed up in this affair, for Leone was almost certain it was he? His aunt Éleusie de Beaufort had alluded briefly to Agnès de Souarcy's meeting with her overlord just before the young woman's arrest.

'Where are you supposed to meet him?'

'At a tavern called La Jument-Rouge, it's . . .'

'I know where it is.'

Leone handed the boy the coins, which quickly disappeared under his tunic.

'I advise you not to go back and warn your client in order to try to get the other silver coin or I'll . . .'

'I know . . . you'll throw me in the Sarthe!'

The boy turned on his heel and vanished before Leone had decided what to do next.

Was Artus d'Authon a friend or foe? Now was not the time to worry about that.

Which of the buildings had Nicolas Florin slipped into? Leone did not believe that he had discovered he was being followed. He could do nothing but wait, crouched in the shadow of a nearby wall. Sooner or later the man would have to come out again.

A good half-hour went by, during which the knight managed to empty his mind of the endless calculations, theories, questions. Not thinking is a strenuous and exhausting exercise for a man of thought. Accepting nothingness, inviting it, becoming the void, is to allow oneself to experience infinity. Time then passes in a random way. The little barefoot girl who lifts her thick cotton dress, tied with a piece of string at the waist, and squats in the gutter to empty her bladder as she stares at you fills the whole universe. How much time passed before she stood up and ran off? A little ball of hemp blown across the cobblestones comes to a stop then rolls on for a few feet* before stopping again then rolling again, until it reaches a wall where somebody's foot treads on it and carries it who knows where;

for a few split seconds that ball becomes the most important thing in the world.

Francesco de Leone almost didn't recognise the beautiful Nicolas. He cut a dashing figure. He was without question one of the finest-looking creatures Leone had ever seen. His willowy body was perfectly suited to lay clothes. Indeed, it appeared Florin was well acquainted with the latest town fashions. He had swapped the black habit and long white cape of the Dominicans for a silk shirt, on top of which he wore a short tunic that set off his dark-purple leggings and breeches. Elegant Parisians referred to these as *hauts-de-chausses* and *bas-de-chausses*. Over his tunic he wore a bodice lavishly embroidered with gold thread, and a jacket of fine dark-green wool gathered at the waist by a belt covered in gold work and with slits in the sleeves to allow a glimpse of the bodice. The whole was topped off by a greatcoat, open at the front and sides, that would have been the envy of the finest lords, and a hood of a softer green than the jacket, which concealed his tonsure, and whose pointed end he wore hanging down in the style of the young dandies at court.

Francesco de Leone recalled the clothes they were given when they joined the Hospitaller order. Besides bed and table linen they received two shirts, two pairs of leggings, two pairs of breeches, a bodice, a fur-trimmed jacket and two coats, one with a fur lining for winter, as well as a cape and a belted tunic coat. Only when the clothes or linen became threadbare did they take them to the administrator, who would duly replace them. In exchange they handed over their fortune to the order, and in Francesco's case this had been a substantial one inherited from his mother. And yet he had no doubt that the bequest would have pleased the remarkable woman who had given birth to him. As for him, leaving behind his worldly goods had been such an immense relief that he had spent the whole night following this final rite of passage wide awake and in a state of bliss. Clearly the inquisitor did not share his fondness for self-denial.

Claire. As he grew older so the memory of his mother seemed to grow clearer. Her elder sister, Éleusie de Beaufort, resembled her, though she was less pretty, less vivacious. Small things – a made-up poem, a beautiful flower, a child's words, the unusual colour of a ribbon – would elicit his mother's ready laugh. And yet that pale and lofty brow concealed such intelligence and wisdom, some of which Leone liked to believe he had inherited. Added to this was her intuition, which Leone had not been endowed with. He saw in this the price he had to pay for his physical strength and masculinity. She had 'sensed' the twisting currents sweeping along all their lives long before they became apparent. As a small boy Leone had been convinced that this mysterious gift came from the angels. Had she also sensed her own slaughter and that of her daughter at Saint-Jean-d'Acre? No. It was unthinkable, for if she had had such a premonition, she would have escaped in time with her child.

There was so much he did not know about that beautiful, noble woman who had held him in her arms and called him 'her brave knight of the white cross' when he was only five or six years old. Had she already known that he would one day join the Hospitaller order? How was that possible? Had they not simply been loving words from a mother to her son?

Lost in such sweet, painful memories, Leone realised just in time that he was stalking his prey too closely, and running the risk of the other man turning round and seeing him. Florin must not be able to recognise him later on. He slowed his pace.

Did the inquisitor rent a bachelor's apartment in this well-to-do, discreet part of town where he could transform himself at his leisure and perhaps even keep the company of ladies?

He had lined his purse well with the blood of others.

Nicolas Florin was hurrying now. He entered one of the neighbourhoods where the passers-by leave as dusk sets in and the peaceable atmosphere dissolves as another type of creature comes to life. The modest corbelled dwellings appeared in places to form arches above the alleyways. The front of each building was occupied by stalls or workshops. Leone began to notice women whose appearance betrayed their calling*, as required by the Church and civic authorities. Their gaudy, low-cut dresses and the absence of the type of jewellery and belts worn by burghers' wives or noblewomen, which they were prohibited from wearing, marked them out as purveyors of the flesh. Leone deduced that there was a bordel nearby, as in the big cities.[34] A strumpet, scarcely older than fourteen, approached Florin. He sized her up from head to toe as he would a horse. The knight flattened himself in a doorway and observed the transaction taking place a few yards away, hardly daring to imagine what the poor girl would be put through in exchange for a few paltry coins, for he was certain that Florin's sexual preferences would also entail violence and torture. They finally moved away, disappearing into a hemp-and-linen draper's stall that must have fronted a house of ill repute.

A good half-hour passed before the inquisitor re-emerged alone, wearing a look of sly satisfaction, and Leone wondered whether the poor girl was still able to stand. The pimps who supplied the wine and candles never interfered with their customers' antics, however abusive, so long as they got their money.

Florin walked back the same way he had come, Leone following behind, only instead of turning into Rue des Petites-Poteries he went straight on until he reached Rue de l'Ange where he slipped through the doorway of a well-to-do town house. Leone waited a few moments before approaching. The ground and first floors were made of stone with a half-timbered second floor above. The newly tiled roof had no doubt replaced the original thatched one, suggesting that the owner was extremely wealthy. The little dormer windows were wooden and protected by oilcloth, and all the interior shutters were closed, apart from those on the first floor. The pipes draining dirty water from the kitchen onto the street were dried up, as were those funnelling human waste into sewers or pits. The handsome-looking dwelling seemed to have been recently abandoned.

Florin must have rented a tiny room in Rue du Croc where he could transform himself into a rich burgher and then come to this smart house. But who did it belong to and why did nobody appear to be living there?

It took Leone one hour and much lying to find out the answers to these questions from the various shop owners on Rue des Petites-Poteries and Rue de l'Ange. Monsieur Pierre Tubeuf, a rich draper, having been very opportunely found guilty of heresy and dealings with the devil, had had his property confiscated by the Inquisition. Terrified that any objection on their part might prompt the inquisitor to charge them with the same crimes, his wife and two children had fled the town. Leone had no doubt that this was what would have happened. Florin had awarded himself a magnificent house at the cheapest price.

The knight left the neighbourhood. Now he knew where Agnès's torturer lived.

Artus d'Authon waited, the barely touched cup of buttered ale in front of him. What was the child doing? He should have reported back long ago. The Comte made a supreme effort to suppress his anger and above all his despair. Had the little beggar boy tricked him? And yet the prospect of another silver coin should have been incentive enough. Perhaps Florin had suspected that he was being trailed and the boy had given up. He felt a flicker of fear for the boy's safety, but reassured himself. Those young street urchins were quick on their feet and catching one would be no easy task. He raged against himself. What could he do now? Florin would recognise him instantly if he took it into his head to follow him. He cursed his ineptitude as a man of honour. He was capable of provoking a duel, fighting and winning, yet scheming and subterfuge were foreign to him, and he felt powerless against a sly snake such as the inquisitor. His chief bailiff, Monge de Brineux, was too much like him to be of any use. The solution came to him in a flash. Clément! Florin had never seen the boy and Clément had already shown that he possessed both courage and intelligence. Moreover, he would do anything to save his beloved mistress. Artus felt a great sense of relief and celebrated by swigging back his beer. He would return to Alençon with Clément the day after tomorrow. Come evening, Florin would be back where he belonged – in hell. The Comte would invoke the judgement of God and Agnès would be freed, her accuser having been struck down by the hand of God. He leapt up, almost overturning the table, and rushed out to the astonishment of the other customers.

The knight Leone found Rue des Carreaux, which led to his meeting place at the Bobinoir[35] Tavern, Rue de l'Étoupée. He was guided there by the crier[36] whose job it was to announce the price of wine served at the tavern.

Landlords were commonly named after their establishments and Monsieur Bobinoir, who was no exception, looked up as the knight walked in and wondered what a smith was doing coming into his tavern, which was a meeting place for haberdashers, a guild that was growing in wealth and status and whose members were now considered to be on a par socially with the burghers. Maître Bobinoir paused. His regular customers did not care to rub shoulders with a member of the lowly professions. Then again, as long as the man was not a tanner whose clothes were impregnated with the stench of rotting flesh, or even a common dyer, he did not feel obliged simply to ask him to leave. Besides, something about the man's appearance intrigued Monsieur Bobinoir – a sort of effortlessness, an ease devoid of arrogance. No doubt the other customers sitting at the tables that day felt it too, for after giving him a second glance they quickly returned to their conversations. The smith looked around the room for a place to sit then turned silently to the landlord, who motioned with his chin towards an isolated table.

When Monsieur Bobinoir went over to take his order he made a point of speaking in a loud voice so as to reassure his regular customers:

'We keep good company here, smith, and Bobinoir is pleased to welcome you today. If tomorrow you still have a thirst, be a good fellow and slake it in the tavern serving people in your own trade.'

The smith's deep-blue eyes gazed up at him and Maître Bobinoir, gripped by a sudden anxiety, had to resist the urge to draw back in order to avoid being humiliated in front of his customers. And yet slowly the man's face creased into a smile:

'You are too kind, Monsieur Bobinoir, and I thank you. I accept your hospitality and will remember that it is an exception.'

'There's a good chap,' the landlord boomed, pleased at having more or less stood his ground. 'Will you take some wine?'

'Yes, bring your finest. I am waiting for a friend . . . a Dominican friar. Like me he is not a haberdasher, but . . .'

'A friar!' interrupted Maître Bobinoir, then pronounced solemnly, 'I am honoured to receive him in my establishment.'

A few moments later, Jean de Rioux, the younger brother of Eustache de Rioux, who had been Leone's godfather in the Hospitallers, walked into the tavern. Monsieur Bobinoir now began to fuss over the Dominican, whose arrival he saw as open confirmation that his establishment attracted the salt of the earth and was far from being a den of iniquity.

As his old friend approached the table, the knight stood up to embrace this courageous, honourable soul who had not hesitated to lower himself to spying if it meant remaining true to his faith and that of his departed brother.

'I am angry at fate, Jean, for my pleasure at seeing you after all these years is spoiled by the circumstances that drove me to request your help. But, most of all, I am eternally grateful to you for not hesitating to offer it, despite your duty of obedience to your order.'

'Francesco, Francesco ... What a joy to behold you, too! As for my help, it is only a mark of the friendship and respect I have always felt for you. Eustache thought of you as a son, and you are like a younger brother to me. No request of yours could be anything but pure, which is why upon receiving your brief missive I did not hesitate for a second to offer you my help, likewise Brother Anselme.'

Jean fell silent as Maître Bobinoir approached and set down a cup of frothy beer in front of him. He nodded politely to the man and waited for him to leave before continuing in a hushed voice:

'As for my duty of obedience to my order, it can never outweigh that which I owe to God. Do not think, dear Francesco, that just because we willingly submit to the rule we become sheep. Do not think that we cease to have minds of our own. Many of us, Dominicans and Franciscans alike, question the bloody path that the Inquisition has taken. What was once firm conviction has turned into ferocious zeal. Defending the faith is one thing, coercive violence another, and it makes a mockery of the Gospels.'

'It was Benoît XI's intention to rein in the Inquisition.'

Jean de Rioux looked at him, incredulous. 'And revoke Innocent IV's papal bull *Ad extirpanda*?'

'Precisely.'

'But the political risk would have been enormous.'

'Benoît was aware of that.'

'A rumour is spreading that he died a natural death from internal bleeding,' Jean de Rioux added.

'It was to be expected . . . And yet he was murdered, he died from eating poisoned figs,' corrected the knight. 'The defenders of the imperial Church are rid of an embarrassing reformer and Christianity is deprived of one of its purest souls.'

They sipped their drinks in silence, then the Dominican spoke again in an almost inaudible voice:

'What you tell me, brother, increases the unease I feel and yet am unable to define. Something is being prepared, something whose true nature is still unclear but which goes far beyond fraudulent trials in exchange for money. Florin feels invulnerable, and that cannot be explained merely by the fee he will receive from that oafish baron.'

'You and I have reached the same conclusion. Only I believe I am able to put a name and a face to this menacing shadow.'

'Who?'

'The camerlingo Honorius Benedetti.'

'Surely you are not suggesting that he is behind the sudden death of our beloved late lamented Benoît XI?'

'I am almost sure of it, although I have no way of proving it and doubtless never will.'

They parted company an hour later at the top of the tavern

steps. Jean had told Leone in detail about the cross-examination of Agnès de Souarcy that he had attended. He was in no doubt as to the trumped-up nature of the absurd charges and of the trial itself. Jean had made special mention of the shameful role played by Agnès's daughter.

They had to act quickly. The preliminary questioning would not go on for much longer, especially now that Florin's key witness, the malicious but foolish Mathilde de Souarcy had made such a bad impression upon the judges.

They shook hands upon parting and Jean held on to Leone's. The knight hesitated for a second before asking:

'Jean, my friend, do you believe as Eustache did, and as I do now, that no act in defence of the Light can be considered profane?'

'It is my firm conviction, and it would hurt me if you were to doubt it,' the Dominican murmured solemnly.

Leone handed him a small package wrapped in a piece of cloth, and advised:

'Do not open it here, brother. It contains your preferential treatment and no doubt Agnès de Souarcy's salvation. There is a note with it. If you feel that . . . Well, the content of the note may endanger your life and I would never forgive myself if . . .'

A faint smile lit up the furrowed face that reminded Leone of his Hospitaller godfather.

'You know as well as I do, Francesco, that danger is a fickle mistress. She rarely appears where we think she will – hence her allure. Give me the package.'

Vatican Palace, Rome, November 1304

IT was strange . . . He who suffered so much from the heat had begun to feel chilled to the bone after Benoît's death.

It was as though the sweet reminiscences that had up until then moved and comforted Honorius Benedetti, the deceased Benoît XI's camerlingo, during his darkest hours had been sucked into a bottomless pit. Where was the memory of the exquisite lady's fan he had put away in a drawer, and the swim in the icy river from which he and his brother had emerged pink with cold and delight, only to discover that their feet were bleeding? Honorius, who had been five at the time, had screamed out that they were going to die. Bernardo had quickly rallied, taking his younger brother in his arms and explaining that the crayfish had cut them, but that they would get their own back by having them for lunch. They had gorged themselves on the grilled creatures before falling asleep. Their mother . . . The intoxicating smell of her hair rinsed in honey and lavender water, which made them want to breathe it in, put it in their mouths and swallow it. What had become of these comforting memories?

Exaudi, Deus, orationem meam cum deprecor, a timore inimici eripe animam meam.[37]

It was Benoît. Benoît had taken them with him when he died.

If only Honorius could resent him for it then his beautiful memories would come flooding back. But he could not. Benoît and his angelic obstinacy. Benoît and his gentle determination.

A wave of sadness filled his eyes with tears. Sweet Benoît.

I loved you dearly, brother. The eight months I spent in your company were my only solace in this palace full of loathsome, sickening fools. Why did you force me to kill such purity, Benoît? I didn't care about the others, mere insects borne by the wind. When I held you in my arms, when you spewed your blood, I knew that this cold would haunt me for ever.

Benoît, did you not see that I was right, that I was fighting for us both? Why should we welcome revolution, we who cherish continuity? Why should we give up everything in the name of a supposed truth, a truth so vague that it can only seduce madmen? I defend the established order, without which men would once more be plunged into the chaos we have saved them from. Surely you did not believe that they loved Truth? That they prayed for Justice? They are weak, dangerous fools.

Oh, Benoît . . . Why did you have to resist me, to oppose me unwittingly. If only we had seen eye to eye, I would have laboured tirelessly to seat you on the throne of God, as I did Boniface* – whom I did not even like. I would have been the indefatigable means for you to reign over our world. God illuminated you with His smile, but He gave me the strength to continue fighting. Why did you have to persist in your dream?

I cried for nights on end before giving him the order to slay you. I prayed for nights on end. I prayed that the scales would finally fall from your eyes. But you were blinded by the light.

Your death throes were the longest hours of my life. Your suffering wounded me so deeply that I vow to obliterate from my vocabulary for ever the words 'torment, affliction, ordeal'.

Without you, Benoît, my world is empty. You were the only one who might have been a kindred spirit, but your love for Him separated us. And yet I, too, love Him more than my life, more than my salvation.

I drugged myself so that my vile executioner might enter the secret corridor leading from my office to your chamber. Even as I drank the bitter potion I prayed it would kill me. But death turned its back on me. They blamed my faltering speech on the opium when I was choking with grief.

Remember how I watched you eat those figs one by one. You beamed at me like a child as you recalled the sweet days spent at Ostia. With each shred of purple skin that you spat out into your hand another drop of life drained from you. I counted the number of breaths you had left, and as the poison spread into your veins so my soul drained from my body.

I have no place in my heart for regret, Benoît. Still worse, I have no regrets because I could never have allowed you to strip away our majesty, our supremacy, in the name of some splendid Utopia. Still worse, because since your death I no longer live, I toil. That is all I have left, together with this terrible emptiness.

If in His eyes and yours I acted wrongly, in the eyes of mankind I did what was right. I will accept my punishment. It can be no worse than my present suffering.

Beloved Benoît, may your sweet soul rest in peace. I implore you even as each fibre of my being cries out for an end to this most fervent of its desires.

Honorius Benedetti stood up and dried his face, which was moist with tears. The room was spinning, and he leaned against his enormous work table to steady himself. Finally the dizziness went away. He paused to catch his breath then pulled the braided rope behind the tapestries that brightened up his study. An usher appeared out of nowhere.

'Show him in.'

'Very good, Your Eminence.'

The cowled figure stepped into the room.

'Well?'

'Archambaud d'Arville is dead, run through with a sword. Leone has slipped through our fingers.'

The camerlingo closed his eyes in a gesture of despair.

'How could that be? Did you warn Arville to be on his guard? Leone is a soldier – one of the finest in his order.'

'He was supposed to drug him in order to render him weak.'

Benedetti grunted and asked:

'Do you think this is another intervention by one of theirs?'

'The idea had crossed my mind.'

'Why have none of my spies succeeded in flushing them out? I might be forgiven for thinking that they enjoy divine protection!'

'No, Your Eminence. God is on our side. Even so, our enemies are accustomed to secret warfare. We forced them back into their caves, crevices and catacombs. They turned this defeat to their advantage. They have become an army of shadows whose strength we cannot gauge.'

'In your opinion, does Leone know that his secret quest was in fact instigated by others?'

'It would surprise me.'

The prelate's irritation got the better of him and he demanded sharply:

'All the evidence suggests that that scoundrel Humeau sold the manuscripts he stole from the papal library to Francesco de Leone. Have you found them?'

'Not yet. But I am searching tirelessly.'

'Indeed! I would prefer it if you searched successfully.'

'Everything points towards Clairets Abbey.'

'What is Leone's connection to the place?' asked the camerlingo.

'The Abbess, Éleusie de Beaufort. Benoît XI appointed her and I am beginning to wonder whether there might not be some other connection between her and the knight which we don't know about.'

'Make it your business to recover the Vallombroso treatise urgently. Without it we are incapable of calculating the dates of birth. And the work on necromancy, too . . . At this stage any help, however subversive, is welcome.'

'You don't intend to . . . I mean, you are not going to use that monstrosity?'

'You speak of monstrosities? And what do you suppose you are guilty of since you began working for me?'

The figure remained silent.

'And what of the woman?' the camerlingo continued.

The figure drew back his cowl. His face broke into a smile.

'At this moment in time, Your Eminence, there can't be much left of her and I wouldn't want to be in the place of what little there is.'

'Her suffering brings me no enjoyment. Suffering is far too precious a sacrifice to be wasted in vain demonstrations. I know one thing,' the prelate murmured, before continuing in a firmer voice: 'Agnès de Souarcy must die, and quickly, but her execution must be made to look like a just one. I have no need for a martyr on my hands.'

'I'll inform her torturer at once. He will be disappointed. He gets drunk on suffering like others do on mulled wine.'

'He has received handsome enough recompense for his obedience,' Benedetti pointed out sharply. 'I detest the enjoyment of torturers. Once his work is done I want him killed. We have no more need of him. His repulsive existence is a stain on my soul.'

'Your wish is my command, Your Eminence.'

Honorius was exasperated and said through gritted teeth:

'You are aware of my wishes, now carry them out – I pay you enough! I would hate to lose patience with you. Now go.'

The threat was plain enough and the figure pulled down his cowl and left.

The camerlingo waited a moment before angrily summoning the usher with an angry tug on the bell rope.

'Has she arrived?'

'Not yet, Your Eminence.'

Disappointment was written all over Benedetti's face and he muttered under his breath:

'Why is she so late? Let me know as soon as she arrives.'

'Very good, Your Eminence.'

Louvre Palace, Paris, November 1304

ONE of Philip the Fair's huge lurchers was gazing at him balefully. Guillaume de Nogaret sat waiting in the King's study chambers, trying his best not to move for fear that the bitch with a white coat and brindled markings on her head might interpret his slightest gesture as a threat. These animals allegedly killed their prey with a single bite. He understood the need for them, though not what induced the ladies to keep the more decorative of these four-legged creature as pets, even going so far as to dress them in embroidered coats to keep them warm in winter.[38] It was true that to Monsieur de Nogaret's mind God's only true creature was man, and to a lesser extent woman, and the Almighty had put all other species on earth for him to use without ill-treating or doing violence to them.

The counsellor saw Philip the Fair's tall, emaciated figure appear at the far end of the gloomy corridor he had been staring down. He stood up to the immediate accompaniment of unfriendly growls from the bitch, which moved forward, sniffing vigorously at the hem of his coat.

'Down,' he ordered in a hushed tone.

This had the effect of making the dog growl even more loudly.

As soon as her master entered the room, she bounded over

to him and placed herself between him and this man whose smell she did not care for.

'There's a good girl, Delmée,' Philip said reassuringly, bending down to pat her. 'Go and lie down, my beauty. Did you know, my dear Nogaret, that she is the fastest of all my hunting dogs, and that she can snap a hare's spine with one bite?'

'A truly fine animal,' the counsellor conceded with such a lack of conviction that it brought a smile to Philip's lips.

'I sometimes wonder what other interests or amusements you have besides the affairs of state and the law.'

'None, Sire, which do not relate to your affairs.'

'Well, how do things stand regarding my pope? Benoît XI, or rather his sudden demise, has left me in an invidious position.'

Nogaret was in no way offended by this remark. And yet if the Pope's unexpected passing had left anybody in a delicate situation it was he. His plan to provide Philip the Fair with a Holy Father who was more concerned with spiritual matters than France's affairs of state was still not ready. Guillaume de Nogaret detested acting hastily, but the forthcoming election gave him no choice. He explained:

'On my behalf Guillaume de Plaisians has approached Renaud de Cherlieu, Cardinal of Troyes, and Bernard de Got,* Archbishop of Bordeaux. These are our two most promising candidates.'

'And?'

'It will doubtless come as no surprise to you, Sire, to learn that they are both, and I quote, "extremely interested in serving our Holy Mother Church".'

'Indeed, it comes as no surprise, Nogaret. The papal crown confers countless benefits, including, I suppose, money. What do they demand for deigning to rule over Christendom?'

'They are both equally greedy . . . Privileges, titles for family members, various gifts and certain assurances from you.'

'What assurances?'

'That their authority in spiritual matters should remain established and that you should no longer interest yourself in the administration of the French Church.'

'The French Church is in France and I am the ruler of France. The landed wealth of the French Church is so vast that it would make even my richest lords green with envy. Why should it enjoy even greater privilege?'

Nogaret equivocated:

'Indeed, Sire . . . But we need a pope who will be well disposed towards you. Let us offer these assurances . . . Do you really think that the successful candidate will come complaining and risk the negotiations that led to his election being revealed?'

Philip the Fair's pursed lips betrayed his ill humour.

'Which one do we favour?'

'If we have considered them both it is because their willingness to serve us is unquestionable. Monseigneur de Got is certainly the shrewder of the two, though like Cherlieu a mild-mannered man, a trait, if I may say so, which influenced our choice.'

'Indeed, we do not want a strong personality. And what do they intend to do about that scourge, Boniface VIII? You are aware, Nogaret, of how keen I am for him to be deposed, albeit posthumously, in revenge for poisoning my existence. He systematically opposed my every order, and I am convinced he even went so far as to instigate the rebellion in the Languedoc by backing that troublemaker Bernard Délicieux.* Boniface . . .' the King said with contempt. 'An arrogant blunder whose memory is a stain on Christianity!'

Their mutual loathing for Benoît XI's predecessor created a further bond between the two men.

'Plaisians has naturally broached the matter with tact and diplomacy. They both appeared to listen carefully to him, and in any event showed no hostility.'

'How will we choose between the two, for we are unable to move two pawns at the same time?'

'I would give my backing to the Archbishop of Bordeaux, Monseigneur de Got.'

'And your reasons?'

'You are better acquainted than I with his skill as a diplomat. Furthermore, the Gascons like him, which will earn us additional votes at no cost and with no need for open intervention. Finally and most importantly, Monseigneur de Got has come out in favour of reuniting all the military orders under one flag, and thus of ending the Templars' autonomy. Our motives may differ, but we seek the same end.'

'Let it be Monsieur de Got, then. We shall back him resolutely and discreetly, and make sure he shows his gratitude.'

Clairets Abbey, Perche, November 1304

*C*ROUCHED *in the corner of a tiny room, dark and dank, stinking of excreta and sour milk. Crouched on the muddy floor that has coated her skimpy dress, her calves and thighs with a foul greenish film. Crouching, straining in the darkness, trying to make sense of the sounds she heard. There had been a voice barking out orders, obscene laughter and cries followed by screams of pain. Then a terrified silence. Crouching, trying hard to merge into the stone walls, hoping to dissolve there, to vanish for ever. Steps coming to a halt outside the solid-looking low door. A voice declaring:*

'At least they say this female's pleasing and comely!'

'She used to be. She looked more like a beggar when I brought her back down from the interrogation room.'

A loud rapping on the door. Why did they keep on when all they needed to do was pull the bolt across? The rapping grew louder and louder. Stop, I say, stop . . .

Éleusie de Beaufort managed to wrench herself free from the nightmare that had ensnared her. Drenched in sweat, she sat up in bed. Agnès. The torture. The torture was about to begin. What was Francesco doing?

Somebody was moving outside the door to her chambers. A voice cried out. It was Annelette:

'Reverend Mother, I beg you, wake up . . . Jeanne . . . Hedwige . . .'

She leapt out of bed and ran to open the door.

Thibaude de Gartempe, the guest mistress, was clinging to Annelette Beaupré's arm. Behind the two women stood Emma de Pathus and Blanche de Blinot, both deathly pale.

'What is it?' asked Éleusie, alarmed, as she straightened her veil.

Thibaude shouted in a rasping voice:

'They're going to die, they're going to die . . . Oh dear Lord . . . I won't stay in this godforsaken place a moment longer . . . I want to leave, now . . .'

The guest mistress, her eyes flashing and in the grip of hysteria, looked ready to hurl herself at the Abbess. Annelette tried to pacify her and snapped:

'That's enough! Let go of me! You're digging your nails into my arm. Let go, I say . . .'

The other woman cried out:

'I want to leave . . . Let me leave. If you . . .'

A stinging slap jerked the woman's head to one side. Annelette was preparing to raise her hand again when Éleusie intervened:

'Will somebody tell me what is going on!'

'It is Jeanne d'Amblin and Hedwige du Thilay. They are terribly ill. The vomiting began just after bedtime.'

The Abbess felt the blood drain from her face. She began shaking and in a barely audible voice asked:

'Yew poisoning?'

'It could be. I'm still not sure, although the symptoms appear to be consistent.'

Without a word Éleusie leapt out into the corridor and ran to the dormitories, followed by the four women.

Jeanne d'Amblin lay between sheets soaked in bloody vomit, her eyes closed, her chest barely lifting as she breathed, her face twisted into a grimace of excruciating pain. Éleusie placed a hand on the woman's icy brow then stood up straight, trying her best to stifle the sobs that were choking her.

Annelette roared:

'Where is the water I ordered?'

A petrified novice handed her a jug, spilling a quarter of the contents on the floor.

A cry rang out from the other end of the dormitory:

'She's leaving us . . . No, it's not possible . . . Somebody, do something . . .'

Éleusie rushed over. Hedwige du Thilay's head had just flopped onto the shoulder of the sister in charge of the fishponds and henhouses, Geneviève Fournier. Beside herself, powerless to accept the truth, she was shaking the treasurer nun's frail little body in an effort to revive her and whispering:

'Please, Hedwige dear, please wake up . . . Come along, Hedwige, come along now . . . Can't you hear me? It's me, Geneviève, remember, with my turkeys, my eggs, my carp and crayfish. Please try, I beg you. You must breathe, Hedwige dear. Look, I'll help you. I'll loosen your nightshirt and you'll feel more comfortable.'

With surprising gentleness, Annelette attempted to free the

poor woman's skinny corpse, but Geneviève refused to let go. Annelette sniffed the bluish lips and stuck her finger in Hedwige's mouth in order to smell her saliva. Then she kissed Geneviève's brow, which was slick with sweat, and murmured:

'She's dead. Let go of her, please.'

'No. No!' shrieked the sister in charge of the fishponds. 'It's not possible!'

She clung on to her sister, almost lying on top of her lifeless body and buried her face in the woman's neck, repeating in a frantic voice:

'No, it's not possible. The Lord wouldn't allow it. He wouldn't allow one of his sweetest angels to be taken like that. I know he wouldn't! No, dear Annelette, you're mistaken – she isn't dead at all. She's fainted, that's all. It's just a nasty turn. You know what a frail constitution she has. Dead! . . . What nonsense!'

Éleusie was about to intervene, but Annelette discouraged her with a shake of her head and instructed:

'We must see to Jeanne now that I think I know which poison we are dealing with.' She added in a whisper so that Geneviève Fournier would not hear: 'Not a word to Jeanne about Hedwige's death. You know how close they were. Our extern sister's life is hanging by a thread and there is no point in weakening her chances by dealing her a terrible blow.'

They turned away for a time from the woman who refused despair, knowing that the respite would be short-lived and that the gentle Geneviève's grief would soon hit her with all the force of an implacable truth.

Jeanne was suffocating. Waves of nausea filled her mouth

with bloody saliva that oozed down her chin. She let out a cry:

'Dear God, the pain . . . My stomach is bursting. Bless me, Reverend Mother, for I have sinned . . . I beg you, bless me before . . . it's too late . . . Water . . . I'm so thirsty . . . Bless me . . .'

Éleusie made the sign of the cross on her brow and murmured:

'I bless you, my daughter, my friend, and hereby absolve you of your sins.'

A faint relief slackened the grimace of pain etched on Jeanne's face. The dying woman managed to whisper:

'Is Hedwige any better?'

'Yes, Jeanne, we hope that she may live,' Éleusie lied.

'We . . . we were poisoned at the same time.'

'I know . . . Rest, preserve your strength, daughter.'

Jeanne closed her eyes and spluttered:

'Damn her . . .'

'She is damned, now try to be quiet.'

Annelette picked up the ewer of water and ordered Jeanne to be held down and her mouth forced open.

The dying woman tried feebly to resist, and groaned:

'Let me die in peace. I am at peace.'

For the next quarter of an hour, the apothecary nun forced her to drink, ignoring her pathetic protestations and the gagging that made her cough and spit. Two novices took turns to fetch water from the kitchens. After Jeanne, whose strength was waning fast, had swallowed several pints of fluid, the apothecary nun stood up straight, the front of her robe soaked in water and bloody vomit. Pointing a threatening finger at Emma de Pathus and Yolande de Fleury, who had been standing silently, transfixed, beside the bed since the nightmarish scene began, she ordered:

'Sit her up and keep her upright.'

The two nuns pulled Jeanne's inert body into a sitting position.

'You two,' she commanded, turning towards the quaking novices, 'open her mouth and keep it open until she starts vomiting.'

They all obeyed, incapable of uttering a word.

Annelette thrust her fingers down Jeanne's throat, faintly disgusted by the fetid yet sweet smell of her breath, and fingered her uvula until the poisoned woman's diaphragm began to contract. She waited until her hand was bathed in a flood of warm liquid from the intestines before releasing her sister, who was gradually regurgitating the contents of her stomach.

Half an hour later when they lay Jeanne back comfortably, her heartbeat was still irregular and her limbs were shaking, but she was having less difficulty breathing.

Éleusie followed Annelette down the corridor. Blanche de Blinot was leaning up against one of the pillars and weeping into her hands. She raised her head when she heard them coming and wailed:

'I'm a coward. A cowardly old woman. I am so afraid of death. I feel ashamed.'

'Blanche, do not be so hard on yourself,' Éleusie sighed. 'Death is a worry to us all, even though we know that a wondrous place awaits us beside Our Lord.'

Turning towards Annelette Beaupré, the old woman asked:

'Will Jeanne die too?'

'I don't know. Hedwige was frailer and older than Jeanne. And she may have swallowed more of the poison. We won't know until we have found out how they ingested it.'

'But why?' whispered the senior nun, sniffling.

'We do not know that either, dear Blanche. And if I had formed a theory it now needs reappraising in light of the two new victims' identities,' the Abbess suggested, thinking of the plans of the abbey locked in the safe.

For if the murderess's aim was to steal them, then why poison Hedwige and Jeanne who did not have the keys? She did her best to comfort Blanche, adding:

'Go and rest for a while. The novices are watching over Jeanne. They will inform us of any change in her condition.'

Château d'Authon-du-Perche, November 1304

H UDDLED up beside the great hearth, the only source of heat in the immense study chamber, Joseph de Bologne and Clément were performing an exercise in smelling. The old physician had pushed a beaker containing a foul reddish-yellow liquid under his apprentice's nose. He said impatiently:

'Come on, be more precise. What does it smell like?'

Stifling a desire to retch, Clément replied:

'Oh . . . I think I'm going to be sick . . .'

'Scientists aren't sick, they consider, they use their noses. More importantly, they remember what they smell,' Joseph interrupted him. 'Use your nose, Clément. It is the doctor's best tool! Come on, what is it?'

'Rotten egg, very rotten egg.'

'And where do we find this unpleasant odour? For let us not exaggerate – there exist far more evil-smelling ones.'

'In the faeces of patients suffering from digestive haem-orrhage.'

'Good. Let's try another more difficult one.'

'Master . . .' interrupted Clément, whom these experiments were powerless to distract from his one obsession, which he thought about day and night, sobbing in his bed when he knew he was alone: 'Master . . .'

'You're thinking about your lady, aren't you?' said Joseph, who had consciously increased the number of experiments and lessons in the hope of offering his brilliant student some reprieve from his torment.

'She scarcely leaves my thoughts. Do you think . . . that I shall ever see her again?'

'I would like to believe that innocence always triumphs over adversity.'

'Do you really believe that?'

Joseph de Bologne studied the boy, and was overwhelmed by an infinite sadness. Had he ever witnessed the triumph of innocence? Probably not, and yet he was ready to lie for the sake of this young girl disguised as a boy whom he had come to love as his only spiritual son:

'Sometimes . . . Though generally when it is helped along. Come, my boy, let us continue,' he said, striving to give his voice a ring of authority.

He crossed to the other side of the vast room and poured some amber liquid into another beaker before submitting it to Clément's olfactory expertise:

'What do we smell? What does that pleasant odour tickling the nostrils suggest?'

'Apple juice. *Pestis!*[39] The smell on plague victims' breath. Well, the majority, others smell of freshly plucked feathers.'

'Try your best to remember both smells. I am telling you, that dread disease has not finished with us yet. And what must you do?'

'If a bubo forms, I must cauterise it with a red-hot knife, taking care to wear gloves, which I must incinerate, and to scrub my hands and forearms vigorously with soap. If the plague has infected the lungs, then there is nothing I can do except to avoid going within two yards of the victim. In effect, the plague victim's saliva forms tiny bubbles, which are expelled into the air and breathed in by the person to whom the sufferer is speaking.'

The old physician's wrinkled face beamed and he nodded. A good master doth a good pupil make.

Suddenly they both jumped. It felt as if a whole army had just invaded the room. Artus called over:

'May I draw near without fear of contracting some deadly disease? What is that evil smell?'

'Rotten egg, my lord.'

'You scientists certainly do engage in some extraordinary activities. Esteemed doctor, I wish to speak to your assistant urgently.'

'Should I leave the room, my lord?'

'On the contrary, I will leave you to your evil smells and take him to my chambers, which are protected from such noxious vapours.'

Once they were inside the little rotunda, Artus went straight to the point:

'I need your help, my boy.'

Clément could tell by the Comte's solemn expression that this related to Agnès. For a split second he froze with fear. No. No. She couldn't possibly be dead. In that case he would be dead, too, for his life depended so much on that of his lady.

'I-is it very bad news?' he stammered, doing his best to stifle the sobs that were rising up his throat.

'It is not good, but no worse than yesterday or the day before, so do not begin to despair yet. Madame de Souarcy is still alive . . . But the torture will begin shortly.'

Artus looked murderously around the room, searching for something he could break, something he could smash to pieces in an attempt to calm his fury. He brought his fist down on the table, upsetting the inkpot in the shape of a ship's hull. Clément stood still, watching the ink run slowly along the grain of the wood and drip on to the floor. Artus stood next to him and they both looked on in awe as the tiny dark stain spread ominously across the floorboards. Black ink, not red, Clément kept saying to himself. Ink, not blood, just ink. Even so, he pulled from his belt the piece of coarse cloth he used as a handkerchief, and rushed over to soak up the inky pool.

Artus raised his eyes, as though Clément's simple gesture had broken the evil spell riveting their gaze to the floor. He continued where he had left off:

'Florin must die, Clément. There is no other solution. He must die, and soon.'

'Give the order to saddle me a horse, my lord, and I'll leave at once. I'll kill him.'

The child's blue-green eyes staring at him conveyed his fierce determination. And, strangely, Artus knew that he was capable of doing it, even if it meant being killed himself.

'I will be the one to wield the sword, my boy. It is an old friend that has never failed me. What I need is someone to trail

Florin, for he knows me. I thought I had found a little helper, but he vanished into thin air.'

Clément grew excited:

'I can replace him. Just give the order, my lord!'

'We leave for Alençon at dawn tomorrow.'

'But it is more than twenty leagues* from here . . . Will we arrive in . . . time?'

Clément stumbled over the last word, which sounded like a death sentence.

'Twenty-three to be exact, and I'll be damned if we don't arrive in time! If we ride our horses hard, we'll arrive the day after tomorrow at dusk.'

THE feeling of agonising numbness that scarcely left Camerlingo Benedetti was cut short by the arrival of an usher:

'Your visitor is here, Your Eminence.'

A sigh of relief stirred Honorius. He felt as though this blessed announcement had finally allowed him to reach dry land, to leave behind the turbulent seas that had been buffeting him for the past few days and nights.

'Give me a moment to say a short prayer and then show her in.'

The other man bowed and left.

And yet, the camerlingo had no intention of spending the time in quiet contemplation. He wanted to savour it, be aware of its every nuance.

Aude, the magnificent Aude. Aude de Neyrat. The mere sound of her name worked on him like a magic charm. The tightness that had gripped the prelate's throat for months abated. He could breathe the almost cool air again, exhilarated. The insistent throbbing pain in his chest vanished, and for the first time in what seemed an age he dared to stand up and stretch without being afraid he might shatter.

To behold Aude, to smile at her. Unable to contain himself

any longer, he rushed over to the tall double doors of his office and flung them open, to the astonishment of the usher, who was waiting outside with Madame de Neyrat.

'Come in, my dear, good friend.'

The woman stood up with an exquisitely graceful movement. Honorius thought to himself that she was even more stunningly beautiful than he had recalled. She was quite simply miraculous. One of those miracles that occur once in a lifetime, and whose perfection leaves the onlooker humbled. A mass of blonde locks framed a tiny, angelic, perfectly oval-shaped face. Two almond eyes like emerald-green pools stared at him joyfully, and a pair of heart-shaped lips broke into a charming smile. Honorius closed his eyes in a gesture of contentment. That graceful figure, that domed forehead concealed one of the most powerful, most sophisticated minds he had ever encountered.

She walked towards him, her feet barely touching the ground, it seemed to him. Honorius closed the doors behind them.

Aude de Neyrat took a seat and smiled, tilting her ravishing head to one side:

'It has been such a long time, Your Eminence.'

'Please, Aude, let us pretend that time, which has scarcely left its mark on you while turning me into an old man, never really passed.'

She consented with an exquisite gesture of her pretty hand, and corrected herself:

'Gladly . . . It has been no time at all, then, dear Honorius.' Pursing her full lips, she declared in a more solemn voice:

'Your letter delighted me at first and then, I confess, I found it troubling.'

'Forgive me, I beg you. But I am plagued by worries, and no doubt it showed through in my words . . .'

The camerlingo paused and looked at her. Aude de Neyrat had led a turbulent life. Only a miracle could explain how she bore no signs of it. Orphaned at an early age, she had been placed under the tutelage of an elderly uncle who had quickly confused family charity and incest. The scoundrel had not enjoyed his niece's charms for long, and had died a slow and painful death while his protégée stood over him devotedly. At the tender age of twelve Aude discovered she had a flair for poison, murder and deception, equalled only by her beauty and brains. An aunt, two cousins who stood to inherit, and an elderly husband had shared the same fate as the hateful uncle, until one day the chief bailiff of Auxerre's men had become suspicious of the series of misfortunes befalling her relatives. Honorius Benedetti, a simple bishop at the time, happened to be in the town during her trial. Madame de Neyrat's striking beauty had made him recall the follies of his youth, during which he would leave one lady's bed, only to fall into the bed of another. He had insisted on questioning her, arguing that his robe would encourage a confession. She had confessed to nothing but had spun a web of lies which, as a connoisseur, had impressed him. In his view such cunning, such astuteness, such talent should not end up with a rope round its neck, still less burnt like a witch at the stake. He had moved heaven and earth, using money, threats and persuasion. Aude had been released from custody and cleared of all suspicion. She had been the prelate's only carnal transgression since his renouncement of the world. He had joined her a week later in the town house she had inherited from the husband she had sent to an allegedly better world. For a moment, Honorius had been afraid that she would not willingly take part in his violation of the rule. He had been mistaken. And, as he had secretly hoped, she did not feel indebted or under any obligation to spend those few hours with him naked and sweating between the sheets. She had done him the honour of offering herself to him because he was a man, not her creditor. During these hours of perfect folly, they had discovered one another, sized one another up like two wild beasts of equal stature. They had made love as one makes a pact. Typically, Aude had considered that the ends justified the means. Had she not confided during the early hours:

'What else was I to do, dear man? Life is too short to allow it to be ruined by spoilsports. If only people were more sensible, there would be no need for me to poison them. I am a woman of my word and a woman of honour – admittedly in my own peculiar way. Consequently, my uncle, who believed he had the right to take away my innocence and my virginity, paid with his life. I had no say in the deal he struck over my young body and therefore I saw no need to ask his opinion regarding his death. Promise me that you are a sensible man, Honorius. I would hate it if you disappeared . . . You are far too special and precious not to be part of my life.'

He had roared with laughter at the charming threat. He had not had many reasons to laugh since; his life had veered out of control and become bleak and joyless. In the end, Aude's cheerful vivacity revived the only memory that allowed him to breathe freely.

'What I am about to tell you, my radiant Aude . . .' he began before she interrupted him with a look of glee:

'Must never leave this room? Surely you know me better than that, my dear man.'

He exhaled slowly. Could he have dreamed of a more perfect confessor than Aude? The one person he could trust. He closed his eyes and continued with difficulty:

'Aude, my wonderful Aude . . . If only you knew . . . Benoît is dead and I am responsible. His death wounds me, gnaws relentlessly at my insides, and yet it had to be done.'

'Why?' she asked, apparently untroubled by his admission.

'Because Benoît was a purist, whose obstinacy threatened to undermine the foundations of our Church. He had a dangerous dream and clung to his idea of evangelical purity at a time when we are threatened from all sides, at a time when, on the contrary, we need to strengthen the authority of the Church in the West. Dialogue, exchange and openness are no longer appropriate . . . Indeed, I ask myself whether they ever have been. A reform of the Church, a display of *mea culpa* would be fatal to us, I am convinced of it. Aude, we are the guarantors of an order and a stability without which mankind cannot survive. We are confronted by forces which I consider to be evil, and which are attempting to undermine our power. A number of European monarchs, including Philip the Fair, are intent upon weakening our authority, my dear. However, they are not my main concern. We will succeed in forcing them back. It is the others, I confess, who make me afraid.'

'The others? What others?' enquired the splendid young woman.

'If I knew who they were, my worries would be over. I can feel them closing in on all sides. I see evidence of them in the proliferation of heresies, in the zealous austerity of some of the mendicant friars, in the benevolent attitudes towards their ideas on the part of nobles and burghers. I seek them out tirelessly . . . Already the hopes of the wealthy and erudite minorities rest with these reformers. The others, the poor, will soon follow suit, seduced by their grotesque theories of equality. We fend off and will continue to fend off heretical movements, but they are merely the outer expression of a deeper hatred of us and of what we stand for.'

'And yet, the Inquisition has never seemed so active,' his guest pointed out.

'The Inquisition is a jack-in-the-box used to scare people. There have been past uprisings against it, proving that the people will react if they find a . . . leader.' Honorius paused before continuing: 'A leader or a miracle. Just imagine, my friend . . . Just imagine . . .'

'What is it you are not telling me? I sense your fear and it alarms me.'

The young woman's perceptiveness convinced him to tell her everything:

'I am involved in a struggle which at times I fear will be in vain. I fear imminent failure. It would only take a miracle – a convincing miracle – to tip the scales.'

'What kind of miracle?'

'I don't know. I doubt whether even Benoît understood the

true nature of it, and yet he was ready to protect it with his life, as is one of his key combatants, the Knight Hospitaller Francesco de Leone.'

He looked at her intently for a moment before continuing:

'If my explanations seem vague and uncertain, it is because for years I have been searching blindly. A text, a sacred prophecy fell into our hands and was spirited away. It contained two birth charts. After long years of futile searching and disappointment, Boniface became aware of the existence of an astronomical treatise written by a monk at the Vallombroso Monastery. The revolution contained within its pages could under no circumstances be propagated. The work was locked away in our private library. We were making headway in our calculations, which would have allowed us to decipher both charts, when the treatise was stolen by a chamberlain and sold to the highest bidder . . . Leone. The fact remains that we were able to interpret the first chart and, thanks to an eclipse of the moon, to find the person it referred to: Agnès de Souarcy.'

'Who is she?'

'The illegitimate recognised child of a lowly baron, Robert de Larnay.'

A disbelieving frown creased Madame de Neyrat's pretty brow.

'What an absurd story. What possible part could a minor French noble play in a clash between the forces of conservatism and reform within the Church?'

'An admirable summary of the chaos into which I have been plunged for years.'

'Moreover, a woman. What are women in the eyes of a

prelate? Saints, nuns or mothers on the one hand, and whores, delinquents and temptresses on the other. What possible importance could a woman have?'

Honorius said nothing as she reeled off her list. He was clever enough to know that she was right. Be that as it may, what other role could a woman play? Was not she, Aude, the charming murderess, living proof of this?

'I am hopelessly in the dark, my dear. All I know about the woman is that she represents a terrible threat, the exact nature of which escapes me. She must die, and quickly.'

'And you want me to carry out her execution?' Madame de Neyrat enquired with a smile.

'No. I took care of that long before I called upon you.'

'What is it you want from me, then, dear Honorius?'

'I need that Vallombroso treatise. I need it urgently so as to be able to calculate the second birth chart and pre-empt my enemies. I engaged the services of a henchman whose incompetence worries me and is beginning to exasperate me. I counted upon his anger, his bitterness, his need to exact revenge on life for the injustice of which he believes he is a victim.'

A brief silence followed this admission. Aude de Neyrat responded thoughtfully:

'Honorius, Honorius, it is wrong to place your trust in fear and envy. They are the attributes of a coward, and cowards are the worst traitors.'

'I did not have much choice, my lovely woman. Will you help me?'

'I told you once that I am a woman of my word and a woman of honour. I always repay my debts, Monsieur,' she replied unsmilingly for the first time. 'Moreover, very few of those I have incurred I hold dear. I will help you . . .' and then, aware that the tone of her conversation had become rather serious, she added light-heartedly: 'And, who knows, I might even be doing our future pope a service.'

He shook his head before replying:

'I prefer to remain in the shadows, my dear. I am waiting anxiously behind the scenes for a man whom I can serve better than I serve myself. Benoît . . . Benoît, though I loved him dearly, was not this man.'

'And what shall I do with your spy?'

'Eliminate him if the need arises; he has given me proof enough of his ineptitude.'

'I find the idea quite appealing, Honorius.'

Aude stood up, and the camerlingo followed suit, clasping her hands before raising them to his lips. She murmured:

'I will remain in Rome for two days in order to rest. Do not hesitate to pay me a discreet visit if you so wish.'

'I think not, my dear. We know each other too well, but above all we like each other too much.'

She closed her eyes and, flashing one of her most dazzling smiles at him, whispered:

'Why would I have given you the same reply had you been the one to make such a brazen proposition?'

'Precisely because we know each other too well and like each other too much.'

H UNCHED behind his wooden work table in the entrance to Nicolas Florin's office, Agnan knew the moment he looked up and saw him. The image of a noble sword flashed through the young clerk's mind. For days he had been praying for a miracle, an unlikely miracle, and now his prayer had been answered in the form of this man staring down at him with his dark-blue eyes, eyes that changed from deep sea blue to sapphire according to the light. Eyes which Agnan knew contained secrets, terrible but noble secrets of which he had no knowledge, but which stirred him to the depths as he sat behind his little table.

'Would you be so kind as to announce Francesco de Leone, Knight of Justice and Grace of the Order of Hospitallers of Saint John of Jerusalem? I have come to ask after Madame de Souarcy.'

Without thinking or really knowing what drove him to act so rashly, Agnan heard himself say:

'Save her, I beg you.'

The other man studied him for a moment then frowned. 'Is it so easy to read my thoughts? You worry me.'

'You are a great comfort to me, knight.'

The young clerk disappeared then reappeared in a flash. He moved closer to Leone and murmured:

'He is more corrupt and dangerous than any incubus.'

'Do you really think so?' replied Leone with a smile. 'The advantage is that this one is mortal.'

Since his clerk had announced the man's arrival, Florin had been wondering what a Knight Hospitaller could possibly be doing at the headquarters of the Inquisition. That Agnès de Souarcy woman had caused him nothing but trouble. Her torture would begin presently and end too soon for his taste in the eternal rest of the accused. Death. A few hours of inflicted pain, of screams, would bring him some compensation at least. He could have strangled her in her cell, of course, and pretended that she had hanged herself in order to avoid being tortured – this was not an uncommon occurrence. No. She had upset and annoyed him enough. Hers would not be an easy death.

Leone followed Agnan into the inquisitor's tiny office. The young clerk immediately left the two men. Contrary to what he had decided, Florin felt compelled to stand up when the knight entered. The man's striking beauty and palpable strength left Florin speechless. The absurd but irresistible idea occurred to him that he would love to seduce this man in order to destroy him. And why not? Of course he preferred to bed young girls, but what a remarkable demonstration of his power if he managed to lead the handsome Knight Hospitaller astray. After all, for him sex was merely a way of confirming his dominance.

'Knight, I am greatly honoured.'

'The honour is mine, Lord Inquisitor.'

Leone was filled with a sense of excitement, which made him feel ashamed. The excitement that precedes the most gruelling battles. Giotto Capella had been a weak adversary. In comparison the man standing before him was one of the most dangerous, most unpredictable he had ever encountered. Giotto Capella was a broken man, Florin a poisonous snake. He frowned at his sudden perverse desire to defeat the lethal creature by using his own weapons.

'Pray be seated, knight. My clerk informs me that you are concerned about the fate of Madame de Souarcy.'

'Not about her fate, Monsieur, for I am sure it rests in the most capable of hands.'

Florin was flattered by the compliment and bowed his head graciously.

'Nonetheless, Madame de Souarcy's mother was a great friend of my aunt's, and since I was passing through your beautiful province on my way to Paris on Hospitallers' business, I thought I might comfort her with a prayer.'

'Hm . . .'

Florin was no longer listening. He was busy trying to think of the best way to seduce this beautiful man opposite him.

'Would you do me the favour, brother, of allowing me to see Madame de Souarcy?' Leone asked in a soft, cajoling voice.

Suddenly sobered by the request, Florin forced a smile:

'Certainly, knight, I feel powerless to refuse you such a simple favour. I greatly appreciate the generosity of some of the representatives of your order.'

Nicolas Florin was seething. Why was this knight meddling in his trial? He had no authority. He was furious at being forced to yield. However, since it was impossible to know whether a Knight Hospitaller travelling alone, especially a Knight of Justice and Grace, held the rank of commander or was a mere soldier, he had best tread carefully. Florin had reached a crucial stage on his ascent up the ladder to power but he knew that he had many more rungs to climb. Only then would he be above everything, above other men and the law. It would be better if he handled this stranger with care and made a show of welcoming his judgement with disinterest and gentle humility. He continued:

'You understand that since you are not a direct relative of the accused this constitutes a breach of procedure. I would therefore request that your visit be brief. Madame de Souarcy's trial is still in progress.'

Leone stood up and thanked him, gazing into the inquisitor's soft brown eyes. Florin asked:

'Will you come and take your leave of me, knight?'

'Naturally, Monsieur . . . I am surprised you even ask,' Leone replied in a hushed tone.

Agnan hurried ahead of him, mumbling unintelligible words of gratitude as he stumbled down the stairs leading to the cells. The young clerk's fingers were trembling so much that Leone was obliged to draw back the bolt for him.

'Go now and be blessed,' the knight thanked him. 'I can find my own way back. I have so little time, but it will suffice . . . for now.'

'I prayed so hard that you would come, Monsieur,' the other man stammered. 'I . . .'

'Go, I tell you. Hurry back so as not to arouse his suspicions.'

Agnan vanished behind a pillar like some benevolent shade.

Leone did not notice the stench that pervaded the jail. Nor did he see the dirt, the deathly pallor, the dark shadows under the eyes of the woman who stood with great difficulty before him. She embodied the strength, the infinite resilience of womankind. Those blue-grey eyes studying him were recompense enough for all his pain and toil. It occurred to him that she was the light, and that he had waited all his life to see her. He fell to his knees in the filthy sludge, gasping for breath, overwhelmed by the emotion raging inside him, and murmured:

'At last . . . You, Madame.'

'Monsieur?'

Her exhaustion had left her too weak to respond. She tried desperately to find some explanation for this extraordinary show of reverence, for this man's presence in her cell. Nothing made sense any longer.

'Francesco de Leone, Knight of Justice and Grace of the Hospitaller Order of Saint John of Jerusalem.'

She stared at him quizzically.

'I have come a long way in order to save you, Madame.'

She tried to moisten her cracked lips and cleared her throat before speaking:

'Pray rise, Monsieur. I don't understand . . . Who are you? . . . Did the Comte d'Authon . . .'

So, Artus d'Authon was one of her friends. The thought comforted Leone.

'No, Madame. I know the Comte only by name and by his fine reputation.'

'They occasionally send clever spies to extort confessions,' she whispered softly, leaving Leone in no doubt as to her own astuteness.

'The Abbess of Clairets, Éleusie de Beaufort, is my aunt or should I say my second mother, since it was she who brought me up after my own mother, Claire, died at Saint-Jean-d'Acre.'

Despite her extreme fatigue, Agnès had a vague recollection of Jeanne d'Amblin mentioning that the Abbess had taken in a nephew after the bloody defeat that heralded the end of Christendom in the Orient. Finally feeling she could relax, she leaned against the wooden partition. He added:

'We have so little time, Madame.'

'How did you manage to persuade that wicked creature to allow you to see me?'

'By playing him at his own game. There are few possibilities open to us, Madame. One is the right of appeal . . .'

She cut across him:

'Come, Monsieur, you know as well as I do that it would be futile. Inquisitors antedate their records to ensure that no appeal ever reaches the bishop in time. And even if it bore fruit, which I doubt, I will be dead before they assign another inquisitor to my case. In addition to which, the man would bear me a grudge for having challenged one of his colleagues.'

Leone held the same opinion. He had only alluded to this legal tactic in order that she accept more readily what was to follow. He looked at her again through the gloom, moved by what he saw, by what she was unaware of in herself. He thanked God for being the one whose life would be sacrificed in order to save this woman, this woman who had no notion of her extraordinary importance.

'The torture will begin presently, Madame.'

'I know. Should I confess my terror? I endured their screams for days on end. That man . . . He must be dead. I despise my cowardice. I fear I will behave ignobly, that I will be reduced to a screaming wreck, ready to confess to the worst sins in order to stop the pain . . .'

'I am sure of my courage, and yet I, too, would feel afraid. However, we may both misjudge ourselves . . . I adhere to the principle of leaving nothing to chance where man is concerned . . . It generally brings disappointment.'

She tried to interrupt, to beg him to explain, to clarify his last remarks, but he stopped her with a gesture of his hand.

'Madame . . . you must endure the pain. You must hold out until tomorrow, for the love of God.'

'Tomorrow? Why tomorrow and not today?'

More than anything she regretted her words, which were born of her anticipation of the suffering to come. But after all she was only flesh and blood.

'Because tomorrow His judgement will be done.'

She did not even attempt to grasp the meaning of the knight's words. She was beginning to feel so strange, so unreal. He continued:

'The judgement of God can be invoked, Madame.'

'Do you still give it credence?'

'Naturally, since I am His instrument. If Florin were to disappear before your torment began, he would quickly be replaced and the trial would continue and might even be extended to include those closest to you who have supported you . . .'

Agnès understood the allusion to Clément and did not even feel surprised that this strange knight should know of the child's existence. She shook her head.

'. . . However, if God smites him down in retribution for your unjust suffering, no one – not even Rome – will want to continue with the accusation . . .'

'Rome?'

'Time is running out.'

He took from his surcoat a tiny ochre cloth bag and emptied its contents into his hand. He held out a greenish-brown ball the size of a large marble.

'Chew this before the torture begins. Chew it, I beg you. You will barely feel the sting of the lash. This substance found its way to me from China after many misadventures. The resin tastes bitter, but it works like a charm if used properly.'

'Who are you really? Why are you risking your life to help me?'

'It is too soon to speak of that . . .'

He added to her confusion by declaring:

'. . . Purity cannot exist without inflexibility, otherwise it leads to sacrifice, and it is too soon for that. You must live. It is my honour, my faith and my choice to protect you until my last dying breath.'

There was a knock at the ominous door. They could hear Agnan's muffled voice behind the thick panelling:

'Hurry, please! He is beginning to get restless and will come down soon.'

'Live, Madame. Oh dear God! Live, I implore you!'

Agnès slipped the little brown ball of paste between her

breasts. After the door had closed behind him, she wondered whether she had been hallucinating. She felt for the ball under her dress in order to convince herself that the meeting had been real.

She lay down and closed her eyes, refusing even to try to comprehend the meaning of their exchange. She was only made of flesh and blood, and the obscure interlacing patterns she was beginning to sense above her made her mind reel.

A clear voice like a waterfall echoed in her head. Clémence. Clémence de Larnay.

Live, my precious. The hideous beast's end is nigh. Live for us, live for your two Clémences.

I will live, my sweet angel, Agnès murmured as she began to fall asleep.

A SHADOW slipped through the darkness of the vast dormitory, hesitating, listening for the sounds of deep breathing and snoring. It glanced at the three rows of cubicles separated by curtains that offered the sisters a little privacy in which to undress. At the centre of each cubicle stood a bed.

Bees. A hive of bees busy doing what? A swarm of insects whose individual existences had no meaning. An unchanging world of rituals, routines and orders. The shadow felt overwhelmed by anger and resentment. How it loathed them all. To leave that place, to flee the mediocre monotony of a life that was no life at all. To live at long last.

The shadow moved forward a few paces. Its bare feet made no sound on the icy floor.

It paused, listening intently, then drew back the curtains to one of the cells.

Prime* had just ended. Annelette leaned over Jeanne d'Amblin's shrunken frame and listened to her still-faint breathing. The extern sister's exhaustion following her fight against the poison had kept her bedridden. And yet, thanks to the care lavished on her by the apothecary, and all the sisters' prayers,

Jeanne had managed the evening before to swallow a little chicken broth without instantly bringing it up. Annelette checked her pulse, which seemed more regular.

'Jeanne, dear Jeanne, can you hear me?'

An almost inaudible voice replied:

'Yes . . . I feel better. Thank you, my dear, thank you for all your care. Thank you all, my sisters.'

'Is your stomach still hurting?'

'Not as much.'

A sigh. Jeanne had fallen asleep again and the apothecary thought that it was for the best. As soon as she had regained some of her strength, she would be told the dreadful news of Hedwige's death. Éleusie had instructed them all to keep quiet about it because of the long friendship between the two women.

The tall, sullen woman was overcome by a deep sense of sorrow. Adélaïde Condeau was dead and so was Hedwige du Thilay. Jeanne had narrowly escaped following them to the grave, and as for Blanche de Blinot, she owed her life to her dislike of lavender tea. The poor old woman was gradually losing her wits and had been plunged into a kind of retrospective terror. The constant expression of fear she wore gave her face the appearance of a death mask. As for Geneviève Fournier, she had become a shadow of her former self after witnessing the shocking death of Hedwige, to whom it appeared she had been a great deal closer than Annelette had previously thought. Indeed, it was as though all the vitality had been drained out of the amiable sister in charge of the fishponds and henhouses. Geneviève wandered through the passageways like a tortured little ghost, scarcely noticing the other sisters as they tried to smile to her.

In contrast, the treasurer nun's gruesome death appeared to have restored the Abbess's determination, which had waned since the arrival of the inquisitor. Annelette felt a nagging concern: what if Éleusie de Beaufort had made up her mind to fight to the death? What if she had foolishly decided to sacrifice herself in order to eradicate the evil beast that was attacking them from within? She could not allow it. The Abbess must not die, and Annelette would do everything in her power to ensure that she did not.

Annelette Beaupré entered the herbarium to make the first of her two daily inspections. The bell for terce* had just rung and she had been excused from attending the service.

She paused in front of the medicine cabinet. A sudden excitement made her almost cry out with joy. She had been right! The mixture of egg white and almond oil she had been preparing each night had worked its magic. A sudden sadness dampened Annelette's enthusiasm. Geneviève Fournier had stopped scolding her hens. Their unreliability and the dwindling number of eggs she found each morning in the nests left her indifferent.

Pull yourself together, woman! Save your tears for when you've trapped this vermin.

Two black footprints were encrusted in the sticky substance. So, somebody had entered the herbarium sometime between compline the previous evening and that morning. Somebody who had no business being there and therefore could only have been up to no good.

The apothecary rushed outside and headed straight for the Abbess's chambers.

Éleusie listened, open-mouthed, hanging on her every word. After Annelette had finished telling her about her trap and what she had discovered, the Abbess said:

'Egg white, I see . . . And what now?'

'Give the order for everybody to assemble in the scriptorium and take off their shoes without mixing them up, and have a novice bring in two warming pans full of hot embers.'

'Warming pans? Do you mean the ones we put in our beds to dry out the damp sheets?'

'The very same. And I want them red hot. It will be quicker than taking everything into the kitchen and unmasking the culprit there.'

A tentative row of white robes waited. The sisters stood in their stockinged feet, their shoes lined up in front of them. Loud whispers had broken out when the unexpected order had been given:

'Take our shoes off? Am I hearing things?'

'What's going on?'

'The floor's freezing . . .'

'I'm sure Annelette is behind this madness.'

'Whatever could they want with our shoes . . .?'

'My stockings are filthy. We don't change them until the end of the week . . .'

'I doubt this is a hygiene inspection.'

'There's a hole in one of mine and my toe's sticking out. I haven't had time to darn it. How embarrassing . . .'

Éleusie had ordered them to be quiet and waited while a bemused-looking novice went to fetch the warming pans she had requested. Finally they arrived from the kitchens, smoking from the embers inside.

Annelette, accompanied by the Abbess, approached the left-hand side of the row of bemused or irritated women. She picked up the first pair of shoes and rubbed them over the lid of the piping-hot pan. She repeated the same procedure with each of the sisters' shoes in turn, ignoring their murmured questions and astonished faces. Suddenly, there was a sound of sizzling, and a horrible stench like rotten teeth or stagnant marshes issued from one of Yolande de Fleury's shoes. Annelette continued brushing it over the pan until a flaky white coating formed on the wooden sole. She felt her face stiffen with rage, but forced herself to continue the experiment until she reached the end of the row of white robes. No other shoe reacted to the heat of the embers. She charged over to Yolande, who was as white as a sheet, and boomed so loudly that some of the sisters jumped:

'What were you doing in the herbarium?'

'But . . . I wasn't . . .'

'Will you stop!' the apothecary fumed.

Éleusie, fearing a fit of violence on the part of the big woman, intervened in a faltering voice:

'Yolande, come with us to my study. You others, go about your tasks.'

They had to drag the reluctant Yolande, who tried to defend herself, insisting that she had not set foot in the herbarium.

Annelette pushed the young woman into the Abbess's study and slammed the door behind them. She leaned up against the door panel as though afraid Yolande might try to escape.

Éleusie walked behind her desk and stood with her hands laid flat on the heavy slab of dark oak. Annelette barely recognised her voice as she exploded:

'Yolande, I am at the end of my tether. Two of my girls are dead and two more have escaped the same fate by a hair's breadth, and all this within a matter of days. The time for procrastination and pleasantries is over. Any other attitude would be recklessness on my part. I demand the truth, and I want it now! If you insist on prevaricating, I shall have no other choice but to turn you over to the secular authority of the chief bailiff, Monge de Brineux, since I refuse to pass judgement on one of my own daughters. I have requested the death penalty for the culprit. I have asked for her to be stripped to the waist and given a public beating.'

Despite the apparent harshness of the punishment, it was in fact relatively lenient for a crime of poisoning; execution was usually preceded by torture.

Yolande stared at her with tired eyes, incapable of uttering a word. Éleusie almost screamed at her:

'I am waiting for the truth! The whole truth! I command you to answer me this instant!'

Yolande stood motionless, her face had drained of colour and was turning deathly pale. She lowered her head and spoke:

'I did not set foot in the herbarium. The last time I went

anywhere near the building, Annelette surprised me and reported my nocturnal outing to you. I've not been there since.'

'You're lying,' said Annelette. 'What do you think those white flakes on the soles of your shoes were? The cooked egg whites, which I spread on the floor in front of the cabinet containing the poisons. What do you think that evil smell was? It was the fetid rue I mixed into the preparation. I found the shoe prints in the mixture this morning – your shoe prints.'

Yolande only shook her head. Éleusie came out from behind her desk and walked right up to her. She spoke in a stern voice:

'Time is running short, Yolande. You are doing yourself no favours. I will tell you the two suspicions I have formed about you. Either you are the murderess, in which case my wrath will follow you to the grave and you will never find peace, or . . . you have developed an excessive attachment to one of your fellow nuns, an attachment that drives you to seek privacy outside the dormitory walls. Such an attachment would result in the two of you being separated, but that is all. I am waiting. You may yet be saved if you confess your sins. Seize this opportunity, daughter. Hell is more terrible than your worst imaginings. Quickly, I am waiting.'

Yolande, her eyes brimming with tears, looked up at this woman she had once so admired and who terrified her now. She closed her eyes and let out a deep sigh.

'My son . . .'

'What?'

'Somebody occasionally brings me news of my son.' A smile lit up the pretty, round face, ravaged with sorrow. She continued: 'He is well. He is ten now. My father brought him up. He passed him off as one of his bastards so that he wouldn't be stripped of the family name. My sacrifice saved him. I thank God for it every day in each of my prayers.'

The other two women received this unexpected confession in stunned silence. The bewildered Éleusie murmured:

'But . . .'

'You wanted the whole truth, Reverend Mother, but some truths are better left unsaid. But now I've started I'll go on. I was fifteen when I fell passionately in love with a handsome steward. The inevitable happened. I fell pregnant by a peasant, outside the sacraments of marriage. The man I was supposed to marry spurned the dishonoured girl I had become. There was no excuse for me, it is true, as I had given myself with complete abandon. My beloved was beaten and driven away. Had he remained he would have been castrated and wrongly branded a rapist. He was so caring, so passionately loving. My father shut me away for the last five months of my pregnancy. Nobody was supposed to know. My son was taken from me immediately after he was born and entrusted to a wet nurse. After that I lived in the servants' quarters, on the pretext that I was no better than a beggar and deserved to be treated like one. And then my little Thibaut, whom I would occasionally glimpse at the end of a corridor, was struck down, and I saw in his illness a sign of God's wrath. I resolved to do penance for the rest of my days to atone for my sins.' She seemed not to notice the tears rolling down her cheeks. She clasped her hands with joy and continued: 'My sacrifice did not go unheeded, for which I am eternally grateful. My little boy is glowing with health. He can ride a horse now, just like a young man, and my father loves him like a son. I pray for him, too. He was so hard and unforgiving. Perhaps the love in his heart has been reawakened thanks to my child.' She straightened up and concluded: 'That is the whole truth, Reverend Mother. You, too, have known sensual joy, the love of a husband. I realise that in the eyes of mankind I was unwed, but I swear to you that when my beloved bedded me for the first time I was convinced that God was witnessing our nuptials. I was wrong.'

The revelation had shocked Éleusie de Beaufort. She felt hurt that Yolande had not confided in her. She attempted to comfort her, aware that it was futile.

'Dear Yolande . . . The Church accepts that its sons and daughters have known physical attraction and the pleasures of the flesh within and even outside wedlock in some cases. It is enough that we vow to banish it from our thoughts for ever when we take the cloth. As our holy Saint Augustine . . .'

'You don't understand!' Yolande cried out, suddenly becoming agitated. 'I would never, do you hear, never have sought the deceptive calm of your nunneries, never have yielded to your stupid rules and regulations if I had not feared for my son's life, if I had married my beloved. Never!'

She flew into a hysterical rage, hurling herself at the desk and sweeping up the papers with both hands, crumpling them, tearing them to shreds, banging her fists down on the oak table and wailing:

'Never, never . . . I hate you! Only the memory of Thibaut and my beloved keeps me alive in this place.'

She turned on the Abbess, her face twisted with rage. She raised her hands to claw the woman she had so respected during the long years spent in the nunnery, the long years of what in her eyes had been a less terrible form of imprisonment than any other simply because Thibaut had survived thanks to her atonement.

Annelette leapt in front of Yolande and slapped her twice hard on the face. The apothecary's deep, gruff voice rang out:

'Control yourself! This instant!'

Yolande stared at her with crazed eyes, ready to pounce. Annelette shook her and growled:

'You little fool. Do you imagine that piety is what brought me here? No, I came here because it was the only place where I could practise my art. Do you think Berthe de Marchiennes took her vows because she longed for a life of contemplation? No. Her family didn't need another daughter. Do you think Éleusie de Beaufort would have agreed to lead our congregation if she had not been widowed? And do you truly believe that Adélaïde Condeau would have chosen the monastic life if she had been well born instead of abandoned in a forest? And the others? You little fool! Most of us come here in order to avoid a life on the streets! At least we are close to God and lucky enough not to be hired out by the hour in some brothel in a town, ending our days riddled with disease and left to die in the gutter.'

The brutal truth of Annelette's tirade brought Yolande suddenly to her senses. She whispered:

'Forgive me. I humbly beg your forgiveness.'

'Who brings you news of your son?'

Yolande pursed her lips and declared categorically:

'I'm not telling you. You can threaten your worst but my lips are sealed. I've made enough mistakes already. I refuse to hurt someone who has shown only kindness by bringing me such solace.'

Annelette could tell from her tone of voice that it was pointless to insist. She wanted, however, to confirm the truth of what she had already deduced:

'And do these secret exchanges take place at night in front of the herbarium, which cannot be seen from our Reverend Mother's chambers or from the dormitory?'

'Yes. That's all I'm going to tell you.'

Éleusie felt appalled by the violence of the scene, but even more so by the discovery of yet another life destroyed. In a voice weak with exhaustion, she ordered:

'That will be all, daughter. Leave us.'

'Will your punishment . . .'

'Who am I to turn my back on you when He opened his arms to Mary Magdalene? Go in peace, Yolande. My only reproach is that it took you so long to tell us the truth.'

Suddenly anxious, Yolande stammered:

'Do you think that . . . if I had confessed sooner Hedwige might have been . . .'

Annelette answered for the Abbess:

'Saved? I doubt it. There's no need for you to carry the burden of her death on your conscience. I suspect that she and Jeanne were a threat to the murderess and she decided to kill them. If we find out exactly why, we will discover who the poisoner is . . . or at least I hope so.'

After Yolande de Fleury had left, the two women stood facing one another for a moment. Éleusie de Beaufort was the first to break the silence:

'I am . . . Is it true?'

'Is what true?'

'That you would never have taken holy orders if you had been able to practise as a physician or apothecary in the world?'

Annelette suppressed a sad smile before confessing:

'Yes, it is. And if your dear husband had not passed away would you be here among us?'

'No. But I have never regretted my choice.'

'Neither have I. Still, it was a second choice.'

'You see, Annelette, despite the climate of resentment towards the Church, these nunneries where we are allowed to live in peace, to work, to act, to make decisions are a blessing to women.'

Annelette shook her head.

'Behind this blessing lies a harsh reality: we women enjoy almost no rights in the world. Those who, like yourself, are better off might be fortunate enough to marry a man of honour, respect and love, but what about the others? What choice do they have? Freedom, it is true, can be bought like everything else. I was prepared to pay a high price for mine, but nobody was interested in my opinion, certainly not my father, who never even asked for it. As an unattractive spinster with no inheritance I could either look after my brother's children – my brother who was a mediocre doctor but a man – or join a nunnery. I chose the least demeaning of the two alternatives.'

'I'm afraid I must agree with Annelette,' a high-pitched voice rang out behind them.

They turned as one. Berthe de Marchiennes was standing uneasily before them. She seemed to have lost her usual air of superiority.

'Berthe . . .'

'I knocked several times but no one answered so I came in. I only overheard the end of your conversation,' she added quickly.

She clasped her hands together, and it occurred to Annelette that this was the first time she had ever seen her stripped of her pious arrogance.

'What is happening, Reverend Mother? It feels as though the world is collapsing all around us . . . I do not know what to think.'

'We are as bewildered as you, daughter,' the Abbess replied, a little too sharply.

The cellarer opened her mouth, seemingly lost for words:

'I know that you don't like me very much, Reverend Mother, nor you, Annelette, nor the others. It pains me even though I know I only have myself to blame. I've . . . It's such a terrible thing to admit that you've never been wanted, loved. Even now at my age I don't know which is harder: to admit it to the rest of the world or to myself. God has been my constant solace. He welcomed me into his arms. Clairets has been my only home, my haven. I confess . . . I was jealous and resented your appointment, Reverend Mother. I assumed that my seniority and the faultless service I had rendered guaranteed my position as abbess – more than that, I felt it was my due. During these past few days I have begun to realise how much I overestimated my abilities. I feel so powerless, so pathetically feeble in the face of these lethal blows raining down upon us, and I am infinitely grateful to you, Madame, for being our abbess.'

This astonishing display of humility must have been difficult for Berthe de Marchiennes, and Éleusie reached out her hand, but the other woman shook her head. She moistened her lips with her tongue before continuing:

'I want to help you . . . I must. I know you don't trust me. I can feel it and I don't blame you; I deserve it.'

'Berthe, I . . .'

'Don't, Reverend Mother, let me finish. I deserve it because I am guilty of telling a cowardly lie in order not to . . . lose face. I cannot even give the excuse that I was afraid of upsetting you. No. My only motive was pride.'

Annelette refrained from intervening, having understood that this confession was not addressed to her. The cellarer took a deep breath before continuing:

'I . . . for a few days I mislaid the key to your safe that was in my charge. Or at least I thought so at the time. I was terrified that you might ask me for it in order to validate some deed. I searched high and low. I couldn't understand for the life of me how I had managed to lose that long leather thong I wore tied round my neck. I found it four days later at the bottom of a little mending basket I keep under my bed . . .'

The two other women stared at her in astonishment.

'I was so relieved that I did not stop to think how strange it was that I should find it there.'

'What do you mean?' Éleusie asked, fearing she knew the answer already.

'I had already twice emptied the contents of the basket onto my bed, thinking that if the thong had come untied the key might have dropped down. The knot on the thong was intact. I am now certain that someone took it while I was asleep and then stuck it in the first hiding place they could find.'

'Not a very good hiding place since you had already looked there,' remarked Annelette.

'On the contrary, sister, a perfect hiding place, and one that shows the thief's contempt for me. She must have known that I had turned my bed, my mending basket, my whole cell upside down and she was counting on my pride, on my relief at having found the key without needing to admit my incompetence. I am therefore guilty of the sin of pride . . . But if that monster thinks I'm a coward she's very much mistaken.'

A GNÈS had been overcome with drowsiness soon after diligently chewing the bitter ball and forcing herself to swallow the mouthfuls of unpleasant saliva it produced. The nightmare she no longer wished to fight against had gradually given way to a sort of waking dream. She had let her body slide down the wall, slowing its descent with her hands.

Crouched in the corner of a tiny room, dark and dank and stinking. Crouched on the muddy floor that has coated her skimpy dress, her calves and thighs with a foul greenish film. Crouching, straining in the darkness, trying to make sense of the sounds she heard. There had been a voice barking out orders, obscene laughter, and cries followed by screams of pain. Then a terrified silence. And yet Agnès felt outside it all. She felt as though she were slowly sinking back into the wall. Crouching, trying hard to merge into the stone walls, hoping to dissolve there, to vanish for ever. Steps came to a halt outside the solid-looking, low door. A voice declared:

'At least they say this female's pleasing and comely!'

'She used to be. She looked more like a beggar when I brought her back down from the interrogation room.'

'Come on, let's take her. At least the women aren't as heavy to carry back as the men after they've fainted.'

The familiar sound of the bolt being drawn back. And yet she did not stir. She felt as though she were drifting, suspended in a foglike stupor.

'On your feet, Madame de Souarcy!' bellowed one of the men who had just walked into her cell. 'On your feet, do you hear?'

She would have preferred to remain like that, sitting in the stinking mud. But she knew instinctively that she must hide the nature of her apathy. Florin must not sense that she felt as if she were floating outside her body since she had swallowed the brownish ball. She managed to raise herself on all fours then rise to her feet. She was swaying like a drunkard. One of the men remarked sarcastically:

'You need less than my goodly wife to reach seventh heaven.'

The other man let out a coarse laugh of approval that Agnès did not understand. What in heaven's name were they talking about?

Her body was weighed down by a pleasant languor and they had to drag her along the corridor.

The other guard, the one who had laughed, declared:

'They shouldn't starve them like that . . . then we wouldn't have to carry them. Look at her, she can barely put one foot in front of the other. I tell you she won't last out the first half-hour,' he predicted, referring to the timing of the torture sessions.

The procedural rules stipulated that there should be no more than half an hour of torture per question. It was an extra-ordinarily meticulous quantification of pain and one many inquisitors did not respect. They only needed to confess and be pardoned by one of their colleagues since each had the power to absolve the others.

They propped her up, holding her under the arms, while one of them opened the door to the torture chamber. What she saw inside made her blood run cold.

A long table, long enough for a human body to lie stretched out on. A long table glistening dark red. Beneath it a trough filled with a curious viscous substance. Blood. Blood everywhere. Blood on Florin's face, blood on his forearms up to his rolled-up sleeves. Blood on the leather apron of the executioner, who was standing in a corner, arms crossed. Blood on the walls, blood on the straps hanging from the table. A sea of human blood.

Nicolas Florin glided towards her. His face was bathed in sweat and his eyes shone gleefully. Suddenly, Agnès understood the nature of his ecstasy: the blood, the screams, the endless torment, the ripped flesh, death.

She stared at him and declared calmly:

'You are damned, beyond atonement.'

He leaned forward and smiled, brushing her lips with his.

'Do you really think so?' he whispered into her mouth.

He turned round, walked gracefully over to the executioner and barked:

'That's enough chatter. There's work to be done and I have a burning desire to begin. What a fitting expression!'

A rough hand tore away the top half of her dress and pushed her towards the table. Another hand shoved her hard in the back and she lurched forward. The congealed blood on the wooden table touching her stomach plunged her into a bottomless pit of despair. She was bathing in the blood of another, in the martyrdom of another who had entered this hell before her. She barely felt the straps tighten across her back.

Florin twisted the mass of auburn locks that had lost their shine and tossed them to one side with regret. He misconstrued the cause of his victim's distress and in a purring voice declared:

'Come, come . . . We haven't started yet. A little nudity is surely nothing in comparison with the rest. You will soon see for yourself. Agnès Philippine Claire de Souarcy, née Larnay, you have been summoned here today before your judges to answer to the charges of complicity in heresy; individual heresy aggravated by latria; the seduction of a man of God, for which you are to be tried at a later date; sorcery and the invocation of demons. I ask you one last time, do you confess?'

The blood smelled of iron. Can a man be identified by the smell of his blood? Can one pray for him with one's mouth pressed into the pool of red liquid that was once his life?

'You do not confess your guilt?' Florin concluded hastily, for the contrary would have driven him to despair.

He felt a warm sensation spread across his belly and a rush of blood to his groin. He had waited so long for this moment. He struggled to hold back his mounting pleasure, to keep his eyelids from closing. He struggled not to hurl himself onto her back and bite into her, ripping at the beautiful pale flesh of his magnificent prey with his teeth until her blood ran down his throat.

'Clerk!' Florin shouted in the direction of an oil lamp that appeared to be floating a few inches above the floor. 'Note down that Madame de Souarcy refuses to confess and chooses to remain silent, a sure sign of her guilt.'

The young man sitting cross-legged on the floor nodded and recorded the refusal.

'Executioner, the lashes, quickly!' Florin snarled, thrusting his hand out towards the tall man in the leather apron. 'Clerk, note down that we are respecting proper procedure by first inflicting upon the accused the punishment reserved for women. If our generosity is not rewarded with a confession we shall consider alternative methods of persuasion.'

Florin turned towards the open fire where some thin-bladed knives were being heated above the flames until they were red-hot.

Her body tensed when she heard the swish of the whip being raised. She cried out as it struck her back with full force. And yet the sting of the thick leather thongs felt bearable. The blows rained down on her for what seemed like an eternity. Her body jolted with each punishing new wave. She could feel her skin splitting, but it seemed relatively painless. Something smooth and warm ran down her sides and dropped onto the table. Her flesh was smarting and yet it almost wasn't hers. A thought flashed through her mind, a soothing thought: her blood was mixing with the blood of the poor soul who had lain on that same table before her. She felt her torturer's hands kneading her raw flesh. She felt the powder being sprinkled onto her wounds. A crippling pain made her cry out despite the little brown ball. Salt. The wicked man was rubbing salt into her wounds.

She felt herself drifting into oblivion and willed it with all her might. Florin's hysterical screams came to her as if in a nightmare. He was gasping with pleasure, crowing as he ordered her to confess her sins. He cried out in a voice quivering with excitement:

'Executioner, this witch refuses God . . . The irons . . . The irons and let them be white hot . . .'

There was a loud knock at the door. Agnès let out a sob before plunging into merciful unconsciousness.

Jean de Rioux stood before the inquisitor. He avoided looking at the tortured woman, feigning disinterest.

Florin was panting, hunched over, his face covered in sweat, his eyes glazed over. The Dominican felt his gorge rise and struggled with an overwhelming urge to kill the man right there in that cellar that he had transformed into an unspeakable playroom for his own enjoyment. But Leone's instructions had been categorical: the judgement of God. He silently handed the missive to the torturer.

As soon as the inquisitor saw the seal, the glazed look in his eyes disappeared. Incredulous and excited, he murmured:

'The halved bulla?'

This message could only have come from one of the two camerlingos, and had almost certainly been sent by Honorius Benedetti himself. He trembled as he broke the seal. How extraordinary. Such was his power that the camerlingo now addressed letters to him in person.

He read and reread the contents, written in Latin:

'It is essential that the correct procedure be applied to Madame de Souarcy so that her trial cannot be judged null and void. We now share the same enemies and this links us definitively. My messenger will recover this missive. H.B.'

A sober Florin gazed up at the tall, grave-faced man. So, he was the camerlingo's secret emissary. This explained his objection to Mathilde de Souarcy's evidence. His mission was to ensure that Madame de Souarcy could not be saved due to some procedural error. Why had he not spoken up? If only Florin had known, he would not have wished him dead for demanding that the foolish young woman's accusation be thrown out. But Jean de Rioux was no doubt sworn to the utmost secrecy.

'We now share the same enemies and this links us definitively.' What a magnificent prospect . . . Rome, greatness would soon be his!

Jean de Rioux's voice almost made him jump.

'Guards . . . Take Madame de Souarcy back to her cell. Have her wounds cleaned and bandaged.'

The astonished guards looked questioningly at Florin, who chivvied them:

'Go on . . . Do as you're told! The half-hour is up. The torture will resume tomorrow.' Then, turning to the Dominican, he added in a hushed voice: 'I shall walk back with you, my brother in Christ.'

Clairets Abbey, Perche, November 1304

A WOMAN *lay face down on the rack, the blood from the gashes on her back oozing to the floor. The woman was moaning. Her long fair hair was sticky with sweat and blood. A hand brushed against her martyred flesh, pouring a grey powder onto her wounds. The woman arched her back and went limp, fainting.*

Éleusie de Beaufort clasped her hands to her mouth to stifle her growing impulse to scream. She fell forward onto her desk in a faint.

The same vision had come back to haunt her. She had mistakenly believed that she was the suffering woman. It was Agnès they were torturing at that precise moment.

She fell to her knees and prayed:

'Dear God . . . dear God . . . Dear, sweet Francesco . . .'

A sudden wave of nausea made her stretch out on the broad dark flagstones where, unable to calm down, she repeated:

'The beast must die, Francesco, he must die! The beast must die, he must die!'

*

Annelette Beaupré sat on her stool in the herbarium, leaning against the cold stone wall with her arms crossed, pondering. Berthe de Marchiennes's confession that morning had baffled her. After the cellarer's departure, she and Éleusie de Beaufort had exchanged glances, unable to make head or tail of her story. The Abbess was adamant: her key had never left her person and she was too light a sleeper for anyone to be able to take it and return it while she was resting. And why replace Berthe's key when all three were necessary in order to open the safe where the seal was kept? Was Berthe lying to cover herself? Curiously, Annelette did not give that theory much credence, despite her dislike of the cellarer nun.

The answer came to her in a flash. Copies! Four days was plenty of time for a good smith to produce one. She suddenly had a worrying thought: what if Blanche de Blinot had also mislaid her key temporarily and said nothing? What if – given her mental deterioration – she had not even noticed its disappearance? What if a second copy had been made of the key for which Annelette had publicly accepted resonsibility? Her hand automatically reached up to touch the top of her robe. The small lump she felt there did not set her mind at ease.

The third and last key was hanging round Éleusie's neck. Assuming the theory of the copies was correct, it placed Éleusie de Beaufort above suspicion since she was free at any time to open the safe and retrieve her private seal. However, since her key was the only one of its kind she would be the next victim.

Something was not right. Some crucial element was missing. Why would the murderess insist on trying to take the seal when so many of them now thought this was her intention? Every deed, every letter would be scrupulously checked and rechecked by the Abbess. Moreover, if the poisoner killed her, her seal would automatically be invalidated.

There were so many loose ends and no clear way of tying them together. The whole affair seemed illogical. Annelette was unable to arrive at the truth. The murderess was both intelligent and extremely cunning. She had discovered the other sisters' weaknesses and strengths, their petty secrets and vanities, their deep resentments and turned them to her advantage. Yolande's Thibaut, Berthe's pride, Blanche's senility . . . But why poison Hedwige du Thilay and Jeanne d'Amblin? What part did these two friends play in these murderous equations? Two friends . . . What if only one had been targeted and their innocent habit of sitting together at mealtimes or taking tea together had sent the other to her grave? Which of the two had been meant to die, then, Hedwige or Jeanne? Hedwige du Thilay? Was her position as treasurer in some way connected? The paymistress managed the abbey's revenue, oversaw and paid the farrier, the singers and the veterinary doctor . . . In short, she was in charge of a good deal of money. It had not been unheard of in the past for monks to make veritable fortunes by falsifying deeds with stolen seals. No, she felt she was losing her way. Enrichment was not the murderess's motive, Annelette would have staked her life on it. And what of Jeanne d'Amblin, whose strong constitution alone had saved her from the poison? Jeanne had permission to leave the abbey in order to make her rounds. She met many of their donors, conversed with them and even became their confidante. Had she seen or heard something that had worried the poisoner? Something whose importance the extern sister had not realised at the time? Think . . . the answer was easily within her grasp.

Thibaut!

Thibaut, the beloved son for whom Yolande had been prepared to lie. Annelette must learn more about him and ask for the Abbess's help in order to do so.

Annelette had suddenly made great headway towards a solution. The poisoner must have discovered that the sister in charge of the granary slipped out at night to meet her informant near the herbarium. She had borrowed her shoes in order to point the finger at Yolande de Fleury. Annelette cursed for the first time in her life, stamping her foot petulantly:

'Zounds!'

Her theory didn't hold water, for it assumed the culprit knew that a trap had been laid for her, and yet Annelette had told no one of her plan, not even the Abbess.

Thibaut, Thibaut . . . The answer, she was certain, lay in the pretty name of that illegitimate little boy.

An insistent ringing sound gradually brought her out of her thoughts: the sisters were being called for vespers.

She left the herbarium, more determined than ever to ingest nothing that she had not prepared herself in the kitchens. For, if her enemy were as clever as she gave her credit for, she would soon realise that Annelette was her most formidable enemy and would not hesitate to crush her.

A figure were crouching behind the hedging laid with chestnut branches that protected the medicinal herb garden from the wind.

Annelette, Annelette, thought the figure, how tiresomely

tenacious you are. How it bores me. How would you like to die, dear apothecary? Just to please me, go on. Die!

Éleusie de Beaufort studied her apothecary daughter in silence.

'What you are asking me to do is so strange, Annelette . . . Do you really think that this little boy can help our investigation?'

'I am convinced of it. We only need to send one of our lay servants. You mentioned that Yolande de Fleury's father lives on his estate in the vicinity of Malassis. It is not so very far from here. A good day's ride there and back.'

'And what is his mission?'

The tall woman sighed. She had no idea. And yet she instinctively persisted.

'I confess that I am not quite sure.'

'Annelette, I cannot send one of our servants out without telling him what I want him to do.'

'I am aware of that, Reverend Mother . . . I want news of little Thibaut.'

'News. Is that all?'

'That is all. I am going back to the dormitory.'

Éleusie de Beaufort had become prey to a strange obsession. Whereas once she had avoided entering the perilous library, now she felt the need to check and recheck its contents several times a day. She was driven by an impulse she was powerless to resist. The abbey plans were locked in the safe, and, unless she was fiendishly clever, the murderess could not possibly know of their existence. Even so, the Abbess always ended up lifting the wall hanging and opening the door leading to the place which at once fascinated and terrified her.

She gazed at the oil lamp sitting on her desk. The feeble light it gave off was not enough to drive out the lingering shadows that seemed to cling to the shelves of books full of revelations. She rushed into the corridor and seized one of the resin candles. She needed a bright light if she was going to check the titles of all those books brimming with terrible truths.

Éleusie sighed wearily. She must remain steadfast. Only when she had finished would she allow herself a few hours' well-earned rest.

She took her time inspecting the books shelf by shelf, raising her candle aloft for fear of setting alight these precious but terrifying works.

The crouching figure's eyes were trained on the high horizontal arrow-slit windows, which for the last few minutes had been visible owing to a flickering light marking them out from the rest of the wall. A triumphant smile lit up the figure's face in the chilly gloom of the garden. The figure had been right and all this surveillance had finally paid off. The camerlingo would be pleased and, the figure hoped, would prove even more generous. The secret library was right next to the Abbess's chambers. The figure would soon be in possession of the manuscripts so coveted by Honorius Benedetti. There was no longer any reason to kill Éleusie de Beaufort in order to appropriate the third and last key. The figure was quite happy to grant the Abbess this pardon. Not because her brutal murder would have saddened the figure, but because Éleusie was a stubborn link in the chain. She formed part of the shadowy spider's web they were at pains to make out. The Reverend Mother might provide valuable information. That is, if she could be persuaded to reveal what she knew. Then again, they had every means of persuasion at their disposal!

Rue de l'Ange, Alençon, Perche, November 1304

NIGHT was slowly falling over Rue de l'Ange. Should he see in this street name a sign or simply another quirk of fate?

Francesco de Leone concealed himself in the porch of the handsome town house belonging to the late Pierre Tubeuf, the draper who had had the misfortune of crossing Florin's path. He waited for a moment then walked across the quadrangular courtyard towards the imposing building. The occasional flickering light of a candle passing behind the drawn curtains of the first-floor windows showed that the beautiful Nicolas was somewhere inside the house he had requisitioned for his own use.

The knight had not allowed himself to follow any plan, any strategy. His actions were guided by a sort of superstitious belief. It seemed essential to him that Florin should be the architect of his own doom, although he did not know where this conviction came from. It was not because he feared feeling any remorse, still less compassion. No. It was more like a vague intuition that nothing relating to or affecting Madame de Souarcy should be tainted or soiled, not even the death of her torturer.

Leone's eyes had filled with tears when Jean de Rioux had described to him the cellar, the outstretched body, the pale lacerated back, the blood dripping from her wounds. It had taken a moment for him to realise that he was crying. A miracle. This woman had already produced a miracle in him. How long had it been since he had felt that overpowering sorrow that was a sign of his humanity, proof that his soul had remained intact despite his being habituated to horror? He had witnessed so much death and suffering, had wallowed in it until it became invisible. Agnès's torment had shocked him into remembering the twisted, burnt bodies, the gaping mouths, the chests pierced by arrows, the amputated limbs, the gouged-out eyes. He was infinitely grateful for these memories which, before he met her, had been packed down so tightly they had become an indistinguishable mass. He no longer wanted to forget; he refused to take the easy escape and become inured to horror.

He walked towards the broad, gently rising steps leading up to the double doors of the hall and rapped with the heel of his hand.

He waited, his mind clear.

A crack appeared in the door before it swung wide open. Florin had changed into a sumptuous silk dressing gown embroidered with gold brocade which Leone was sure had once kept Monsieur Tubeuf warm on chilly evenings.

'Knight?' he asked in a deep voice.

'I shall be leaving Alençon shortly, and . . . the thought of not saying farewell . . . saddened me.'

'I would have been equally . . . sad had you left without saying farewell. Pray come in. Would you care for some wine? The . . . My cellar is well stocked.'

'A glass of wine, then.'

'This hallway is icy. Let me take you upstairs, knight. My principal rooms are on the first floor. I will join you directly.'

The vast reception room with its roaring fire was magnificent. An abundance of candelabra cast a harmonious, almost natural light. The exquisitely carved chests, the elegant pedestal tables imported from Italy, the tall bevelled mirrors and the lush tapestries hanging on the walls were evidence of the former owners' wealth. Leone sat in one of the two armchairs drawn up in front of the stone hearth. Florin returned carrying two Venetian glasses – a rare and splendid luxury seen only at the tables of the most powerful princes.

He pulled the other chair up to face his guest and sat down, brushing his knees against those of Leone, who did not recoil. The inquisitor was filled with a new kind of excitement. He had hooked his fish, and what a fine catch he was. If he managed to seduce this man, who could possibly resist him? The complexity of this game, the subtlety it required, intoxicated him more assuredly than any alcohol. He murmured in a deep, soft, seductive voice:

'I am . . . I was going to say honoured but suddenly the word displeases me.'

'Moved?' suggested Leone, leaning imperceptibly towards him.

'Yes. Moved.'

'As for me, I am stirred to the depths,' Leone confessed, and the sincerity Florin perceived in the knight's voice thrilled him since he misunderstood the reason for it.

'Stirred to the depths?' the inquisitor repeated, rolling the words greedily on his tongue. 'Is it not remarkable that our paths should have crossed like this?'

'Not really,' Leone corrected, narrowing his bright-blue eyes. 'Do you believe in fate?'

'I believe in desire and in satisfying desire.'

The long, slender hand, responsible for such torment, moved towards the knight's face. He watched it caress the air, the flesh transparent and orange against the firelight. Leone closed his eyes for a moment and a smile spread across his face. He took hold of Florin's wrist and stood up. The inquisitor followed suit and took a step forward so that his body was almost touching the Hospitaller's.

A sigh.

Florin's eyes, as deep as pools, widened and his mouth fell open without emitting any sound. He staggered backwards, staring down at the hilt of the dagger protruding from his belly, and gasped:

'But why . . .'

Leone did not take his eyes off him. The other man pulled out the lethal blade and a flow of blood soaked the front of his fine dressing gown, making the gold brocade glisten.

'You should be asking who, not why. For the sake of the rose. So that the rose may live.'

'I don't . . . You said . . . Stirred . . .'

'I am stirred to the depths of my soul. She has stirred me for eternity. I was not mistaken.'

Florin grasped the back of his chair with both hands to stop himself from falling. His thoughts were racing but he could make no sense of them.

'Agnès?'

'Who else? Do not even attempt to understand for it is beyond you.'

'The camerlin—'

'That evil pig, that vile executioner. There was no letter from the camerlingo. Jean de Rioux wrote the orders you received and the seal was taken from an ancient document in the library of a nearby abbey.'

A crimson bubble burst at the corner of the inquisitor's mouth, then another, followed by a string of ephemeral bright-red pearls. He coughed and a trickle of blood appeared and dangled from his chin. His features were twisted as the pain searing his insides exploded with renewed vigour. He groaned, stumbling over his words:

'It hurts . . . It hurts so much.'

'All those tortured ghosts will finally be at peace, Florin. Your victims.'

'I . . . I beg you . . . I'm bleeding to death.'

'What? Should I put you out of your misery? What compassion have you ever shown that you should merit mine? Give me a single example. I ask no more in order to spare you the agony of a slow death.'

The blood was draining from the face that had once been so seductive. Leone wondered how many women, and men, had succumbed to the perfect mirage, only to discover the nightmare concealed within. How many had perished after an eternity of pain suffered at those long, slender hands? An infant's cries brought him back to the man now lying crumpled up before the hearth.

'It hurts . . . It hurts so terribly . . . I'm going to die, I'm so afraid . . . For pity's sake, knight.'

The image of those blue-grey eyes encircled by sickly shadows flashed through his mind. For her sake, for the sake of the incomparable rose whose petals he had once sketched in a big notebook, Leone picked up the bloodstained dagger. He leaned over the dying man, loosened the neck of his gown and with a single movement slashed his pale throat.

A rattle, a sigh. Florin's body shook violently then went limp.

Francesco de Leone paused to consider the torturer's corpse, searching deep inside himself to see whether this execution had given him any pleasure. None. Only a fleeting sense of relief. One beast was dead, but others would replace him, of this he was certain.

He picked up his glass from one of the little Italian pedestal tables and placed it carefully on the mantelpiece. Florin had fallen on top of the other and the purplish wine had mingled with the red of his blood. He stooped to pull off the luxurious rings that adorned the dead inquisitor's fingers. He kicked over one of the chairs, which fell on its side. He opened the blood-soaked dressing gown, baring the slender chest. This would give the appearance of a lovers' tryst that had gone wrong or a bloody burglary. Leone considered the scene he had staged, then removed his soiled surcoat and threw it on the fire before walking out into the night.

God would judge.

As for his fellow men, the knight was counting on their tongues loosening now that they no longer needed to fear the inquisitor, and on their thirst for revenge.

God would judge.

Fʀᴏᴍ the table perched on a dais that allowed a good view over the refectory, Éleusie's gaze swept over the sisters, who were seated at two long planks of wood resting on trestles, their faces lit up by the flickering flames of the resin candles.

The vast room would normally have been alive with the sound of whispering, inappropriate since meals were supposed to take place in silence. The odd misplaced giggle would normally have rung out, occasioning a call to order from the Abbess. The senior, cellarer and treasurer nuns would normally have shared the Abbess's table, but Blanche de Blinot rarely left her steam room now and Hedwige du Thilay was dead. The only one left was Berthe de Marchiennes, who, divested of her habitual air of superiority, resembled the ageing, pathetic woman she really was.

Éleusie de Beaufort had suggested to Annelette Beaupré that she occupy Hedwige's empty seat so as to spare her daughters a further painful reminder, but the apothecary nun had declined her offer. It was easier for her to survey the others, to observe their reactions from her end of one of the trestle tables, and she was sure that the murderess would be more cautious of the hierarchy sitting up on their dais.

Annelette Beaupré was keeping a close watch on Geneviève

Fournier. The sister in charge of the fishponds and the henhouses was deathly pale, and the almost blackish-purple shadows under her big brown eyes betrayed the fact that she was not sleeping and not eating either, as she had swallowed next to nothing since Hedwige du Thilay's horrific death. This stubborn refusal to eat, which many attributed to the close friendship the two women had enjoyed, troubled the apothecary nun. Undeniably they had been close, as were many of the other sisters, but surely not to the point of starving herself to death. Annelette glanced along the table and felt a pang of grief when her eye alighted on the sprigs of autumn flowers marking Adélaïde Condeau's empty place, and that of Jeanne d'Amblin, who was recovering but still too weak to leave her bed.

Annelette watched Geneviève lift her bowl of turnip, broad bean and bacon soup to her lips, only to set it down abruptly on the table, her hands trembling. She looked around fearfully before lowering her head and pressing the crumbs of black bread between her fingers. The apothecary nun had seen enough; Geneviève was starving herself to death because, despite all the precautions they had taken, she was terrified. Two novices were posted as lookouts at the entrance to the kitchens while the new sister in charge of meals, Elisaba Ferron, prepared the food. Elisaba had just completed her noviciate and taken her final vows. The middle-aged woman, the widow of a rich merchant from Nogent-le-Rotrou, had received Annelette's backing for this post. She was burly enough to knock out anyone attempting to meddle with her pots. As for her stentorian voice, it struck fear into the hearts of more than a few when she placed her hands on her generous hips and boomed: 'My name is appropriate. It means joy in the house of God the Father. Don't forget it, God is joy!' Nobody in their right mind would contradict Elisaba for, despite her loud generosity, she was made of stern stuff, having spent her married life shaking up lazy clerks and putting impudent customers in their place.

Annelette perceived the worried, suspicious glances. They were all surreptitiously sizing one another up in an attempt to discover which familiar friendly face concealed the wicked beast. She watched the furtive glances flying around the room, pausing occasionally and silently wondering. Would their hitherto peaceable, relatively harmonious congregation survive the insidious sickness of suspicion? Annelette was unsure. Indeed, if she were honest she would have to admit that what kept them together was, above all, the shared conviction that this enclosure protected them from the outside world. But death had climbed in among them by stealth, shattering the stout ramparts and their belief that the world's madness could never enter there. In reality, though, what were the majority of the sisters most afraid of? Being poisoned or finding themselves alone and destitute on the outside with no household willing to take them into service? Faith had unquestionably guided the majority in their choice. And yet, even they must have realised by now that the abbey had been their only refuge. And what would she, proud Annelette, do? She preferred not to think about it. Nobody was waiting for her on the outside. Nobody cared what became of her. Her sole existence, her sole importance was concentrated within these walls. This diverse congregation of women, whose members infuriated, amused and only occasionally interested her, had become her family. She had no other now.

The meal ended in an uneasy calm. Only the sound of the benches scraping against the floor broke the oppressive silence. Annelette was the last to leave the table and she followed Geneviève Fournier. Once outside the refectory the sister in charge of the fishponds turned left, cutting through the guest house and across the gardens to go and check her fish and poultry once more before going to bed. She walked slowly, stooped forward with her head down, oblivious to her surroundings. It was dark, and Annelette followed at a few yards' distance, taking care not to give her presence away. Geneviève crossed the cloisters and went past the relics' room. She walked alongside the stables until she reached the henhouses, which were near the entrance to the orchards. She stopped in front of the makeshift wooden fence and stood watching her beloved hens. Annelette, who had also come to a halt, was filled with a strange tenderness. What was her sister thinking about as she stood in the dark, chill night? About Hedwige? About death? Finally Annelette took the plunge. She strode over to Geneviève, and placed her hand on the woman's shoulder. The sister in charge of the fishponds and the henhouses jumped and stifled a cry. Annelette could see a look of terror in her eyes. Geneviève quickly regained her composure and let out a feeble laugh:

'How fearful I must seem. You gave me such a start . . . Are you taking the air, dear Annelette?'

The other woman studied her in silence for a moment before declaring:

'Don't you think the time has come?'

'Pardon?'

'Why are you so afraid of being the next victim that you are starving yourself?'

'I don't know what you're talking about,' the younger woman snapped.

'You know, or think you know, the cause of Hedwige's murder and Jeanne's near-fatal poisoning and that is why you fear for your life.'

'I don't . . .'

'Be quiet! Can't you see that as long as you say nothing the murderess will want to eliminate you? But the more of us you let into your secret the less reason she will have to silence you.'

A huge tear rolled down the face of the sister in charge of the fishponds and henhouses, and she stammered:

'I can't go on . . .'

'Then tell me your secret. It is your only protection.'

Geneviève studied her. She so longed to believe her but was still so afraid.

'I . . . I saw you take my eggs, a large amount of them. At first, I was so upset that I even considered telling our Reverend Mother. But I waited. I asked Hedwige's opinion. It was only later, during the incident in the scriptorium when I saw you rubbing the soles of our shoes on the heating pans, that I understood the necessary part my eggs had played in the trap you had laid.'

'I see. Hedwige knew about my . . . borrowing from your hens, and as she was good friends with Jeanne she almost certainly mentioned it to her.'

Geneviève nodded nervously and murmured in a faltering voice:

'I am to blame . . . It's my fault they were poisoned.'

'No. Get that silly idea out of your head. Go back now, Geneviève. Go back and eat something. I will inform our Reverend Mother of this conversation. I advise you . . . I advise you to confide in some of the sisters about what has been worrying you.'

'But the poisoner . . . I might tell her.'

'That's precisely what I'm hoping. If she planned to get rid of you in order to stop you from talking, she'll realise it's too late and give up.'

A look of relief appeared on the diminutive sister's face and she flung her arms around Annelette who, embarrassed by this effusiveness, carefully extricated herself, smiling apologetically:

'I am not accustomed to such displays of affection.'

Geneviève nodded and confessed:

'Dear Annelette. I think that many of us have misjudged you. You seem so severe . . .' she added with a sigh. 'And yet you are without doubt the bravest, most intelligent woman I have ever known. I wanted to tell you that.'

With this she left, heading towards the gloomy buildings silhouetted against the moonlit sky.

Annelette stayed behind, watching the hunched figures of the hens asleep in their shelter. She did not doubt for a second the veracity of Geneviève's story. And yet she felt convinced that it didn't stand up either. Assuming Hedwige had mentioned Geneviève's concerns about her eggs to Jeanne, it followed that Jeanne must then have told somebody else in order to explain why both women had been targeted by the poisoner. Unless the two had shared food or drink that was only meant for Hedwige. The apothecary decided to put her mind at rest before going to bed. She went up to the dormitory, still deserted before compline, and entered Jeanne's tiny curtained cell. The extern sister was dozing. Annelette's foot knocked against something that made a hollow sound. She looked down and saw an empty soup bowl. Good. Jeanne was eating again and would soon recover her strength. She picked it up and went over to the sleeping woman's bedside. Something cracked under the thick leather sole of her shoe, and she was concerned lest the sharp noise rouse her sister. The hubbub of the other sisters returning to their cells after compline was sure to wake her and she would come back to talk to her then.

She left quietly, pulled the drapes closed behind her and went to the kitchen to return the soup bowl. It was then that she became aware of something squeaking as she walked. She looked under her shoe, assuming she must have picked up a pebble from the garden. A tiny object glistened in the darkness. She tried to dislodge it and cried out in pain. At first she saw nothing. It was only when she went and stood under one of the lights in the kitchen that she noticed that her finger was bleeding. Upon closer inspection of her shoe she realised that the pebble was in fact a thick shard of glass. How had it got there? There was very little glass in the abbey. Only the scriptorium windows were glazed, and as far as she knew none of them was broken. Holding her finger above the sink, she doused it with water from a ewer, then bathed it with liquor made of thyme, rosemary, birch and sage,[40] a phial of which she carried in her belt at all times. A discreet cough made her swing round. A shy novice leaned forward and murmured:

'Our Reverend Mother wishes to see you. She is waiting in her study.'

The young woman disappeared immediately and Annelette spent a few moments dressing the tiny wound with a strip of linen before joining the Abbess in her study.

When she walked in, Éleusie rose to her feet, an inscrutable look on her face. Annelette raised her eyebrows quizzically.

'I have just received a most astonishing piece of news. I still do not know what to make of it. It feels as though the more we progress, the less I understand.'

Annelette waited. Something in the Abbess's manner intrigued her, alarmed her even. Éleusie raised her impossibly dainty hand to her brow and sighed:

'The child . . . little Thibaut de Fleury . . . He died nearly two years ago, a few months after his grandfather.'

Annelette felt her knees go weak. She slumped down onto the chair opposite the desk and breathed:

'Oh dear . . . But . . .'

'That was my first reaction, too, daughter. We have come up against a series of impossibilities. Why bring tales of a thriving happy childhood to his mother in that case? Who would be capable of such a monstrous act? And why did nobody notify her of her father's and then her son's deaths?'

'I am at a loss,' Annelette confessed. 'Above all, I don't

know what to do. Should we inform Yolande that she is the victim of a grotesque farce?'

'And risk it killing her?'

'And risk it killing her . . . but also perhaps forcing her to give us her informant's name,' corrected the apothecary.

'Do you think that this informant is acting out of spite or is she simply passing on to Yolande information communicated to her by a third person?'

'I have no idea, and the only way of finding out is to discover her identity.'

Another silence descended. Annelette tried to bring order to the chaos of her thoughts, to find a link between the disparate, seemingly nonsensical elements. Éleusie de Beaufort was overwhelmed by an intense fatigue. She felt herself withdraw. Her world was gradually being reduced to ashes and she could only contemplate the wreckage. By dint of a supreme effort of will, she ordered:

'Go and fetch Yolande.'

Annelette found the sister in charge of the granary in the steam room folding bed linen with the guest mistress, Thibaude de Gartempe. Yolande stared at her coldly when she passed on the Abbess's request. The little woman, who had always been so cheerful, had not forgiven the apothecary nun for her suspicions. She followed her in silence and, much to Annelette's relief, did not even ask the reason for the interview.

Éleusie was standing, leaning back against her desk as

though steeling herself for an attack. Yolande could tell from the concern on her face that something terrible had happened.

'Reverend Mother?'

'Yolande . . . my dear child . . . Your . . . Your father died nearly two years ago.'

Yolande lowered her eyes and murmured:

'Dear God . . . May his soul rest in peace. I hope he found it in his heart to forgive me . . .' Suddenly she asked: 'But . . . What about my son? What about Thibaut? Who looks after him now? I was my father's only child.'

'Your informant did not tell you, then?' the apothecary nun cut in.

Yolande turned towards her, a hard, inscrutable expression on her face, before saying through gritted teeth:

'I would prefer not to have to talk to you. I've never liked you, although I never expected to have any reason to distrust you.' She turned back to the Abbess, her voice softening again: 'Reverend Mother, pray tell me, who is looking after Thibaut?'

It was Éleusie's turn now to lower her gaze. Annelette barely recognised her voice as she uttered the terrible words:

'He joined your father shortly afterwards.'

Yolande did not understand what her Reverend Mother had just said to her. She insisted, puzzled:

'He joined him . . . how? Where? I . . .'

'He is dead, my dear child.'

An eerie smile appeared on the lips of the sister in charge of the granary as she leaned towards the distressed woman and asked:

'I don't . . . What are you saying?'

Éleusie felt a wrenching pain in her chest and she repeated in an almost aggressive tone:

'Thibaut is dead, Yolande. Your son died nearly two years ago, a few months after his grandfather.'

Annelette had the impression that Yolande's life was draining out of her as she watched the woman crumple. A strange sound like wheezing bellows filled the room, followed by a moan that gradually grew louder and louder until it exploded into a scream. Yolande whirled round in ever-faster circles, clawing at her face, unable to stop the piercing scream rising from her throat and pervading the room seemingly without her needing to take a breath. She slumped to her knees, panting uncontrollably as though she were choking to death. Annelette and Éleusie stood motionless, staring at her dumbstruck. How many minutes passed, filled only by the frenzied sobs of a grieving mother, the groans of a dying animal?

Suddenly the groaning stopped. Yolande looked up at them with crazed eyes, her face twisted with rage. She got to her feet using both hands. Éleusie rushed over to assist her, to embrace her, but Yolande leapt backwards, pointing her finger at her and snarling:

'How could you . . .? Cruel traitress, you're no better than your henchwoman, the apothecary. A couple of nasty, evil madwomen.'

Éleusie, incredulous, stepped back from her daughter. Yolande continued raging at her, and Annelette, afraid she might attack the Abbess, prepared to intervene.

'How dare you invent such a despicable lie? Did you have

to sink to such depths? Do you think I am a fool? You made up this monstrous story in the hope that I would give you the name of the kind friend who brings me news. Never! I can see through your wicked ploy. And do you know how? Because my little boy is with me every second of the day. Because if he had died I would have died instantly in order to be with him. Wicked monsters! You will be cursed for this!' She interrupted herself, clasping her hand to her mouth to stifle a hysterical laugh. 'I demand, Reverend Mother, that you request my immediate transfer to another of our order's abbeys. I wish to flee as soon as possible the stinking pit you and your disciples have dug in this place. I am sure I will not be the only one to demand a transfer. Others have seen through your despicable scheming.'

Annelette thought that Yolande had finally tipped over into madness. She interceded to try to calm her:

'Yolande, you are mistaken. We . . .'

'Shut up, you demented poisoner! Do you suppose I don't know that you are the culprit? Oh, you are very clever and cunning, but you can't fool me.'

This accusation so took the apothecary nun by surprise that she was incapable of reacting. She tried, however, to reason with her sister:

'You don't understand . . . If I am right, your informant . . . well, it wouldn't surprise me if she was the poisoner we are tracking down. If so, then your life is in danger.'

The other woman hissed:

'A clever try, to be sure, but you'll have to do better than that to convince me. Murderess!'

Yolande flew out of the Abbess's study as if the devil were on her tail.

Annelette turned to Éleusie and murmured:

'I think she has lost her mind.'

The Abbess let out a sob and groaned:

'Dear God, what have we done?'

Annelette grappled with her own panic. For the first time in her life the tall imperious woman doubted herself. The accusations hurled at her by the sister in charge of the granary – during an unconvincing fit of grief – were unimportant. What was important was the crippling pain she and the Abbess had inflicted upon her. What mattered was the plan Annelette had thought up in order to force her to confess the name of her informant. She was filled with an excruciating sense of shame and heard herself say, almost imploringly:

'Reverend Mother, may I as an exception sleep in your chambers? I will make a bed on the carpet in your study. I realise that . . .'

Her apothecary daughter's eyes, brimming with tears, her trembling lip and quivering chin spoke louder to Éleusie than any words. She agreed in a faltering voice:

'I dared not propose it myself. We are so alone tonight. And yet, Annelette, there is a battle raging outside, a merciless battle. I bitterly regret the pain we have caused Yolande, but she had to face the terrible truth, no matter what. Thibaut is dead and her informant has been lying to her for two years for reasons that are still unclear to me. In addition . . . And may God forgive me for what is not heartlessness on my part, for I assure you that my heart bleeds for that poor grieving mother . . . May God forgive me, but we are all in peril and Yolande's loss changes nothing. That poor little boy joined his Creator two years ago . . . Our lives are in danger today or perhaps tomorrow. We will mourn our dead later. The beast must be killed first, and quickly.'

Annelette sighed and walked over to her Mother Superior, hands outstretched, and whispered:

'Thank you for voicing what I no longer dared to think.'

Adèle de Vigneux, the granary keeper, woke up shivering. The thin coverlet had slipped off her bed. She felt for it in the gloom, stifled a yawn and blinked, groggy from sleep. The dormitory was quiet except for the sound of breathing echoing from one end of the huge, icy room to the other. Occasionally somebody moving or coughing broke the monotonous rhythm. A loud snoring rose above the other sounds. It was Blanche de Blinot. Adèle de Vigneux smiled. Age seemed to protect Blanche from troubled dreams.

The young granary keeper pulled the coverlet over her and curled up snugly. Just as she drifted back into oblivion, a silhouette appeared behind the curtains around her cell.

Night was still keeping dawn at bay when they awoke to prepare for lauds.* Adèle pulled on her robe and adjusted her veil, her eyelids heavy with sleep. She drew back the curtain round her tiny cell and was surprised by the silence that prevailed in the neighbouring cell. Yolande de Fleury was still asleep. She had seemed so agitated the night before that Adèle had enquired after her wellbeing, only to be sharply rebuked. The other woman was so overwrought that the younger woman had not insisted. Yolande had said:

'Those two madwomen think I'm a fool but they'll soon discover how wrong they are. I would have felt it, you see. Those are things that a . . . I mean they are in the blood. Good night, Adèle. Please don't ask me to explain. I am in a foul mood and would hate to lose my temper with you, who have done nothing.'

Adèle paused. Perhaps a good sleep had helped her sister regain her composure. She pulled aside the drape and whispered:

'Yolande dear, Yolande . . . It's time to get up.'

There was no reply. She took a step forward. Something about the position of the sleeping woman alarmed her. She touched the hand lying on top of the coverlet.

A scream rang out through the dormitory. The nuns all stopped what they were doing and looked at one another. Berthe de Marchiennes was the first to emerge from this dreamlike trance. She rushed over to Adèle's cell. The young woman was repeating the same words, like a litany:

'Her hand is ice cold . . . Her hand is ice cold, it isn't normal, she's ice cold, I tell you . . .'

Berthe drew back the cover sharply. Yolande de Fleury was lying with her mouth wide open. Purple-red scratch marks disfigured the pale skin on her neck. One of her legs was dangling over the side of the bed.

The cellarer nun closed the dead woman's eyes, turned to Adèle de Vigneux and said in a soft voice:

'She is dead. Please be so good as to fetch our Reverend Mother and Annelette Beaupré.'

Adèle stood rooted to the spot, her eyes moving between Berthe and the ice-cold corpse.

'That's an order, Adèle. Go and inform our Reverend Mother immediately.'

The young woman suddenly seemed to emerge from her stupor, and disappeared. Berthe sat down on the edge of Yolande's bed. She clasped her hands together in prayer:

'We are your humble devoted servants. Do not forsake us.'

Alençon, Perche, December 1304

T HE horses were exhausted and their riders scarcely any
fresher by the time they reached the town of Alençon at
dusk. The destrier, Ogier, was tossing his head and snorting; a
cloud of vapour surrounded the stallion's flared nostrils and his
chest heaved with the effort of breathing. Clément's mare,
Sylvestre, quivered with tiredness, almost prancing as she walked,
as though she were nervous of stumbling. Artus patted the neck of
his magnificent mount and murmured:

'Steady! Steady! My brave steed. Our journey is done and I
have found fine lodgings for you. My heartfelt thanks, Ogier.
You are an even hardier beast than when I broke you in.'

The horse raised his head, shaking his pitch-black mane and
flattening his ears in exhaustion.

Clément jumped down from his mare and stroked her
muzzle – he was no less grateful to her for this punishing race
against time, which was running short.

The ostler arrived to take the exhausted animals to be
groomed. He tugged roughly on Ogier's bit and the horse
threatened to rear up.

'Whoa, you oaf! Nobody manhandles my faithful steed's
mouth like that!' Artus shouted. 'Show him a little respect or
he'll buck you at the first opportunity, and quite rightly. The

same goes for the mare. Be careful. You can't ask an animal to give its all and then treat it like a beast of burden. These creatures have nearly killed themselves to get us here at breakneck speed. Treat them in the manner they deserve – and for which I am paying you handsomely – or you'll have me to answer to.'

The ostler did not need telling twice and gently cajoled the two mounts until they consented to walk on.

Clément followed Artus d'Authon through the streets of Alençon. How tall he was and what big steps he took, the child thought, as he did his best to keep up. All of a sudden Artus stopped, almost causing Clément to slam into his back.

'He should come out soon. I'll point him out to you. Follow him, and when you've discovered where he lodges make your way directly to La Jument-Rouge,' he said, gesturing towards a nearby tavern, 'and don't try anything, do you hear?'

'Yes, my lord.'

'. . . I'm warning you not to disobey me and try anything foolish, Clément. You may be brave, but you're not big or strong enough to take him on. I am. You will greatly harm your lady if you do not follow my instructions. Do you understand that if he slips through our fingers tonight, tomorrow Madame Agnès will die a thousand deaths?'

'I know, my lord. And then will you kill him?'

'I will. He has left me no other choice. It is a small matter in the end and I probably should have done it sooner. I could kick myself for hoping I could convince him.'

The Inquisition headquarters were strangely abuzz with activity when they arrived. Clerks were darting in and out of the place and men-at-arms with sullen faces rushed about for no apparent reason. Amid the general mayhem, the Comte d'Authon, flanked by Clément, walked towards the main entrance and went in. A skinny young friar, whom Artus did not recognise, came running up to them.

'M-my lord, my lord,' he stammered, giving a quick bow. 'He is dead. God be praised for doing justice. The wicked beast is dead.'

Sensing the Comte's bewilderment, he added:

'Agnan, my name is Agnan. I was chief clerk to that evil inquisitor. I was there when you came and tried to reason with him. I knew it was a waste of precious time. But it doesn't matter any more. He died as he lived, like a wicked sinner.' Agnan almost shrieked: 'God has passed judgement! His ineffable verdict has come down to earth like a revelation. The innocent dove, Madame de Souarcy, is free. Nicolas Florin's other victims, too. The judgement of God requires all his cases to be closed, permanently.'

'How did he die? When?'

'Last night. At the hands of a passing drunkard. It seems he invited the man into his house, the house he extorted from some poor soul whom he tortured to death. There was a struggle, ending in that devil's murder. Monsieur . . . We have witnessed a miracle . . . God intervened to save Madame de Souarcy, and . . . but it comes as no surprise to me. I looked into that woman's eyes, she reached out and touched me with her hand and I understood . . .'

'What did you understand?' Artus asked calmly, for the young man's exalted speech troubled him.

'I understood that she was . . . different. I understood that this woman was . . . unique. I am unable to describe it in words, my lord, and you must think me out of my mind. But I know. I know that I have been touched by perfection and that I will never be the same again. He also knew. He emerged from her cell stirred to the depths, his eyes shining with the indescribable light.'

'Who?' insisted Artus, sure that the young man had not lost his mind, that his garbled speech concealed a profound truth.

'Why, the knight of course . . . The Knight Hospitaller.'

'Who?' the Comte d'Authon almost cried out.

'I assumed that you knew one another . . . I can tell you nothing more, Monsieur. With all due respect, please do not ask. No man has the right or the power to question a miracle. Madame de Souarcy is waiting for you in our infirmary. She has been through a terrible ordeal, but her courage is matched only by her purity. What joy you will feel in her presence! What joy . . . What joy I felt. Just imagine . . . She touched me, she looked straight into my eyes.'

Agnan wriggled free from Artus's restraining hand and ran off, leaving Artus and Clément speechless.

Agnès was raving, although the friar who was looking after her reassured them as to her physical health. Lash wounds were quick to heal. On the other hand, Madame de Souarcy was suffering from a fever that required her to spend a few days in bed, where she would receive the best care. Clément and Artus sat at her bedside. Occasionally, she would murmur a few incomprehensible words before sinking back into semi-consciousness. Suddenly, she opened her eyes, sat up straight and cried out:

'Clément . . . No, never!'

'I am right beside you, Madame. Oh, Madame, I beg you, please get better,' sobbed the child, his head in his hands.

Artus's heart was in his throat and his soul in torment; he was overjoyed that an alleged drunkard, whom he was certain was the Knight Hospitaller, had slain Florin, and at the same time devastated that the knight had got there before him. What a fool! He had tried to negotiate, to buy the man, when he should have stopped wasting time and unsheathed his sword. He had not saved Agnès, he had not earned her gratitude, and he would never forgive himself for it. He would have given his life for her, without hesitation. He was angry at the knight even as he felt grateful to him. Her other saviour had preceded him by a few hours, that was all, a few hours that had made all the difference. And that young friar Agnan, whose words Artus had not understood. Agnan, whose life had been illuminated because Agnès's hand had brushed against his hand or cheek. And suddenly Artus understood. He understood that this extraordinary woman who had stolen his heart and soul was unique, just as the young clerk had said. He understood that her attraction went deeper than her outward intelligence, courage, charm and beauty. And yet even as he held her slender hand between his, he could not help but ask who this woman really was. Everyone who knew her had been transformed in a way that could not be explained by love: Agnan, Clément, the knight, he himself . . . to name only those he knew. Who was she really?

In the days that followed tongues began to wag. Artus and Clément had found satisfactory lodgings at La Jument-Rouge. Everyone was talking, gossiping and conjecturing. The streets were alive with rumour and speculation. Even the local stoker and potter had revelations to make, tales to tell containing a mixture of truth and hyperbole. Nicolas Florin's brutality, his cruelty, his corruption, his taste for riches became common knowledge. He was even accused of sorcery, of having sold his soul in exchange for power, and it was rumoured that he had held frequent black masses. The humble folk unleashed themselves upon this man whom they had at first adored, then feared and finally come to hate. The episcopate, which had hitherto turned a blind eye, finally intervened, decreeing that the Grand Inquisitor's remains would not be buried in consecrated ground. This declaration reassured the masses, who, up until the day before, had bowed to Florin, also turning a blind eye to his notorious dealings, but now, no longer fearing reprisals, they turned against him as one.

Agnès's scars soon healed thanks to the constant attention of those around her. A few days after the death of her would-be executioner, she got out of bed and walked a few paces. Clément scolded her for rushing matters and Artus implored her not to overexert herself.

'Come now, dear gentlemen, I'm not as fragile as you think. It would take a lot more than this to finish off a woman like me. Any doubts I might have had about that have been dispelled.'

Despite the supplications of Artus, who longed for her to accept his hospitality, she decided to return directly to her manor in order to reassure her people and attend to the affairs she had been obliged to neglect.

Château de Larnay, Perche, December 1304

THE girl shied away in terror. Her cheek was stinging and Eudes's anger made her fear for her safety. A second blow sent her crashing into the door frame and she felt the blood streaming from her nose. She implored:

'Master . . . I've done nothing wrong . . . kind master.'

'Out of my sight, you whore! Vile whores, all of you!' shrieked Eudes, screwing up the letter the servant had just brought.

The young girl fled as fast as she could to get away from the madman's fists.

Eudes de Larnay was trembling with rage and regretted dismissing the servant girl. Beating her more would have brought him some relief.

The fools! The unutterable fools!

That wretch Florin had been handed this trial on a plate and had not managed to bring it to a successful conclusion. The fool had got himself stabbed by some brute – some drinking or orgy companion he had pulled from the gutter or from a cheap tavern. As for his gormless niece, who had nothing better to do than flutter her eyelids and prance about in her finery, she was too inept and stupid to have been seen fit to repeat what he had taken such pains to din into her. And as for that strumpet

Mabile, who had led him on, made a fool of him, extorting his money with her lies. His entire household was useless, cowardly and stupid!

A sudden wrenching pain dispelled his anger.

Agnès . . . my magnificent warrior. Why must you detest me so? I hate you, Agnès, for you are always in my thoughts. You haunt me. You dog my days and my nights with your presence. I wanted you dead, yet what is there left for me if you die? He stifled the sob that threatened to choke him and closed his eyes. I love you, Agnès. Agnès. You are my festering wound and my only remedy. I hate you, I truly hate you.

He snatched up the pitcher from the table and drank without filling his goblet. The wine trickled down his striped silk doublet. The alcohol stung his insides, reminding him that he had not eaten since the day before. But the effect of the liquor soon sated him.

I have not finished with you yet, my beloved.

He would think up some other ruse. Quite apart from his resentment and his insatiable lust, he had no choice. He had no choice. His own survival depended on it.

YOLANDE de Fleury was resting in the ground. Every day Éleusie went to her grave to pay homage to her memory. Her grief was eased slightly by the thought that after a few moments of terrifying despair, the sweet Yolande had realised that her little Thibaut could not be dead. At least this is what the Abbess hoped Yolande had continued to believe until the very end.

Éleusie de Beaufort felt sure that Annelette was right. The sister in charge of the granary must have told her informant about the terrible scene that had taken place in the Abbess's study. She must have assured her that she had not revealed her name to them. It had never occurred to her that the kindly bringer of good news was none other than the murderess. Yolande had not suspected for a moment that by relating these events she was signing her own death warrant, for the informant could not risk being denounced.

The poor little angel had joined her son, and the day Yolande's coffin had been scattered with earth Éleusie had made a promise to herself. She would find out who had lied to Yolande and why. She felt that her daughter would not find peace otherwise. She felt that little Thibaut, whom she had never met, was pleading with her to do it for his mother's sake and his own. Suddenly, doing God's work in however small a measure and standing firm against the tides of evil seemed more important to her than anything else. Yolande de Fleury's informant was none other than the murderer of Adélaïde, Hedwige, Yolande herself, and of the Pope's emissaries. And yet, curiously, it was the lies the accursed woman had told in order to lull Yolande into a false sense of security that had come, in Éleusie's eyes, to represent an unforgivable sin. The Abbess had first wanted to eliminate any danger, to drive it outside the abbey's walls, and then, if she could, to see that justice was done. Now, she demanded atonement for these sins. Nothing less than execution.

The early-morning frost crunched beneath her feet as she walked back towards the main buildings. Before, an eternity ago, she had loved the peaceful indifference of winter. She would smile at the stillness of the snow that appeared to muffle every sound. The cold had not seemed to her unrelenting as it could be warded off by sitting beside a hearth or swallowing a bowlful of hot soup. That morning, she felt the deadly chill pierce her to the bone. She thought of all the deaths, all the creatures in the nearby forests that would perish before the advent of better weather. Death. Death was sliding, creeping, slipping all around. Her existence had become a graveyard and no amount of life would ever change that. She was the sole survivor in the mortuary that had implanted itself in her mind.

A few snowflakes pricked the skin on her hands before melting. She paused. Should she go to the herbarium to see Annelette? No, she hadn't the energy. Her study, however unwelcoming it might feel since the dreadful scene with Yolande, was still the only place where she could reflect.

The bells of Notre-Dame Church were pealing out. Sudden cries and an acrid smell made her turn her head in the direction of the guest house. She ran towards the building. Flames were rising out of the arrow-slit windows and she could hear the blaze roaring inside. Fire. A bevy of nuns was following Annelette's instructions and racing to fetch heavy pails of water. A human chain quickly formed. Pails, pans, every sort of receptacle passed from one pair of hands to the next. Annelette finally saw the Abbess and ran over to her, crying out:

'It's a diversion, I am sure. She is trying to divert our attention, but to what evil end I do not know.'

It came to Éleusie in a flash: the secret library. She ran in the opposite direction as fast as her legs would carry her.

The moment she opened the door and stepped into the cold room she sensed something was wrong. Her gaze fell upon the thick tapestry obscuring the tiny passageway and the door leading into the secret place. It seemed to be moving as though the biblical scene had come alive.

Who? Who had discovered her secret? Who had entered there? Dear God, the forbidden works, the notebook belonging to Eustache de Rioux and Francesco! It must under no circumstances fall into enemy hands. So, she had been right all along. The sole intention of the poisoner was to lay her hands on these works.

She searched frantically for any object she could use as a weapon. Her eye fell upon the stiletto knife she used to cut paper. She seized it and ran towards the hidden opening. A figure dressed in a heavy monk's habit, a cowl drawn over its face to avoid recognition, turned towards the Abbess, then made a dash for the door leading into the main corridor. Éleusie gave chase, still brandishing the knife, but the figure aimed a blow at her throat that left her fighting for breath. The Abbess struggled to seize the volumes wedged under the figure's arm, but to no avail. Bent double and gasping, Éleusie watched as the shadowy figure vanished at the end of the corridor. A sudden rush of energy she no longer thought herself capable of roused her, and she hurtled outside as though her life depended on it. She shouted at all the sisters she encountered who were on their way to help fight the fire:

'Go and instruct the porteress nuns[41] not to allow anybody out of the abbey under any circumstances. Failure to obey will be severely punished. This instant! Nobody must leave the abbey. That's an order!'

She herself raced to the main door and stirred the porteress, demanding that she bolt the heavy doors at once. The panic-stricken woman obeyed.

Éleusie sighed and dug her fingers into the painful stitch in her side to try to ease it. She bent double in a fit of nervous laughter and gasped:

'You'll not escape, you wretch! You thought you had got the better of us, didn't you, you vulture? I've got you now. I'll crush you like the vermin you are!' She turned towards the ashen-faced porteress and commanded: 'I am reinstating the strict cloister without exception. Nobody is to leave here without an order signed by me and only me. Every, and I repeat *every*, sister whom I authorise to leave must have her body as well as her bundles and cart thoroughly searched. Without exception.'

Éleusie suddenly turned on her heel and ran towards her daughters who were busy fighting the fire, snarling to herself:

'The manuscripts will stay in the abbey. Hide them . . . hide them as best you can, I will find them! You'll take them over my dead body.'

Manoir de Souarcy-en-Perche, December 1304

AGNÈS, who was still pallid and frail, looked at Clément and asked:

'What are you saying?'

'That we need to pay a visit to La Haute-Gravière, your health permitting.'

'I shall decide whether my health permits. Stop fussing over me like a mother hen.'

A joyous smile flashed across the child's face:

'So, Madame, you are my baby chicken now.'

Agnès laughed and ruffled his hair. She loved him so much. Had he not constantly been in her thoughts she would never have survived her imprisonment at Alençon.

'A big fat baby chicken, indeed!' She grew serious again, continuing: 'But we know nothing about the place, dear Clément.'

'Indeed we do, Madame. I learned from my remarkable teacher, the physician Joseph de Bologne.'

'Joseph again,' Agnès joked. 'Do you know, I think I am going to end up being jealous of that man?'

'Oh, Madame, if only you knew him . . . You would immediately fall under his spell. He knows everything about everything.'

'Gracious me! What a flattering description. You miss him, don't you?'

Clément blushed and confessed:

'Never when I am with you, for that is where I always wish to be.' She could see him fighting back the tears. 'I was so afraid, Madame, so terribly afraid that I would lose you and never find you again. I thought I would die of sorrow a thousand times. And so if I must choose I prefer to stay here with you.' He paused before adding: 'Even so, Monsieur Joseph's teaching is without parallel. The man has studied the world with his mind, Madame. He has so much knowledge of science. Is it not wonderful and incredible that he should consider me worthy of receiving it and be willing to answer so many of my questions? Moreover . . . he knows.'

'What does he know?' demanded Agnès, alerted by Clément's sudden seriousness.

'That I am not . . . I mean that I am a girl.'

'Did you tell him?'

'Of course not. He found it out. He claims you can already see a woman's eyes in those of a child and that only a fool would confuse them with a man's eyes.'

Agnès grew anxious.

'Do you think he will tell the Comte?'

'No. He holds his lord in high esteem, but he gave me his word that he would say nothing. And you see, Madame, you and he are the only two people whose word I completely trust.'

Agnès felt relieved and quipped:

'Don't say it too loud. You'll upset a lot of people.'

'Why should I care if I make you happy? Getting back to the subject of La Haute-Gravière, which is part of your dower, plenty of nettles grow there.'

'And little else,' the lady agreed with a sigh. 'Even the oxen won't graze there. I was thinking of buying some goats at the next livestock fair. At least we could make cheese from their milk.'

'Nettles thrive in ferrous soil.'

Agnès understood immediately what the child was implying. 'Really? Is Maître Joseph sure of this?'

'Yes. According to him, an abundance of nettles means the soil is rich in iron ore. We must find out, Madame. Is it the soil's composition or do the plants point to a deposit?'

'What must we do? How does one go about finding an iron-ore deposit?'

Clément pulled out of his thick winter tunic what looked like a dark-grey sharpening stone, and declared:

'By means of this wonderful, inestimably rare object Joseph lent me in order to help you.'

'Is it a piece of carved rock?'

'It is magnetite, Madame.'

'Magnetite?'

'A very useful stone that comes from a region of Asia Minor known as Magnesia.'[42]

'How can it help us, my dear Clément?'

'This little piece of stone you see here has the power to attract iron, or soil containing iron. It sticks to it. We don't know why.'

Rising from her bench, Agnès commanded:

'Saddle a horse! You will sit behind me on a pillion. You are right, we must find out immediately.'

Clément left at once. A smile spread across Agnès's lips, and she muttered to herself:

'I have you, Eudes. If, God willing, this is an iron mine, you will soon pay for the suffering you caused me.'

She drove out the images flooding into her mind, of Mathilde; her tiny nails when she closed her baby fist round her mother's finger; charging through the corridors at Souarcy, shrieking whenever a goose came up to her flapping its wings.

She must banish from her thoughts these happy memories that wounded her like a knife.

Where had the strange, beautiful man disappeared to, the Knight Hospitaller who had saved her, for she suspected that Florin's death had been more than fortuitous. If the story of the ill-fated encounter with a drinking or orgy companion had convinced those who wanted to destroy the inquisitor's already monstrous reputation, it had left Agnès sceptical. She had pondered for hours their brief exchange, attempting to reconstruct every detail, every word spoken. She had the bewildering certainty of having come close to a mystery that had then rapidly eluded her. Francesco de Leone was Éleusie de Beaufort's nephew, or rather her adoptive son. Would the Abbess agree to tell her more, to enlighten her about him?

Had Mathilde remained at Clairets, would her uncle have been able to corrupt her like that? Had she, whose only thought had been to protect her daughter, been at fault?

Stop!

Mathilde. Her cold eyes, her pretty fingers adorned with Madame Apolline's rings. Her lies aimed at sending her mother to the stake and Clément to the torture chamber.

No. She would cry no more. She was beyond tears.

APPENDIX I
HISTORICAL REFERENCES

Ballads of Marie de France. Twelve ballads popularly attributed to a certain Marie, originally from France but living at the English court. Some historians believe she was a daughter of Louis VII or the Comte de Meulan. The ballads were written before 1167 and Marie's fables around 1180. Marie de France was also the author of a novel *Le Purgatoire de Saint-Patrice*.

Benoît XI, Pope, Nicolas Boccasini, 1240–1304. Relatively little is known about him. Coming from a very poor background, Boccasini, a Dominican, remained humble throughout his life. One of the few anecdotes about him demonstrates this: when his mother paid him a visit after his election, she made herself look pretty for her son. He gently explained that her outfit was too ostentatious and that he preferred women to be simply dressed. Known for his conciliatory temperament, Boccasini, who had been Bishop of Ostia, tried to mediate in the disagreements between the Church and Philip the Fair, but he showed his disapproval of Guillaume de Nogaret and the Colonna brothers. He died after eight months of the pontificate, on 7 July 1304, poisoned by figs or dates.

Boniface VIII, Pope, Benedetto Caetani, *c.*1235–1303. Cardinal and legate in France, then pope. He was a passionate defender of pontifical theocracy, which was opposed to the new authority of the State. He was openly hostile to Philip the Fair from 1296 onwards and the affair continued even after his death – France attempted to try him posthumously.

Calling. See Prostitution.

Chrétien de Troyes, c.1140–c.1190. Poet from Champagne, sometimes described as the creator of the modern novel. He travelled widely and possibly visited England. He was closely associated with Countess Marie, daughter of Eleanor of Aquitaine who became Queen of England. Devoted to Ovid, he translated his *Art of Love* and reinvented narrative romance, injecting an element of psychological insight. He played with symbolism and crafted subtle plots, and in *Cligès* introduced elements of mythology. His best-known poem is probably *Perceval or The Story of the Grail*, but he also wrote *Lancelot, the Knight of the Cart*; *Yvain, the Knight of the Lion* and *Eric and Enid*.

Clairets Abbey, Orne. Situated on the edge of Clairets Forest, in the parish of Masle, the abbey was built by a charter issued in July 1204 by Geoffroy III, Comte du Perche, and his wife Mathilde of Brunswick, sister of Emperor Otto IV. The abbey's construction took seven years and finished in 1212. Its consecration was co-signed by the commander of the Knights Templar, Guillaume d'Arville, about whom little is known. The abbey is only open to Bernardine nuns of the Cistercian order, who have the right to all forms of seigneurial justice.

Délicieux, Bernard. Franciscan monk who fiercely opposed the Dominicans and their Inquisition. He was a good public speaker and his independence of spirit drew enormous crowds. He organised a demonstration against Philip the Fair when the King visited Carcassonne in August 1303. He went as far as to participate in a plot to enflame Languedoc against the King. He was arrested several times and ended his days in prison in 1320.

Got, Bernard de, *c.*1270–1314. He is best known as a canon and counsellor to the King of England. He was, however, a skilled diplomat, which enabled him to maintain cordial relations with Philip the Fair even though England was at war with France. He became Archbishop of Bordeaux in 1299 then succeeded Benoît XI as pope in 1305, taking the name Clément V. He chose to install himself in Avignon, because he was wary of the politics of Rome, which he knew little about. He was good at handling Philip the Fair in their two major differences of opinion: the posthumous trial of Boniface VIII and the suppression of the Knights Templar. He managed to rein in the spite of the sovereign in the first case, and to contain it in the second case.

The Hospitallers of Saint John of Jerusalem were recognised by Pape Pascal III in 1113. Unlike the other soldier orders, the original function of the Hospitallers was charitable. It was only later that they assumed a military function. After the Siege of Acre in 1291, the Hospitallers withdrew to Cyprus then Rhodes, and finally Malta. The order was governed by a Grand-Master, elected by the general chapter made up of dignitaries. The chapter was subdivided into provinces, governed in their turn by priors. Unlike the Templars and in spite of their great wealth, the Hospitallers always enjoyed a very favourable reputation, no doubt because of their charitable works, which they never abandoned, and because of the humility of their members.

Inquisitorial procedure. The conduct of the trial and the questions of doctrine put to the accused are adapted from the work of Nicholas Eymerich (1320–1399) and Francisco Peña (1540–1612) – *The Inquisitor's Manual.*

Knights Templar. The order was created in 1118 in Jerusalem by the knight Hugues de Payens and other knights from Champagne and Burgundy. It was officially endorsed by the Church at the Council of Troyes in 1128, having been championed by Bernard of Clairvaux. The order was led by a Grand-Master, whose authority was backed up by dignitaries. The order owned considerable assets (3,450 châteaux, fortresses and houses in 1257). With its system of transferring money to the Holy Land, the order acted in the thirteenth century as one of Christianity's principal bankers. After the Siege of Acre in 1291 – which was in the end fatal to the order – the Templars almost all withdrew to the West. Public opinion turned against them and they were regarded as indolent profiteers. Various expressions of the period bear witness to this. For example, 'Going to the Temple' was a euphemism for going to a brothel. When the Grand-Master Jacques de Molay refused to merge the Templars with the Hospitallers, the Templars were arrested on 13 October 1307. An investigation followed, confessions were obtained (in the case of Jacques de Molay, some historians believe, with the use of torture), followed by retractions. Clément V, who feared Philip the Fair for various unrelated reasons, passed a decree suppressing the order on 22 March 1312. Jacques de Molay again stood by the retraction of his confession and on 18 March 1314 was burnt at the stake along with other Templars. It is generally agreed that the seizure of the Templars' assets and their redistribution to the Hospitallers cost Philip the Fair more money than it gained him.

Medieval Inquisition. It is important to distinguish the Medieval Inquisition from the Spanish Inquisition. The repression and intolerance of the latter were incomparably more violent than anything known in France. Under the leadership of Tomas de Torquemada alone, there were more than two thousand deaths recorded in Spain.

The Medieval Inquisition was at first enforced by the bishops. Pope Innocent III (1160–1216) set out the regulations for the inquisitorial procedure in the papal bull *Vergentis in senium* of 1199. The aim was not to eliminate individuals – as was proved by the Fourth Council of the Lateran, called by Innocent III a year before his death, which emphasised that it was forbidden to inflict the Ordeal on dissidents. (The Ordeal or 'judgement of God' was a trial by fire, water or the sword to test whether an accused person was a heretic or not.) What the Pope was aiming for was the eradication of heresies that threatened the foundation of the Church by promoting, amongst other things, the poverty of Christ as a model way to live – a model that was obviously rarely followed if the vast wealth earned by most of the monasteries from land tax is anything to go by. Later the Inquisition was enforced by the Pope, starting with Gregory IX, who conferred inquisitorial powers on the Dominicans in 1232 and, in a lesser way, on the Franciscans. Gregory's motives in reinforcing the powers of the Inquisition and placing them under his sole control were entirely political. He was ensuring that on no account would Emperor Frederick II be able to control the Inquisition for reasons that had nothing to do with spirituality. It was Innocent IV who took the ultimate step in authorising recourse to torture in his papal bull *Ad extirpanda* of 15 May 1252. Witches as well as heretics were then hunted down by the Inquisition.

The real impact of the Inquisition has been exaggerated. There were relatively few inquisitors to cover the whole territory of the kingdom of France and they would have had little effect had they not received the help of powerful lay people and benefited from numerous denunciations. But, thanks to their ability to excuse each other for their faults, certain inquisitors were guilty of terrifying atrocities that sometimes provoked riots and scandalised many prelates.

In March 2000, roughly eight centuries after the beginnings of the Inquisition, Pope John Paul II asked God's pardon for the crimes and horrors committed in its name.

Nogaret, Guillaume de, *c*.1270–1313. Nogaret was a professor of civil law and taught at Montpellier before joining Philip the Fair's Council in 1295. His responsibilities grew rapidly more widespread, He involved himself, at first more or less clandestinely, in the great religious debates that were shaking

France, for example the trial of Bernard Saisset. Nogaret progressively emerged from the shadows and played a pivotal role in the campaign against the Knights Templar and the King's struggle with Pope Boniface VIII. Nogaret was of unshakeable faith and great intelligence. He would go on to become the King's chancellor, and although he was displaced for a while by Enguerran de Marigny, he took up the seal again in 1311.

Peña, Francisco, 1540–1612. In citing this name, the author has knowingly committed an anachronism. Francisco Peña is the specialist in canonical law whom the Holy See charged, in the sixteenth century, with producing the new edition of *The Inquisitor's Manual* by Nicholas Eymerich.

Philip the Fair, 1268–1314. The son of Philip III (known as Philip the Bold) and Isabelle of Aragon. With his consort Joan of Navarre, he had three sons who would all become kings of France – Louis X (Louis the Stubborn), Philip V (Philip the Tall) and Charles IV (Charles the Fair). He also had a daughter, Isabelle, whom he married to Edward II of England. Philip was brave and an excellent war leader, but he also had a reputation for being inflexible and harsh. It is now generally agreed, however, that perhaps that reputation has been overstated, since contemporary accounts relate that Philip the Fair was manipulated by his advisers, who flattered him whilst mocking him behind his back.

Philip the Fair is best known for the major role he played in the suppression of the Knights Templar, but he was above all a reforming king whose objective was to free the politics of the French kingdom from papal interference.

Prostitution was reasonably well tolerated as long as it stayed within the limits imposed by the powers that be and religion. The canonical lawyers of the thirteenth century conceded that it was not immoral in certain circumstances, as long as the woman 'engaged in it only out of necessity, and did not derive any enjoyment from it'. In towns 'pleasure girls' had to live in particular districts and wear certain identifiable clothes. These attitudes to prostitution might seem contradictory. But when the mentality of the day is considered, they do make sense. For in those days men had many more options than women, and it was recognised, although not necessarily publicly, that women only fell into prostitution because they had no choice. So although the Church regarded prostitutes as sinners, it also considered men who married them to be doing a good deed. Prostitutes could be 'washed' of their old lives if they married or joined a convent. The rape of a prostitute was considered a crime and punished as such.

Valois, Charles de, 1270–1325. Philip the Fair's only full brother. The King showed Charles a somewhat blind affection all his life and conferred on him missions that were probably beyond his capabilities. Charles de Valois, who was father, son, brother, brother-in-law, uncle and son-in-law to kings and queens, dreamed all his life of his own crown, which he never obtained.

APPENDIX II
GLOSSARY

Liturgical Hours

Aside from Mass – which was not strictly part of them – ritualised prayers, as set out in the sixth century by the Regulation of Saint Benoît, were to be said several times a day. They regulated the rhythm of the day. Monks and nuns were not permitted to dine before nightfall, that is until after vespers. This strict routine of prayers was largely adhered to until the eleventh century, when it was reduced to enable monks and nuns to devote more time to reading and manual labour.

Matins: at 2.30 a.m. or 3 a.m.

Lauds: just before dawn, between 5 a.m. and 6 a.m.

Prime: around 7.30 a.m., the first prayers of the day, as soon as possible after sunrise and just before Mass.

Terce: around 9 a.m.

Sext: around midday.

None: between 2 p.m. and 3 p.m. in the afternoon.

Vespers: at the end of the afternoon, at roughly 4.30 p.m. or 5 p.m., at sunset.

Compline: after vespers, the last prayers of the day, sometime between 6 p.m. and 8 p.m.

Measurements

It is quite hard to translate measurements to their modern-day equivalents, as the definitions varied from region to region.

League: about two and a half miles.

Ell: about 45 inches in Paris, 37 inches in Arras.

Foot: as today.

APPENDIX III
NOTES

[1] Francisco Peña.*

[2] Treatise for the Use of Inquisitors.

[3] Francisco Peña.

[4] Paris, 1290.

[5] Otherwise known as 'bastard hand', it was used in the writing of deeds, letters, ledgers and any manuscript written in the vernacular.

[6] Ballad by Marie de France.*

[7] Chrétien de Troyes.

[8] Although these men did not take vows of poverty, chastity or obedience they enjoyed the privileges of the order in exchange for working on the land as craftsmen or servants at the commandery.

[9] A piece of land given to a tenant farmer by a lord in exchange for rent and/or labour.

[10] Preceptor was the name given in Latin texts for the commander.

[11] Bread was an indication of social status. As such a distinction was made between rich men's bread, knights' bread, equerries' bread, menservants' bread . . . poor men's bread and famine bread.

[12] Greetings O Queen, Mother of mercy; our life, our love and our hope.

[13] A guild of wealthy merchants who sold fabric, clothing, *objets* and even gold work to the wealthy classes. They also dyed precious fabrics, like silk, which ordinary dyers did not deal in. Haberdasher became one of the most respected professions in the society of the time.

[14] In 994, Raoul le Glabre described it as 'an illness which attacks a limb and consumes it before separating it from the body'.

[15] Due to lysergic acid diethylamide, or LSD.

[16] This direct link was not generally acknowledged until the seventeenth century.

[17] Ergotamine is still used to treat migraine and headaches related to

vasomotor function.

[18] Haemorrhages due to fibroids.

[19] Root vegetables (carrots, turnips, celeriac, etc.) were the food of peasants; the nobility ate only leaf vegetables.

[20] A galliass or galleass was a heavy low-built vessel with sails and oars, larger than a galley, from where the word originates.

[21] Granted in 1256 by Alexander IV and confirmed by Urban IV in 1264.

[22] Those sentenced by a tribunal to pay money which was then distributed among the poor.

[23] Aconite is no longer used to treat these symptoms, except in homoeopathy, owing to its extreme toxicity.

[24] Malefactor who broke seals in order to change the wording on deeds.

[25] Parchment. Hide prepared in Pergame. It remained in use after paper became more widespread and was used by the nobility for title deeds and official deeds until the sixteenth century.

[26] Foxglove.

[27] Hemlock, used for thousands of years to treat neuralgia.

[28] Yew. Extremely toxic and used from ancient times onwards to coat arrow heads.

[29] Species of flowering plant *Thymelaeaceae*, once used as a purgative but which fell into disuse due to its toxicity.

[30] It was equally used as an antiseptic and to bring on periods.

[31] Latria: the worship given to God alone. Here it refers to the worship of the devil as though he were God.

[32] Dulia: inferior type of veneration paid to saints. Here it refers to the act of praying to demons to intercede with the devil.

[33] Poisoner.

[34] Paris boasted approximately fifteen such establishments.

[35] Winding frame.

[36] Landlords employed criers to announce the price of the wine and sometimes the food they served in exchange for the right to drink there.

[37] Listen to my prayer, O Lord, deliver my soul from fear of mine enemy.

[38] The custom of ladies dressing their pet dogs to protect them from the cold began in the fourteenth century.

[39] Plague. It is thought to have been rife, particularly in China, for three thousand years. In any case, the first known pandemic occurred in AD 540 on

the shores of the Mediterranean where it also affected Gaul. The second pandemic, known as the black plague, lasted from 1346–1353. It started in India and killed 25 million people in Europe and probably as many in Asia.

[40] Plants with antiseptic qualities that were used in the old days as well as lily, climbing ivy, bilberry and arnica.

[41] Nuns or lay people in charge of opening and closing the doors to the enclosure or the buildings within the enclosure.

[42] Wherein the word magnetism. The Greeks were familiar with magnets, which did not reach Europe until the twelfth and thirteenth centuries.

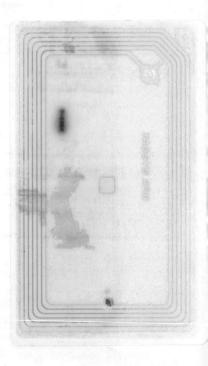